REDCOAT JUSTICE

"Fire the house and barns," Tavington told his Dragoons. Raising an arm above his head, he made an official proclamation for all to hear. "Let it be known: Those who harbor the King's enemies will lose their homes."

A Redcoat came out of the house carrying Gabriel's satchel.

"Rebel dispatches, sir."

Tavington opened the bag and began examining its contents. Martin took the opportunity to glance at Gabriel. To his horror, he saw that his son had retrieved his blue uniform jacket and was putting it on.

"Who carried this?" Tavington demanded.

When no one answered, the cold fury that was always just below Tavington's surface erupted. "WHO CARRIED THIS?" he screamed.

"I did, sir," Gabriel stepped forward. "I was wounded. These people gave me care. They have nothing to do with the dispatches."

"Seize him," Tavington ordered. He handed the dispatch case down to the lieutenant of the infantry as evidence. "Take that man to Camden. He's a spy. He will be hanged and his body put on display."

THE PATRIOT

A novel by Stephen Molstad

Based on the screenplay by Robert Rodat

HarperEntertainment
An Imprint of HarperCollins*Publishers*

HarperEntertainment
An Imprint of HarperCollins*Publishers*
10 East 53rd Street, New York, NY 10022

ISBN 0-06-102076-1

First Printing: June 2000

Printed in the United States of America

Visit HarperEntertainment on the World Wide Web
at www.harpercollins.com

00 01 02 03 04 ❖/   10 9 8 7 6 5 4 3

Robert Rodat did the hard part when he created this powerful story. He also made time to discuss it with me. Kirk Petruccelli, Victor Zolfo, and Suzanne Fritz showed me Fresh Water Plantation. York County historian Sam Thomas did the same at Historic Brattonsville. As usual, I leaned on the Kerns, the Markintys and my wife, Elizabeth. Everything might have crumbled without the constant encouragement, support, and good judgment of Dionne McNeff and Lisa DiSanto. Thanks.

1

On a warm spring day in March 1776, a young horseman hurried down a red clay road through the South Carolina low country on the most important errand of his brief career. In his leather satchel were bundles of letters requiring delivery that very day to the four elected members of the Provincial Assembly who lived in Berkeley County. His journey began before dawn in Charles Town, the colony's capital, and took him through some of the most lush and beautiful landscapes he had ever seen. He crossed the Cooper River by ferry in darkness, then clattered along the raised wooden boardwalks of the coastal tidewater marshes, surrounded by endless fields of sea grass and great blue herons as tall as a man. At sunrise, he climbed into the rolling green hills and followed the twisting road through primeval forests of towering trees. Long beards of Spanish moss hung from the branches of ancient gnarled oak trees that grew to twenty feet in circumference. Birds of dazzling color shrieked and swooped through the air, and broad-leafed plants of every description grew in abundance. A thousand clear streams laced the hills, gathering in small lakes or spilling into the flood plains to form black-bottomed swamps. Majestic cypress trees rose out of the water to incredible heights and were reflected in the mirror-smooth surface of the water. South Carolina, with its moist, warm, subtropical climate and rich red soil, had some of the most fertile land on earth and seemed a sort of paradise to the Europeans who arrived there to farm.

On his way toward the upcountry, the messenger passed

sprawling plantations that ran to the thousands of acres and tiny villages that consisted of only a few rough houses and a church. He was a stranger to the area and though he carried a map, there were few landmarks to guide him. It was a requirement of his job to stop from time to time and ask directions of the people with local knowledge. Almost everyone he talked to along the way was an African slave. He came across them working in the rice paddies of the plantations or walking the streets of the small towns where they'd gone to run errands. Forbidden by their masters to travel much past the borders of the property, most of them couldn't point him very far ahead. And even if they knew, they were reluctant to tell a stranger, especially a white one.

There were, of course, letter carriers who knew the area well. But this particular rider was part of a new and ambitious enterprise called the Continental Mail Service, organized out of Philadelphia by a printer named Benjamin Franklin. Franklin required his men to be "stout, honest, astute, and indefatigable." It also helped if they were Patriots, as this man was. In fact, it was the rider's political views that had led the Speaker of the Assembly to choose him for this mission. He'd fired the usual man because he was a Tory, one who sympathized with England and the King, and couldn't be trusted to deliver letters filled with Patriot ideas—ideas that were, in their way, more explosive than dry gunpowder; ideas that threatened to radically change the relationship between the colonies and the mother country; ideas that had already led to the outbreak of war farther north.

Franklin's men kept notes of their deliveries in the logbooks he issued to them, and it was recorded that at three in the afternoon on March 19, the rider arrived at Fresh

Water Plantation and handed his letters to "a Negress calling herself the name Abigale." In the margin of the page, he added his own observation, "a very splendid farm."

There are certain places that seem set apart and sheltered from the ordinary world, places that achieve, at least temporarily, a sort of perfection. Fresh Water Plantation was, by all accounts, such a place. Belonging to a man named Benjamin Martin, it was four hundred acres of open, fertile land with another hundred acres of fruit orchard, all of it nestled on the banks of a meandering river, a tributary of the Santee. A dozen different crops grew in carefully manicured fields that were laid out like a well-planned quilt, to take natural advantage of the land. Berry brambles wove themselves through the sturdy split-rail fence that surrounded the property. The outbuildings were well built and painted white every spring. The smell of horses and freshly turned earth hung in the air.

Rice and indigo were the region's two principal crops and they yielded spectacular profits for Martin's neighbors, but neither was grown at Fresh Water. Harvesting the blue indigo dye caused a horrible stink and drew so many flies as to make a place unlivable, and for rice to be grown at a competitive price all but required slave labor. As elsewhere, Africans did the field labor at Fresh Water, but not one of them was a slave. Everyone knew that Benjamin Martin would hire only freedmen to work at his place—a policy that did not endear him to many of his fellow planters. Instead, he grew pumpkins, squash, peas, barley, brown top millet, pearl top millet, tobacco, asparagus in the winter, and field after field of that miracle plant of the New World—corn. Indeed, the farm's two most important crops were corn and children, and both of them grew straight, tall, and in abundance.

Benjamin Martin had not grown up a farmer but had diligently taught himself the craft over the course of two decades. Through a combination of careful planning and good luck, his yields continued to increase and the new year promised to be better than the last. By mid-spring, the early corn was already shoulder-high to a tall man.

A pair of remarkably large oak trees dominated the property. One of them shaded the farmhouse while the other stood off by itself, down past the barns, surrounded by a white picket fence.

The house was small by comparison to the extravagant mansions at Middleton Place or the Blake Plantation, but it was admired throughout Berkeley County for its proportions and outstanding craftsmanship. Painted white with dark shutters and a gray shake roof, it was a roomy, two-story structure built in the traditional four-over-four architectural style, surrounded on three sides by a wide inviting porch. It radiated comfort and opulence without sinking into pretense or ostentation. Sitting at the top of a gentle rise in the land, it afforded the family a commanding view of the surrounding acreage.

Soon after the post rider passed between the brick pillars that marked the edge of the property, a pair of young white boys who were working alongside the African field hands began shouting and waving their hats in the air. Soon they came sprinting across the field, chasing the rider toward the house.

Margaret Martin, nine years of age, was sitting on the porch that afternoon delivering a reading lesson to her six-year-old brother, William. She closed the book and went to the front steps when she noticed the rider approaching. A moment later, the door opened behind her and Abigale came outside, wiping her hands on a rag. Both of them wore plain, well-made dresses with fitted bodices and full skirts of unprinted cotton. Abigale, a modest, middle-aged woman, kept a neckerchief tied around her throat.

"I have an urgent letter for Mr. Benjamin Martin," the man announced, leaving his horse at the edge of the dirt yard. "Is he here?"

Abigale glanced in the direction of the barns. "Today is Thursday," she pointed out. "Mr. Martin works every day but the Sabbath. Is Mr. Abernathy ill? He's the one usually brings the letters."

He reached into his satchel and brought out a stack of papers tied together with a string. "He has news from Boston and Philadelphia. And an urgent letter from the Speaker of the Assembly himself." He looked over his shoulder and saw the two boys running closer, waving their arms and shouting.

"I understand," said Abigale, "but it can't be helped. Mr. Martin has his routines. He opens his letters in the evening, right after supper and never before." She reached out for the package. The rider was apprehensive about turning the letters over to an African, but since Abigale appeared to be in charge of the place, he handed them over. "Are you hungry?" she asked. "Today's our baking day. Come in and have something." Post riders were excellent sources of news and gossip, and Abigale never missed the opportunity to pry what information she could from them. But the man declined, saying he had three more deliveries to make before dark, and asked for directions to the town of Pembroke. As he was leaving, the two boys finally arrived, sweating and gasping for air. In their excitement, they nearly crashed into the visitor. The older one, eleven-year-old Nathan Martin, slid to a stop and breathlessly stated the obvious.

"A post rider!" Like his father, he had a strong jaw, plenty of thick dark hair, and a sturdily built frame.

"Will there be war?" asked the younger boy, Samuel. He was ten, skinny, and showed his mother's fair complexion. "Is something happening?"

"I'll say something is happening," Abigale snapped at the boys. "This gentleman is doing his work, just like everybody around here except for two boys named Nathan and Samuel who look like they've been swimming in the river."

"We've been working!" the boys protested.

Abigale looked them over and shook her head. She didn't believe them, but left the matter alone and headed back into the house as the rider mounted his horse and started for his next destination.

"How'd she know?" Samuel asked when she was gone.

The boys stood and watched the rider gallop away before an idea occurred to them both at the same time. They tore off in a new direction, heading toward the barn where their father was working.

Like all of the buildings at Fresh Water Plantation, Benjamin Martin had designed and built the barn himself, accepting help from his neighbors and the freedmen who worked for him. It was a handsome and unusual building. The upper walls and roof were made in the customary manner of pine boards that had been milled on the property, but the lower walls were built of large stones cemented in place. Martin had unearthed them when the fields were first being cleared and, rather than leaving them laying about, wanted to put them to use. The back half of the barn was used to keep the goats and horses, while the front half served as a furniture maker's workshop.

That afternoon, Benjamin Martin stood at his lathe, all concentration, running a small chisel down a length of spinning ash wood. The shaft was already cut precariously thin, but he continued shaving off a few more tiny curls of wood with each stroke of the tool, taking care not to apply too much pressure with his enormously strong and steady hands.

His steadiness was his most outstanding feature, the thing people noticed about him first. It was evident in the measured way he walked, in the way he shook a man's hand and looked him square in the eyes, in the way he conducted himself as an Assemblyman, and in the peace and quiet of the farm he had built.

He was of average height but thicker through the chest and shoulders than most men. He had blue eyes, good teeth, a strong jaw, and a well-shaped nose—a set of facial features that, twenty years before, had caused the ladies of Charles Town to fairly swoon.

In his early forties now, he was still handsome but time and hard labor had started to take their toll. He began to find the occasional strand of gray in the long dark hair he wore pulled back and tied in a queue. His skin was tanned and tough from long exposure to the sun, and there were lines around his eyes when he smiled. His doctor and his wealthy friends urged him to work less strenuously than he did. They suggested he hire a manager to run the farm and buy a home in Charles Town where he could enjoy a life of culture, but Martin would have none of it. He spent less time behind a plow than he once had, but continued to supervise the work in the fields and to work in his shop each day making furniture. He was happy with his life at Fresh Water Plantation and had no intention of leaving.

As he worked at the lathe, he wore a distressed leather apron and a pair of old socks pulled onto his wrists to keep his shirt cuffs from catching in the spinning mechanism.

There was a smile of guarded optimism on his face, a smile that showed itself more and more as he came closer to completing his current project.

This time, he was sure he had it right. The long, thin spindle of wood he was so carefully shaving was, he hoped, the final piece to a puzzle he'd been trying to solve for many years—the three-pound rocking chair. It stood in the middle of the shop floor, an elegant spider web of wood fitted tightly together without benefit of glue or nails. The seat, the arm rests, the rails, and the spindles were made of straight-grained ash for maximum strength. The three-pound rocking chair was the ultimate test of his skill, the Holy Grail of the furniture maker's craft. And after so many failed attempts, this time he was pretty sure he'd gotten everything right.

After his parents died, Martin had been turned out to a local minister and, after that, apprenticed to a furniture maker. He was a Swiss gentleman named Rosenast who carried on long conversations with himself and laughed like the devil whenever he bruised his thumb with a hammer, but he was known as the finest cabinetmaker and wood-turner in South Carolina, and he had taught young Benjamin well. Rosenast had tried once or twice to scale the lofty heights of the three-pound rocker, but had come away in defeat. Martin thought of him as he worked, surrounded by a fastidiously organized workshop that held every tool a man of his profession might need: chisels, gouges, and rasps of every size hung from hooks on the walls; there were crosscut saws, rip saws, dovetail, miter, fret, and coping saws; he had jack planes, toothing planes, babetting planes, and heavy wooden clamps. Cabinet drawers held scribes and squares, dividers and rules, and an assortment of augers and gimlets for boring holes. There were hammers and boxes of nails, both broads and brads, which he'd made himself at the iron forge just behind the building. But by far the best tool he owned, the crowning glory of his shop, was the one he was using to finish the spindle: the grand lathe. It had been imported from Holland and was one of the finest pieces of equipment in all the colonies. The main wheel stood over six feet tall and was connected, by means of a leather belt, to the lathe shaft. His assistant, Abner, stood at the wheel, slowly turning the hand crank that spun the spindle of ash at a terrific rate of speed.

"It's going to break if you take off any more," said Abner, a gray-haired man with a long, fleshy face covered by a stubble of gray beard. He wore a work apron and his favorite hat, an old beat-up thing made of straw. He was Abigale's father. Born in Africa and sold into slavery, he had no way of knowing exactly how old he was, but had figured it pretty close to sixty. He had come to Fresh Water several years before when the Martins had helped Abigale buy him away from the man who had owned him. Now he was a freedman.

"Steady," Martin answered, continuing to work. "Keep turning."

"He's right, Mr. Martin. You been eating too well to sit in that little chair," said Joshua, another African, with a laugh. "I'm not saying you're getting heavy, but . . ." Abner chuckled at the comment.

Joshua was a thin, muscular man in his twenties who was known for his sense of humor and his tendency to flirt. He was carrying racks of tobacco plants up into the loft and hanging them to dry.

"Thank you for your opinion," Martin said, raising his eyes from his work and giving Joshua a withering look, "but you're wrong. This chair is strong enough to hold two men."

"Oh, I believe you, Mr. Martin," Joshua said, starting up the ladder. "Just warn me before you test it, so I can get out of the way."

Refusing to be distracted, Martin made several more passes with the chisel, removing imperceptibly small amounts of the wood. Then he ran his bare fingertips along the spinning wood, closing his eyes and feeling for the slightest imperfections.

Abner rolled his eyes and looked across the shop at the youngest of Benjamin Martin's children, three-year-old Susan. She sat at one of the worktables, surveying the scene like a hard-to-please foreman. The look she shared with Abner made it clear that neither the old man nor the little girl held out much hope of the chair proving to be a success.

"Fine," Martin announced with satisfied optimism. He stepped back from the machine and went to the bench where his daughter was sitting. "I think it's going to work this time," he said. "Don't you?"

He didn't expect an answer and she didn't give him one. Susan was a lovely, golden-haired child with a pair of eyes that were so large they made her seem as if she were in a perpetual state of being startled by the world around her. She showed signs of being quite intelligent, and in most ways was developing normally. But she was not a normal child. At nearly three years old, she was still not talking, and her father was at a loss over what to do about it.

As he began fitting the final piece of the chair into place, there was a disturbance at the open barn door. Nathan and Samuel raced up and slid to a stop in a cloud of red dust.

"Father!" Nathan gasped, "A post rider just came to the house!"

"Yes," Samuel said, "he brought a whole stack of letters."

Martin used a mallet to tap the top rail into place atop the back supports, taking care to keep it level. "Did you finish planting the south field?" he asked without looking at the boys.

"Yes!" Samuel answered. "I mean, no. Well, some."

"More than half," Nathan assured him.

Martin stepped back to appraise his handiwork. "Those swimming breaks really cut into the workday, don't they?"

Samuel winced. "How does everybody know—"

Nathan's hand clapped down over his little brother's mouth before he could finish the question. "Are you going to test the chair, Father?"

Martin dismissed them with a jerk of his head. The boys moved away reluctantly, pretending to start back toward their work in the field, but then raced around to the barn's rear entrance instead. They'd heard their father talking about the chair for days and wanted to see if it would hold.

Now that it was completely fitted together, Martin lifted the chair and hung it on a bailing scale. It seemed to float effortlessly in the air. When the gauge came to rest, Martin announced with great satisfaction that it measured precisely three pounds. He said he imagined they sat on chairs such as this in heaven.

Susan, Abner, and Joshua all exchanged another skeptical look.

The moment of truth had arrived. Martin circled the chair, making a final inspection. Before he could sit down, another of his sons rushed into the doorway. Thirteen-year-old Thomas was panting for breath after a long run, his mop of brown hair hanging down to his eyes. He carried a rifle in one hand and a pair of freshly killed birds in the other.

"Father, a post rider! We spotted him as we were coming back through the orchards. There's mail."

"Yes, I heard." The tone of his voice told Thomas the issue was already settled—the mail would be opened at the usual hour and no sooner. It was a tone the children knew well and respected. Still, the boy began to protest that this was no ordinary batch of letters and therefore deserved extraordinary attention. Before he could say much, however, yet another of Martin's sons came to the door and put his arm over Thomas's shoulder.

Gabriel was the oldest child, already eighteen, and even more handsome than his father had been at that age. His blond hair, tied back with a ribbon, came out from under his cocked felt hat and hung to his shoulders. He, too, carried a rifle and the wild birds he'd shot that afternoon—six quail and four good-sized pheasants. Along with Thomas's two kills, it was enough meat to feed everyone at Fresh Water that evening.

"Let's go, General," Gabriel said, calling his brother by his nickname and pulling him toward the house. "We'll have to wait until after supper." Gabriel, more than any of the others, had inherited his mother's patience and good judgment.

"No, wait!" Thomas growled, shaking free. More than any of the others, he had inherited his father's naturally quick temper and excitability—traits Martin labored every minute of every day to hold in check. "There may be news that cannot wait. Father, we could read them while you're working and tell you what they say!"

Martin gave Thomas a stern look that melted the boy to obedience.

"Come," said Gabriel, leading him away. "Oh, and by the way, Father," he said with the slightest of grins, "your chair looks very solidly made this time." Martin thought he could hear the boys giggling as they tromped away.

Unfazed, he took a deep breath and lowered himself steadily, gingerly into the seat of the chair, adding his weight an ounce at a time.

Not a creak.

He leaned back ever so carefully and when the three thin spindles of the back rest supported him, he allowed himself a smile, wishing old man Rosenast were there to see. He began to rock back and forth, tentatively at first, but then with greater and greater confidence. Suddenly he threw his head back and laughed. He'd done it, he'd climbed to the top of the mountain. With a scant three pounds of wood, he had manufactured a piece of furniture so precisely fitted together and so strong, it could—

He stopped laughing suddenly and cocked his head to the side, listening. His smile transformed to a scowl when he noticed a tiny squeaking noise. He pushed back with greater energy and heard the squeak again. Under his breath, he muttered a few words unfit for little Susan's ears and pushed back farther still, to the very tips of the curved rails below. It was a tiny, almost imperceptible sound, one that other men might not have noticed at all. But Martin noticed it. He had taken too many pains in the building of the chair to tolerate a loose and squeaking joint. Determined to find the source of the irksome sound, he leaned far to the side, twisted himself sideways in the seat and pushed back one final time.

One of the slender rear legs snapped cleanly in two, throwing Martin a few inches to the side. For a single desperate moment, he teetered in the air with a shocked look on his face before the other rear leg gave way. He kicked his legs out, trying to regain his balance, but it was too late.

The other parts of the chair collapsed at once, splintering into pieces and dumping Martin unceremoniously on his rump. He ended up with his legs dangling over his head in an extremely awkward position.

Susan's eyes popped open wider than usual. Abner turned away to cover a laugh, and from up in the loft, Joshua squealed as if he'd been sat on.

"Damnation!" Martin roared so loudly they heard him in the south field. He scrambled to his feet in frustration, snatched up a handful of chair, and flung it against the wall of the barn. He reached down for one of the arm rests and was preparing to hurl it with all his strength when he noticed Susan giving him The Disapproving Eye, a talent she'd inherited from Elizabeth, her mother. The effect of the Eye on Martin was swift and complete. He let the wooden arm rest drop from his hand and became very still. He was no less angry or frustrated than he had been the moment before, but the Eye helped him regain his steadiness and composure.

"I'm sorry," he said crisply, to no one in particular. He smoothed his work apron against his chest, walked deliberately over to the woodbin, and pulled out a new piece of wood. Very calmly, he brought it to the lathe and fitted it on the shaft, ready to start again from scratch.

"Abner, would you assist me please?"

Eighteen years earlier, in a letter dated July 9, 1758, Elizabeth Putnam Martin wrote to her aunt, Prudence Putnam, a wealthy spinster living in Newport, Rhode Island.

> *Dearest Aunt,*
> *You must think me terribly ungracious for taking so long to answer your letter and thank you for your gift. In my defense, I*

can only tell you that I have been busier than I ever thought it possible to be. Our wedding was held on Saturday, first of June, at Scots-Presbyterian on Meeting Street. Reception was at our home. We were greatly surprised and even alarmed by the number of persons who attended. Father complained loudly that half of Charles Town had closed up their shops for the chance to feast on the free food he provided. Knowing him well, I'm sure you understand he meant not a word of it but was thrilled to be at the center of a storm such as we had that day. Most of them were strangers to us who had come to have a look at Benjamin. He is the toast of Charles Town since returning a hero from the frontier war, and is a much sought-after dinner guest at the finest homes in this city. He is recognized on the street by shop-keepers, tradesmen, and even slaves who stop to shake his hand and ask questions. His reputation has, I suspect, grown larger still with the news that he, a carpenter from the upcountry, would marry into our respected Putnam family.

I will try to satisfy the request in your letter to know more about him.

His parents died when he was quite young, the particular cause of which I do not know. He was bound out to the care of a local parson, a Quaker sent down from Philadelphia, until the age of twelve when he was apprenticed to a furniture maker, a Swiss gentleman whom he describes as quite mad but extremely capable. His service completed, he came to Charles Town to search for work, but soon left for the war.

I would not blame you for thinking I had lost my senses in marrying a man of such description. It was, until fairly recently, the last fate in the world I would have chosen. We met at the Gadsden home where we had each been invited for a music recital given on the pianoforte by the well-known Mr. Robert Maudley of London. Benjamin caught my eye immediately, for he was a coarse and boorish man surrounded by dignified com-

pany. His clothing was ignorant of fashion, his hair poorly trimmed, and he had brought a flask of applejack cider with him and proceeded to share it around. I considered him ill-tempered, loud, excitable, completely unskilled in the art of conversation, and lacking in manners. To my great mortification, he rose from his chair middle way through the concert and came to talk with me, viva voce, *asking my name,* et cetera.

When he arrived at our door on the following afternoon bearing gifts, I relied on Father to send him on his way. The two of them retired to the study and stayed there for some hours, laughing and taking their dinner in camera. *When they emerged, they stank of liquor and Father's arm was draped over the shoulders of his future son-in-law. The two of them continue to behave like schoolboys when they are together, giggling over impolite jokes and arguing loudly over politics or business.*

He continued to call on me until my resistance began to weaken. One evening he came bearing flowers he'd snatched up from our neighbor's yard and some very bad love poems of his own manufacture. In one of them, he likened himself to a sailing ship lost on a cloud-covered sea and me to the North Star that emerges to guide the vessel to safe harbor. Drivel! When I offered to call Father, he sank to a knee! and informed me that he had decided to make me his wife, that there could never be another woman for him, et cetera, et cetera. *More drivel! My answer was to slam the door in his face.*

I have many reasons to complain! And yet, I admit I have developed an inexplicable fondness for him, one that I am sure will last to the end of my life. Indeed, my opinion of him has reversed itself so thoroughly I now hold him in an esteem that verges on the sin of idolatry. He is industrious and intelligent, exceedingly handsome, ambitious and kind. Though hot-tempered and loud in company with his male friends, I have found him malleable enough when we are alone. We work together well and agree on most questions of household philosophy, such as children. We plan to have only one, or at most two.

We are building a new house on land Benjamin accepted from the governor in reward for his military service. It is an arduous day's ride from my beloved Charles Town, but it is one of the loveliest tracts of land I have seen. Open fields on the banks of a river where two old oaks lean toward one another from a distance. With the help of our country neighbors and friends from Charles Town, we have raised the frame. We also have help from a woman named Abigale. She is a slave woman given us as a wedding gift by Father's business partner, Mr. Van Heynis. As you know, I share your abhorrence of slavery, as does Benjamin, and we have made application to the governor's office to have her legally freed. At present, we are quartered in a two-room cabin Benjamin built by himself. The curtains you sent for our wedding are too fine to hang in such a modest dwelling, but they will be splendid in our house when it is built.

This letter grows overly long and I am called to dinner, having been at this writing for longer than my other duties should allow. I dearly look forward to seeing you again. Please visit us here if you can so that you may judge for yourself whether the southern branch of the Putnams has taken leave of its senses.

Ever your devoted niece,
Elizabeth Putnam Martin

Post Script, my sister Charlotte insists that I add her warmest greetings to you and that I tell you how well she adores Benjamin, both for his handsome looks and for his sense of humor. She is growing fast and is nearly as tall as I.

That evening, the Martin family took their evening meal as they usually did, around the large farm table in the kitchen. A large brick oven built into the wall dominated the room and Abigale had used it to prepare a meal of pheasant stew and boiled corn with a pair of fruit pies for dessert. There was a place set for her at the table, but she was too busy fussing over everyone else to sit down and eat with the family. When the meal was finished, the older boys helped clear and wash the plates while the little ones headed upstairs to play and prepare for bed. Martin, as he often did at that hour, went outside by himself to think.

A full moon cast a butter-yellow glow on the fields. He stepped off the porch and looked into the sky to locate the North Star, a thing he did by habit every night. When he was certain the children were occupied with their tasks, he slipped away from the house and followed the trail that ran behind the barns. The horses snorted to him in greeting and followed him as far as they could along the corral fence. Crickets sang everywhere in the tall grass. He continued down to where the second of the farm's two towering oaks stood by itself, enclosed by a white picket fence. He pushed the gate open and went inside, letting the weighted chain pull it closed behind him.

This small yard was his retreat and his sanctuary. Spanish moss hung in heavy clusters from the tree's twisting branches, and he could hear the river in the distance. The trunk of the tree was so big that when he and Elizabeth had stood on opposite sides of it and reached around, their fingertips barely touched. It was under this tree that she had finally accepted his proposal to marry and, later, where Gabriel had been conceived. Although the two of them had never discussed the matter, he knew it was the place where she would have liked to be buried. Her slate headstone was there, just a few paces from the base of the tree. Martin had carved it himself and it had taken him many tries to get it right. At the top, there was a perfectly round area that looked like the face of a clock, but was actually a miniature map of the night sky with Polaris, the North Star, at its center. It was a design he'd painstakingly copied from her favorite piece of jewelry. Chiseled below were the words:

In memory of ELIZABETH Putnam MARTIN
Who departed this life Feb, the 19th
AD. 1773 In the 35th year of her age.

Of all the fine objects Martin had made in his life, he never took more care than he had with that headstone. He sat down in the grass and leaned against the oak, thinking through the events of the day, and apologized out loud for having lost his temper in the barn. She was still very much alive to him.

Their marriage had been full of love but was not an easy thing. After one year of intoxicating happiness and the birth of their first child, the honeymoon had ended abruptly when Martin, drunk on rum, gave in to her persistent questioning and told her some things about his days fighting the French and Indian War, things he knew he should never speak of. After that, she had turned away from him. For four long years, she barely spoke to him and made him sleep away from her. Martin spent those years finishing the construction of the house, planting the fields, and learning to control his thirst for liquor and dangerous excitements. He never blamed Elizabeth for her reaction to what he'd told her and he was willing to do whatever it took to win back her respect and affection. Eventually, she came back to him and Thomas was born. But even then, they were both strong-willed people willing to defend their principles and they argued and loved with equal intensity. Even during their spats, however, Martin continued to rely on her intelligence and sound judgment to guide him.

Her seventh pregnancy was the smoothest one yet. Elizabeth joked with her friends that after so much practice, she would deliver the child without noticing. But when the labor began, Susan was turned the wrong way in the womb and Elizabeth began to bleed. The midwife assured Martin there was no reason to be alarmed, but she sent Martin to retrieve the doctor just in case. When he returned a few hours later, Elizabeth was dead and Susan had been born.

That had been three years ago. It was common practice in the colonies for people who had lost their spouses to remarry quickly, especially if there were children, but Martin wasn't ready for that. Elizabeth was still alive to him and he continued to summon her spirit when he needed advice in difficult situations. And that night he needed her help.

He was concerned about the letters that had been delivered. He already knew, more or less, what they would say, and their arrival was one more indication that the fighting in the northern colonies continued to spread. With each new decree of the English parliament and each rebellious response from the radical colonists, the conflict grew stronger and threatened to move closer. The previous war, the fight against the French and Cherokee, seemed to him, in hindsight, an ill-advised struggle. But this new war was different. It was being fought for something more than mere real estate. It was a battle of principles, and Martin, a veteran, a war hero, and one of the colony's elected leaders, found himself squarely on the Patriot side. The people of South Carolina had already started choosing sides, joining with the Tories, who supported England, or the Whigs, who favored independence. Bitter disputes arose between neighbors, and political arguments tore families apart.

Although the shooting had not yet begun, it seemed more and more inevitable that it would. As that day approached, a certain question became more urgent and difficult to answer: What was he going to do when the war came to South Carolina?

When he had been sitting under the oak for about twenty minutes, his attention was drawn back to the house by the sound of laughing, shouting children. He reached over and patted his hand on the earth, then stood up and headed back.

"Do you want to know how to find her?" Margaret asked.

Little Susan remained silent as usual, but seemed to nod her head. The girls were at the window of their room, illuminated by a single candle and by the moonlight pouring in, dressed in their sleeping gowns and caps. Neither of them noticed their father come to the doorway behind them.

"First, you start from the front two stars of the Big Dipper, there and there," she said, pointing. "That's the handle. Then you put your fingers in front of you like this. No, that's too close. Like this. Good. Now count up five fingers, and that's her. The North Star. She's always there to protect us."

Martin cleared his throat and stepped inside.

Without a word, the girls came away from the window, knelt at the side of the bed they shared, and prayed for a moment in silence before climbing under the covers. He tucked little Susan in first, then came around to Margaret's side. She looked up at him and whispered.

"I think she understands. It helps her to know Mother's there."

Martin nodded with a thin smile. He sat down on the edge of the feather-stuffed mattress and looked at the nine-year-old girl. She was a beautiful and helpful child who had been acting like a responsible adult for the last three years. Elizabeth's death seemed to affect the girls more than it had the boys. It had put an abrupt stop to Margaret's childhood and, Martin suspected, was the reason Susan didn't talk. It seemed to him that the girl could speak if she wanted to, but had decided to remain mute. He wished the girls good night, picked up the candle, and went down the hall to check on the boys.

Martin had learned the hard way not to go inside the room shared by Nathan, Samuel, and William without first taking various precautions. Ambushes were not uncommon. To his neighbors, Benjamin Martin was known as a man of education and philosophical gravity, an accomplished craftsman and an elected statesman, but the moment he stepped into the boy's room, he was fair game. The three mongooses who lived inside often attacked as a pack, and pillows were their weapons of choice. But on that night, they had all fallen asleep. Nathan and Samuel were in their beds while young William had dozed off on the floor while playing with a wooden horse. Martin set his candle aside and lifted the boy to his bed. As he was leaving, Samuel stirred and struggled to lift his head off his pillow.

"Mail, Papa . . ."

"Sleep now," Martin said softly before closing the door behind him.

When he came down the stairs and into the living room, he found a squadron of Redcoat soldiers deployed for battle against an equal number of Patriots. Thomas, nicknamed "the General" by his siblings, was stretched out on his stomach near the fireplace directing the troop movements. The English cannons fired, throwing a few of the rebels under a chair. But a brave Patriot infantryman raced forward and used his bayonet to dispatch the entire corps of English bombardiers. Thomas quietly provided the men's dying screams.

The living room was where the three of them gathered each night. Beeswax candles burned in the reflective wall sconces, and Gabriel had built a fire in the fireplace. On the mantle was a set of blue and white Merriman plates, each one decorated with part of a rhyming verse, and on the walls there were a few small oil paintings, including one of Elizabeth and her sister, Charlotte, as girls. Wood-slatted venetian blinds hung over the windows, and there was plenty of comfortable, elegant furniture, all of it made on the premises.

"Who's winning?" Martin asked, stepping over Thomas and the battlefield on the way to his desk.

"The Patriots, of course!" answered the boy, stealing a glance at the table in the hall with the unopened mail.

Martin uncorked a bottle of rum and poured himself half a cup before settling into his favorite chair with a deep sigh. He sipped his drink and looked across the room at his oldest son. Gabriel sat stiffly in an armchair, pretending to be engrossed in a copy of Jean Jacques Rousseau's *A Discourse Upon the Origin and Foundations of Inequality Among Mankind.* Martin grinned and glanced away at the fire just as Gabriel peeked over the top of the book. For a few excruciating minutes, the room was silent except for the soft crackling of the fire.

Finally, Martin cleared his throat and casually asked, "What was in the mail?"

Tiny soldiers scattered and Jean-Jacques Rousseau went flying as both boys made a mad dash toward the hallway table. Gabriel got there first. He untied the package and began to quickly sort through the papers, handing the less important news over to Thomas. Eagerly, he unfolded a broadside printed in Boston and brought it back to the living room.

"The New York and Pennsylvania assemblies are debating independence and a vote is expected by the middle of March."

"Middle of March? That's now," Thomas noted. "They must have voted already."

"What about New England?" Martin asked.

Gabriel seemed amused by what he read. "In the town of Chestertown, they burned the Customs House and tar-and-feathered two magistrates. They died of their burns."

"Foolish men," Martin said darkly.

Gabriel looked up. "Who, the rioters or the magistrates?"

Martin ignored the question. "Anything about the Continental Congress?"

Gabriel nodded as he read the notice, a smile spreading slowly across his face. "It says here they'll make a declaration of independence by July."

"Independence!?" Thomas said a little louder than he should have. The sound of the word made him so happy, he broke into a little dance. He set his hands on his hips and executed three steps of a contra jig before stopping short and suddenly returning to his letter. He could feel his father's hard stare and knew that unbridled behavior of that sort was the quickest way for a child of the Martin family to find himself sent to his room. Still, he was smiling wildly as he tried to concentrate on his reading.

Martin extracted a delicate pair of reading glasses from a wooden pocket box and motioned for Gabriel to hand him the remaining letters. He angled his chair to catch the light and began to read.

"Father," Gabriel said, "do you remember my friend Peter Cuppin?"

"From Orangeburg?"

"The same. He writes that a recruiting officer came to his town."

"Yes?"

"And he joined the militia. With his parents' permission."

"Yes?" Martin gazed evenly at his son, as if waiting for him to get to the point when, in truth, the point was very clear to everyone present. Thomas looked furtively between the two men, sensing a possible confrontation. After a moment of tense silence, Martin considered the matter closed. He unfolded a new letter and began to read.

But Gabriel gathered his courage and pressed the issue a bit further. "Peter Cuppin is seventeen, Father, a year younger than I."

Martin continued to read, offering no reaction. Though outwardly calm, it took a considerable act of will to resist telling Gabriel he would *never* be given permission to leave the family and join the war.

Gabriel gave up and returned to the letter in his hands. The three men spent the next few minutes in silence, passing the pages to one another as they finished.

The last letter Martin opened was the one from the Speaker of the Assembly. When he'd finished with it, he made an announcement. "Boys, the Assembly is being convened in emergency session the day after tomorrow. I've been called to—"

"Charles Town?" they interrupted.

He nodded. "We'll leave in the morning and stay with your Aunt Charlotte."

"Charles Town?!" Thomas said loudly. The name of the city stirred him to the same happy reaction the word independence had a moment before. "We're going to Charles Town!" he said as his hands found his hips and his feet started flying below him. This time, he added a song to his performance. "We're going to Charles Town! We're going to Charles Town!"

"Gabriel, will you please walk down to Abigale's place and ask her to come with us. And you, General, upstairs! Without waking the young ones."

Thomas started at once for the stairs, but he took his time about it. He continued dancing as he walked and under his breath he sang, "We're going to Charles Town. We'll see Aunt Charlotte. We're going to Charles Town . . ."

2

As the first light of day silhouetted the trees on the eastern hills, Abigale left the row of cabins where the freedmen lived and carried her traveling bag up to the farmhouse, walking with her father and Joshua. They found Benjamin Martin outside the house wearing a fine suit of gentleman's traveling clothes. He had hitched one horse to a wagon and another to a two-wheel buggy. Margaret, his helper, brought blankets and food, put them in the wagon, then went to wake the other children. They stumbled downstairs rubbing their eyes and buttoning their clothes, expecting to be served breakfast. But their father was ready to leave and after a quick conference with Abner and Joshua, who would look after the farm for the next few days, they set off. Martin led the way in the buggy with Samuel by his side. The others rode in the wagon Gabriel was driving.

By the time the sun broke over the treetops, they had climbed to the top of the Wakefield overlook and stopped, as they always did, to admire the view. Behind them was the valley they called home. Ahead was the town of Wakefield, its chimneys smoking with morning fires, surrounded by a patchwork of small fields.

Thomas, who had been so excited, was now less than thrilled to be traveling. Unable to sleep the night before, he curled up with a blanket over his head and tried to ignore the bouncing of the wagon, the squeaky rattle of the wheels, and the ever-louder screaming of the birds.

The children came awake slowly, in rhythm with the day. By the time they reached Rankinsburg, they were wav-

ing to passersby and shouting the exciting news that they
were headed to the capital. But it was a long trip and soon
their spirits flagged. By the time they started across the vast
Joseph Blake Plantation, a long trip in itself, they had run
through every traditional song, sailor's ditty, lullaby, and
church hymn they knew. They fell quiet for a while, then
turned impatient.

"How much longer, Father?"

"A little ways yet."

"Are we nearly there, Father?"

"Nearly there."

When they came to the broad Cooper River, they drove
the wagons onto a ferryboat and paid the crew to take them
across. Soon after, they rode up onto a high spot in the road
and caught sight of the great city.

Founded a hundred years before, Charles Town sat on a
narrow spit of land shaped like a pointing finger at the
place where the Cooper and Ashley Rivers joined. A deep
natural harbor was sheltered from the sea by a series of
coastal islands, visible in the distance. It was a compact city,
full of tall private homes and taller commercial buildings,
where more than half the narrow streets were paved with
stone or brick. It was a place of industrious merchants and
the wealthy families that owned the plantations. It had
recently surpassed Boston and Philadelphia to become the
richest city in the colonies.

With growing excitement, they rolled through the outly-
ing neighborhoods, then into the city proper, following the
street that ran along the harbor. It was crowded, dirty, loud,
and brimming with life. Ship bells clanged and dock work-
ers shouted to one another in Dutch and Spanish as
winches groaned and raised crates from the holds of the tall
ships tied to the wharves, their masts and rigging towering

overhead. Dogs yipped and ran alongside the wagon. Dirty little boys, some of them as young as William, worked side by side with grown men, cleaning the boats or passing boxes, hand to hand like a fire brigade, in lines that extended from the water to the warehouses. People of all colors and nationalities were moving in different directions, too concentrated on their business to greet one another. A pair of sunburned men in black suits and long, powdered wigs, one of them carrying a money box and the other a stack of ledger books, walked into the path of the wagon without looking and nearly got themselves run over. Farther on, they passed a slave auction where nervous, shackled Africans were being inspected by a horde of potential buyers. Abigale, who was riding next to Gabriel, kept her eyes straight ahead as they clattered past, the cobblestones jostling the wagon this way and that. The odors of fish, urine, sea water, and cooking food hung in the air, and the crowds grew thicker the closer they came to the Exchange Building, the heart of Charles Town's commercial area. A striking example of Palladian architecture, the Exchange Building dominated the harbor and was surrounded by an open square paved with bricks. It was here that the British had levied their hated taxes on imports and exports. Two months earlier, angry mobs had rioted and chased the King's tax men out of town.

A group of unruly men was digging a hole deep enough to erect a liberty pole, which was nothing but a tall straight tree stripped of its branches. Liberty poles were already common in the radical northern towns, serving as a gathering point for Patriot speeches and recruiting, but until now had not appeared in the South.

From the open square of the Exchange, they turned into the narrow confines of Tradd Street, a canyon of two- and three-story mansions built right up to the narrow dirt road. Through gaps in the high walls and gates, the Martins caught occasional glimpses of the sumptuous private gardens that surrounded the homes. Before they reached the end of the block, the children spotted their Aunt Charlotte's house.

Built directly across the street from the Charles Town Society Club by the children's grandfather, Charles Putnam, it was a two-story brick mansion with twenty rooms. In the custom of the city's homes, it was situated behind iron gates and turned sideways to the street. Two long balconies, one above and one below, ran the length of the house and looked out over the garden.

"Matthew! Hello, Matthew!"

Shouting and waving their arms, the children caught the attention of a dignified butler standing on the upper balcony helping one of the other servants beat the dust out of a rug. He smiled when he saw them and responded with a tightly controlled wave of the hand. He folded his rag carefully and set it where it belonged before going into the house.

"Miss Charlotte, the children are here."

He found her reading on a sofa in the upstairs parlor, surrounded by framed artwork and a six-foot-tall harp. She had been awaiting their arrival all day. Though she had received no letter from them, she knew the Assembly would convene the following day. She set down her book and hurried out into the hallway to check her appearance in the mirror on the wall.

She was a tall, attractive woman in her early thirties with strawberry-blond hair pinned up in a bun. She wore a beautiful snug-fitting dress that showed off her very feminine figure. It had lacy sleeves, a large bow below her bosom, and a pale blue color that brought out the blue in her eyes. Naturally beautiful, with smooth rosy skin, she wore no makeup. She leaned close to the mirror and lifted the corners of her small mouth as if she were smiling, inspecting the area around her eyes for wrinkles. There were a few, but they were still barely visible. In general, she was pleased with what she saw and nodded to herself in approval. The only thing she would have changed about her appearance was a certain underlying sadness in her expression that she found it difficult to conceal. It came as a result of having lost too much during the previous few years. First, her husband of five years, John Selton, had drowned during an early-season hurricane. A few weeks later, her father had passed away in his sleep, and shortly after that, her sister had died unexpectedly in childbirth.

She was popular in Charles Town society and had many friends, but more and more she found herself staying at home, reading her books and broadsheet newspapers, with only Matthew and her other servants for company.

The children raised a tremendous ruckus as they came up the stairs and ran toward her. Thomas and Nathan led the way and nearly knocked Charlotte over in their exuberance to put their arms around her. She laughed and recovered her balance as the rest of the Martin brood crowded around.

"Welcome!" she cried, greeting each child in turn and paying each one a compliment. When she looked up and saw their father coming along the balcony, she exclaimed, "They're huge! What have you been feeding them?"

"They're from good stock," Martin said, "on their mother's side, of course."

She thanked him for the compliment with a sweet smile and did her best to curtsy with so many little bodies hanging on hers. For a moment, she let her eyes linger on Martin and he allowed his to linger on her. He stepped up and began peeling the children away from their aunt one at a time.

"Come inside, children," Charlotte said, gesturing to the parlor behind her. "Wait until you see what I have for you."

"Presents!?" they asked in unison. Needing no further encouragement, they moved as a group through the doorway, squealing in anticipation. As they did, they pushed the two adults together, chest to chest. They separated themselves more slowly than they could have.

Charlotte ducked into the room just long enough to retrieve a rag doll, bringing it to Susan, who was in Abigale's arms, wearing a sunny yellow dress and a thin white bonnet.

"I have this for you, Susan. It belonged to your mother."

The girl accepted the doll with a serious look that seemed to belong to a much older child, but said nothing. Charlotte stroked her arm gently before Abigale carried her inside.

"She's still not talking?" Charlotte asked.

Martin shook his head, at a loss about how to help the child. But then he stepped back and looked Charlotte over with a warm smile. "It does me good to see you," he told her.

She nodded to show that the feeling was mutual and led him into the noisy parlor.

That evening, they gathered in Charlotte's spacious dining room and feasted as if it were a Christmas dinner. There was a crown roast of pork, medallions of beef, fresh oysters from the bay, a roast goose as large as any they'd ever seen, two cheese pies, two egg pies, four fruit pies, a brick of chocolate, loaves of freshly baked bread, beer, Pennsylva-

nia cognac, and quality French wine. The servants continued bringing dish after dish until the children moaned and
begged them to stop. The windows were left open for the
view they offered onto the well-tended flower garden, illuminated by a pair of torches, but they also let in the sounds
coming from the street, the sounds of high-spirited men
laughing and talking as they made their way toward the
Exchange.

"Thank you for a fine meal," Gabriel said before dessert
and tea were served. "May I be excused? I'd like to go outside for a walk."

The conversation came to a swift and total halt as all
eyes turned to Martin for his reaction. He finished chewing
the food in his mouth, then washed it down with a long
slug of beer. Although he was the steadiest and most pre-
dictable of men, he managed somehow always to be full of
surprises.

"I don't see why not," he said.

As Gabriel smiled and stood up, Thomas moved immediately to follow, but before he could so much as push his
chair away from the table, his father put a quick, viselike
grip on his arm, pinning it in place.

"Gabriel, we'll expect to see you back here in one hour's
time."

"Yes, Father."

"Don't you worry, Thomas," said his Aunt Charlotte,
"we have a fine view of the square from here. We'll go up to
the balcony after the meal."

The moment Gabriel stepped into the street, he felt a sense
of danger and opportunity. It was a warm, humid night and
half of Charles Town seemed to have come out of their
houses. He looked down Tradd Street and saw the

Exchange square glowing with light and crowded with foot traffic, and before he knew it, he found himself hurrying in that direction to become a part of it.

A loud, chaotic carnival seemed to be underway. Dozens of fires had been built in the square and a hundred pitch torches hung in iron rings on the buildings. Young boys circulated through the crowd hawking political tracts by local writers. Vendors had set themselves up outside the warehouses, selling beer and grilled beef on sticks. Everywhere he looked, people had gathered in clusters to hear men on wooden crates making loud political speeches. The crowds cheered huzzah when they liked the speakers' opinions and hooted when they disagreed. Every social class was represented, from the wealthiest plantation owners down to the coarsest of slaves. On the steps of the Exchange Building, a band of musicians sang bawdy, satirical songs that poked fun at King George and the unpopular members of Parliament, bringing gales of laughter from the hundreds who listened.

Anti-English feelings were nothing new in Charles Town. They'd been brewing for years, then grown suddenly stronger with the spate of hateful, retaliatory tax acts passed in London. But since the arrival of Colonel Burwell and his army of Continental soldiers a few days before, the entire population had become infected with a political fever, mostly of the patriotic strain.

Gabriel noticed a group of well-dressed gentlemen standing apart from the rest of the crowd and went to listen. He slipped past several men until he was close to the man addressing the group. He was a heavyset gentleman with a thick double chin that jiggled as he spoke.

"Admiral Peter Parker has already landed in North Carolina," shouted the speaker, "and will soon be here with his armada of ships to attack our city. Meanwhile, foolish Colonel Moultrie is out on Sullivan's Island constructing a fort from which he expects to shell the British ships. Gentlemen, I have seen his fort. It is nothing but palmetto logs covered with sand brought up from the beach! Let me assure you, it will not stand longer than twenty minutes under Parker's guns." The crowd nodded and said amen. "These damn Whigs have reduced our situation here to anarchy! And the situation is made worse by the arrival of Burwell and his six hundred men. They will be brave enough, I am sure, until the moment when the guns begin to roar! Until the cannonballs fly in the air and our property is destroyed! Until our very lives are in jeopardy along with those of our families! And what will our brave Patriot soldiers do when they have brought this misery down on our heads?" Gabriel glanced around nervously, realizing he was surrounded by Tories, English loyalists. He was surprised by what he saw. They looked like ordinary men, not the devils they were made out to be in the Patriot pamphlets he had been reading for the last several months. Still, he was uncomfortable among them and was anxious to leave. "They will turn and run!" thundered the speaker, answering his own question. "And Parker's men will have control of the town before the luncheon hour!" He unfurled a scroll of paper and showed it to his audience. "Sign this document, gentlemen. It is an oath of loyalty to the crown, and if you value your property and your security, you'll add your names to it."

As Gabriel snaked through the group, making his escape, he heard a man call out, "I've already signed the Patriot petition. Can I sign this one as well?" Some of the listeners laughed, but the speaker invited the man to come forward.

"I strongly recommend that you do. It can't hurt your chances."

Alone once more, Gabriel started off toward the Exchange Building and the Liberty pole, where the brighter fires and larger crowds were gathered. There was a palpable tension in the air, a feeling that the orderliness of the normal world had melted away and anything was now possible.

Soon his attention was drawn to the sound of heavy footsteps that shook the street as they marched past the wharves. A mounted officer of the Continental Army, one of Burwell's men, led 120 blue-uniformed soldiers into the square at a double-time march, their feet lifting and falling together with a precision that was exciting to see. They were followed close behind by a hundred more men, volunteer militia, both blacks and whites, dressed in their own clothes. The officer shouted a command that brought the Continentals to an orderly stop. Their discipline drew applause from the crowd.

The officer shouted that they were heading out to Sullivan's Island to assist Colonel Moultrie and asked for volunteers from the crowd. Each time a young man stepped forward to join them, there was cheering from the Whigs and derisive hooting from the Tories.

Gabriel searched the faces of the Continentals, looking for his friend Peter Cuppin without success.

"Do your duty," one of the soldiers called to him, "join us."

Gabriel shook his head. If it were up to him, he would have gone with them in an instant. He looked over his shoulder and saw the top floor of his Aunt Charlotte's house, only partially obstructed from where he stood, and felt a sudden rush of indecision. The soldiers in line saw it, and all began to shout.

"Do your duty! Come and help!"

Although he believed strongly in liberty for America, "the Glorious Cause," as General Washington called it, his father had taught him that his duty was to his family. Gabriel wondered if his duty would ever allow him to leave Fresh Water Plantation. Did it mean he couldn't join the war? How long would he allow his father to make his decisions for him? With these questions on his mind and the soldiers' shouting in his ears, he turned and walked away.

He went to the Liberty pole he'd seen the Patriots erecting that afternoon and was alarmed to see a number of British officials laying unconscious on the ground with ropes around their necks. When he came closer, he saw they were only effigies, skillfully constructed scarecrows, dressed in English costumes to resemble Lord Dunsmire, Lord General Cornwallis, Governor Lyttelton, and other detested officials. A group of Patriot men were entertaining the crowd with humorous speeches that were peppered with the coarsest language Gabriel had ever heard spoken in a public place. Still the people roared with laughter, especially when the speakers made rough jokes of a sexual nature about King George and his various cronies. Gabriel quickly had his fill of their humor and moved off in a new direction.

He stopped where a small crowd was listening to a one-legged man in an old-fashioned powdered wig. Gabriel recognized the man instantly. It was Mr. Peter Howard, who lived less than ten miles from Fresh Water, in the town of Pembroke. About fifty years old, Howard had a soft, fleshy face lined with delicate wrinkles. Like Benjamin Martin, he was an elected representative to the Provincial Assembly, and the speech he was making left little doubt as to which way he would vote when the body assembled the next day. Balancing his weight on his crutch, he illustrated his points with large, dramatic gestures.

"I lost most of my hearing," he declaimed, pointing to his ear, "while fighting for the Crown in the French and the Indian War. And how does King George reward me? By turning a deaf ear to my pleas that our colony have a voice in the Parliament!" He paused dramatically, as if speaking to an assembly of children. "I lost this leg defending the King's interests in that same war, and how does he repay me? He cuts off my other leg with his taxes!" His hand cut through the air like a scythe.

Gabriel couldn't help but smile at the man's oddly formal style. As he did so, he looked across the crowd and saw a luminous young lady staring back at him. She was about fifteen years old, with smooth white skin that glowed like marble in the light of the torches. She had a high, noble forehead, a graceful figure, and sharp, intelligent features. It took him a moment to realize that she was staring at him in anger. The fierce expression on her face made it clear that, in her opinion, the gentleman speaker had said nothing that warranted a silly grin. Chastened, Gabriel reached up and wiped the smile off his face with the back of his hand, then asked with his eyes if his new expression met with her approval. She nodded that it did, then turned her attention back to the speech. But Gabriel continued to watch her, quickly falling in love with the way she held her scarf against her shoulders, the way she responded to the ideas the old gentleman put forth, and every subtle expression that flashed across her beautiful face. Each time she smiled, Gabriel thought lightning had flashed through the sky. He was sure he had never seen a creature quite as lovely as she.

But then it occurred to him that perhaps he had. He narrowed his eyes and studied her face, which began to look familiar. She caught him staring at her and flashed him a wickedly sharp look in return. The moment she wrinkled her nose, Gabriel recognized her as Mr. Howard's daughter, Anne.

It seemed impossible. The last time he'd seen her, she was a skinny little duckling with wild hair and perpetually skinned-up knees. How could she have transformed so completely to become the woman he saw before him? He recalled with a cringe the last time they'd seen one another. He'd gone into Pembroke with his mother, who left him in the care of the Howards while she attended to some business. Plain little Anne, then about eleven years old, told Gabriel that she loved him, and he had repaid her affections by playing a cruel joke—one he could only hope she'd forgotten. Gathering his courage, he moved through the crowd until he was at her side, then pretended to notice her for the first time.

"Ah, Miss Howard, isn't it?"

Without turning, she said icily, "You know very well who I am, Gabriel Martin. The last time you saw me I was eleven and you put ink in my tea."

Apparently, she hadn't forgotten.

Gabriel straightened himself and spoke with adult dignity. "I believe that was one of my younger brothers. Perhaps Samuel or Nathan."

"It was you," she said. "And it turned my teeth black for a month."

"I was . . . perhaps it . . . I never meant . . ." After stammering like a fool for a moment, he recovered enough to say, "Your father is a fine speaker."

Though she was still angry about his prank, Anne smiled at him more than once, and each time she did,

Gabriel felt a shock of excitement go through him. For the next several minutes, he stood and gawked at her, admiring her soft shoulders and the bright perfection of her eyes. He was still looking at her as Mr. Howard finished his speech and led his family away. As Gabriel watched them go, he was already thinking of all the errands that might require him to visit Pembroke that summer.

In all the dizzying excitement of the square, he'd lost track of time. Realizing that his hour of liberty had expired, he hurried back toward Tradd Street. He stopped on the way to look around him and take one last drink of the intoxicating atmosphere. When he did, he noticed that something was missing. There was not a single English soldier or police constable anywhere in sight. The great throng of people milling through the square had no authority to govern their actions, but seemed to be doing a pretty fine job of governing themselves. He decided that if the loud, rowdy, opinionated, free-wheeling mob around him was any indication of what democracy might look like in the colonies, it was definitely something worth fighting for.

"Look! Here comes Gabriel," Nathan called out.

When the others saw him in the street below, they called his name and waved. Martin noted with satisfaction that his son was more or less on time. Gabriel waved back as he came through the gate and into the house. The Martin clan had gathered on the topmost balcony of Charlotte's house to watch the action in the street.

Directly across Tradd Street, another crowd was hoisting effigies of their own up the sides of the Society Club building. Like the others, the mannequins were dressed to resemble unpopular representatives of British rule. Soon after they were set aflame, men standing below them reached up and beat them with sticks, knocking the stuffing out of them. The Martin children stared at the scene in a mixture of fear and fascination.

"What happened? What did you see?" Thomas demanded when his brother joined them on the balcony.

"I'm sorry if I'm late," he said to his father. "I was listening to Mr. Howard. He made a very fine speech in the square."

"Old Mr. Howard from Pembroke?" Nathan asked.

"The same. His wife and his daughter were with him. I hadn't seen her in a long while."

Thomas and Nathan didn't care to hear about Mr. Howard, who lived near them. They wanted to know about the soldiers they'd seen marching past and whether the English would attack soon.

"Father," Gabriel said, "General Burwell is here recruiting. Governor Lyttelton has vowed that if the Assembly votes a single shilling to the Continental Army, he'll dissolve the body."

"If he did so," Charlotte asked, "wouldn't that force John and Edward Rutledge, our delegates in Philadelphia, to vote for independence?"

Martin nodded. "Yes, and send us to war alongside Massachusetts."

The boys greeted the possibility with an enthusiasm their father did not share.

Across the street, the crowd cheered wildly when muskets were turned upward and began firing into the burning effigies. As the shooting erupted, Martin's boys all leaned over the balcony rail for a better view, but their father quickly pulled them away.

"Inside, all of you," he said.

The older boys moaned in disappointment. They

wanted to stay and watch, but Gabriel took over the task of moving them into the house. He shepherded them to the doorway, but before stepping through it, he paused to look back at where his father was standing with his aunt and smiled knowingly at them.

Martin stared down at the wildness in the street until he felt the persistence of Charlotte's gaze on the side of his face. When he turned to look at her, he couldn't help noticing the smooth bare skin of her arms and throat. Uncomfortable with his feelings, he scrambled to change the subject.

"Are you warm enough?" he asked awkwardly. "Would you like a shawl?"

"I'm fine," she said. "It's quite warm enough."

"Well, yes. Yes, I . . . it is warm, isn't it?"

"From what I hear," she said, "the Patriot side has a clear majority for tomorrow's vote in the Assembly."

Martin nodded. "I believe that's correct."

"General Burwell will be counting on your vote. He'll likely expect you to be the first man to enlist."

"Yes, I imagine so." He sighed, wondering how he could possibly balance all of his conflicting responsibilities. There was no easy answer. His duties to his children, to his farm, and to the approaching war required different things of him.

From inside the house came the sound of a herd of little feet running down a hallway, followed by the sound of something heavy hitting the floor with a thud. Martin shook his head and apologized for his "tribe of heathens."

Charlotte laughed at the remark but then became serious.

"When John was alive," she said with a sad smile, "we dreamed of having children as fine as they. You're a wonderful father to them, Benjamin, but they have long needed a woman in their lives, a mother, especially Susan." Her voice and the vulnerability in her eyes made it plain she was asking to be that woman.

Martin swallowed hard. Charlotte was a beautiful, intelligent woman whom he cared for deeply. Often, as he lay in his lonely bed, he had imagined how sweet it would be to have her there in his arms. For many reasons, coupling with her seemed the only natural thing to do. It was a possibility that always lurked in the corners of the room when they were together, something both of them wanted but couldn't ask for. Until that moment, it had gone unspoken. As he looked at her, he had to admire the courage it had taken to finally bring up the subject. She had a strength of character that reminded him powerfully of her sister.

"Charlotte," he said as tenderly as possible, "I'm not ready for this."

"I know." Though wounded, she forced herself to smile. Leaning forward, she kissed him softly on the cheek before going into the house.

3

On the morning of the meeting, Martin rose early, took a light breakfast, then sequestered himself in the library to reflect. Nathan and Samuel went to the door and strained to hear as their father paced the floor, muttering to himself. It was their only chance to hear the speech he would deliver that day, a ringing and unforgettable denunciation of the British. They knew their father had been making a close study of a revolutionary pamphlet called "Common Sense" published in January of that year.

Soon after the bells of the city's churches tolled ten o'clock, Martin finally showed himself and came out into the garden, where Charlotte, Thomas, and Gabriel were waiting to escort him to the meeting.

It was the fashion among assemblymen to dress themselves simply and somberly to reflect the gravity of their business together. Martin came down the steps in a black coat and black trousers with a white cravat tied around his throat above the white ruffles of his shirt.

Charlotte praised him on his appearance, but it was she who deserved the compliments. She wore a finely tailored yellow dress that was perfect for the occasion. Snug in the torso and loose at the sleeves, it was formal and pretty but in no way pretentious. Her hat was a stiff circle of lace that seemed to float atop her strawberry-blond hair.

Thomas wore a dignified jacket and tie that made him look like a junior member of the Assembly, but Gabriel had on the same jacket he'd worn during the previous day's ride through the country. It was dusty and a bit frayed at the edges, but it had the great advantage of being blue—the color of the Patriot cause—and he wished to leave no doubts about where his loyalties lie.

It was the most exhilarating morning of Gabriel's young life, and there was a bounce in his step as the family went into the street and started toward the Assembly Hall. He was fairly certain the Assembly would vote that day to break its bonds with the mother country and join the rebellion of the northern colonies. It was an historic moment, the birth of a new nation, and he felt the monumental privilege of being present to witness it. He threw his shoulders back and looked passersby squarely in the eyes without regard for their social class or skin color, already practicing for the egalitarian form of government that would soon be established. Several of the gentlemen they passed along the way recognized Benjamin Martin and tipped their hats to him. Each time it happened, Gabriel and Thomas exchanged a look, proud to be walking with their father, who had always taught them to be vigilant about their own freedom, and respectful of the freedom of others.

They heard the roar of voices coming from the square long before they turned the corner and saw the Assembly Hall. Hundreds of people had gathered along the iron fence that surrounded the building's courtyard, all of them, it seemed, talking at once. The presence of Burwell's Continental Army added immeasurably to the excitement. The soldiers stood at their posts, rigidly erect and holding their long muskets to their shoulders, as civilians clamored to inspect them.

The entrance to the grounds was through the covered archway of a gatehouse. Martin led the way past the soldiers guarding the entrance and started up the path to the meeting chamber. An energetic mob of finely dressed, well-educated people stood three deep on either side of the path, leaving barely enough room for the Assem-bly-men and their guests to pass. They held copies of the hated Stamp Act and waved them in the air, shouting words of encouragement to the Patriot representatives and words of anger at the Tories. Martin ignored them and strode steadily ahead.

The architecture of the building was an expression of South Carolina's emerging power. Three stories tall, it featured a set of massive stone columns and a working mechanical clock on the face of a triangular pediment. Near the foot of the stone staircase, the Continental Army had set up a recruiting table. Thomas turned to the soldier who was there and saluted.

"Sir, I'll be reporting for duty immediately following today's vote." He meant it only as a joke, but the soldier took him at his word and said he'd be welcome. Somewhat alarmed, the boy quickly followed his family toward the entrance.

Just outside the doors to the meeting chamber, Martin stopped to greet a pair of his fellow assemblymen, Mr. Simms and Mr. Wilkins, neither of whom appeared to be in very good spirits.

James Wilkins was well known to the Martins. He owned a large, very profitable plantation in Berkeley County about two hours' ride from Fresh Water, but had been raised in Charles Town, where his family attended the same church as the Putnams. He was a tall, handsome man with enormously broad shoulders and a snobbish, superior attitude. Being a slaveowner and a leader of the conservative Tory party made him Martin's enemy on most issues that came before the Assembly. Still, the two of them held a grudging respect for one another and shook hands as cordially as they could manage. Mr. Simms, also a Tory, was a heavyset merchant residing in Beaufort. Like many of the older assemblymen, he wore a stiff, powdered wig on his head. As Martin introduced the man to his sons, Gabriel noted the man's thick double chin and realized Simms was the same man he'd heard speaking near the Exchange the night before.

"Father," Gabriel said as they stepped away, "those men are Loyalists, Tories."

Martin ignored the comment and led the way inside.

The shouting inside the meeting chamber was deafening. It was a large room with slender pillars supporting the weight of the ceiling, and large oil portraits of the most recent Royal Governors. It smelled of wool clothing, candle wax, and perspiration. Forty elected representatives and three times that number of spectators had crowded inside. They were the wealthiest and most powerful people in the colony, and all of them were keenly interested in the question to be decided that day. The outnumbered Tories had gathered on one side of the aisle while the Patriots of the Whig party went to the opposite side.

The Speaker sat in a high-backed chair on a raised platform at the head of the aisle, flanked by his two Chief Secretaries. He pounded his gavel and shouted for order, but the arguments continued to rage. After leading Charlotte and his sons to chairs in the visitors' gallery, Martin found a place on the Patriot side of the aisle. He sat down between Francis Salvador, the first Jew to win elected office in North America, and Colonel William Moultrie. Moultrie was not an assemblyman, but was directly responsible for the city's military defense. He was a slow and deliberate man who parted his thinning hair on the right so that a curling lock swept down over his left eye.

As Gabriel surveyed the dignified madness of the room, he spotted Mr. Howard. His large stiff wig shook as he jabbed a finger in the air and added his voice to the storm of noise. Behind him, sitting beside her mother, was Anne. When she turned her bright eyes toward him and smiled, Gabriel felt himself go a bit dizzy with excitement.

"Order! Gentlemen of the Assembly! Order!" bellowed the Speaker, pounding his gavel repeatedly until, at length, the representatives began to settle into their seats. When he could be heard, the Speaker announced that the English, led by Admiral Sir Peter Parker and General Clinton, had landed within the last fortnight at Wilmington, North Carolina, with a force of fifty warships. The news brought more shouting from the Assemblymen and more pounding of the Speaker's gavel. "The issue before us today is the question of whether South Carolina shall levy a tax in support of a standing army. Our first order of business—"

"And our last, if we vote a levy!" interrupted Mr. Simms.

"Order! Order! Mr. Simms, you do not have the floor. Our first order of business is an address by our distinguished visitor from Virginia, Colonel Henry Burwell of the Continental Army. You have the floor, Colonel."

Burwell, a lanky six feet tall, lifted himself slowly from his chair and moved into the center aisle at a very deliberate pace. He had a naturally commanding presence that was accentuated by his military uniform. Like Martin, he was in his early forties and wore his long hair tied back in a tail. He inspected the room with a pair of soft, expressive eyes that were buried in a rock-hard face etched with worry. By the time he reached the center of the room, everything had fallen silent except for the sound of his boots on the floorboards.

"You all know why I am here," he began quietly, folding

his hands behind his back. "I am not an orator, and I would not try to convince you of the worthiness of our cause. I am a soldier, and we are at war. From Philadelphia, we expect a declaration of independence soon. Eight of the thirteen colonies have levied money in support of a Continental Army. I ask that South Carolina be the ninth."

"Colonel Burwell," said Mr. Simms, rising, "Massachusetts and Virginia may be at war, but South Carolina is not."

"Hear, hear!" agreed his fellow Loyalists.

One-legged Mr. Howard and several others shot to their feet and shouted angry rebuttals across the room. Burwell quieted them with a scarcely perceptible gesture.

"Gentlemen," he said, "this is not a war for the independence of one or two colonies, but for the independence of one nation."

Mr. Wilkins cleared his throat. "And what nation is that?"

"An American nation!" cried Mr. Howard.

"There is no such nation," Wilkins spat back, adding with a hint of threat, "and to speak of one is treason."

Mr. Howard was ready with his answer, but paused when he realized he did not have the floor. "Colonel Burwell, with your permission?"

Burwell granted it with a squint of his eyes.

"We are citizens of an American nation!" Mr. Howard began.

"We are Englishmen!" Wilkins yelled, slapping a pair of gloves across the palm of his hand. His fellow Tories loudly agreed.

Mr. Howard went on. "And our *rights* as citizens of an American nation are being threatened by a tyrant three thousand miles away!"

"Would you tell me, please, Mister Howard," Martin

interrupted, rising to his feet, "why should I trade one tyrant, three thousand miles away, for three thousand tyrants one mile away?" Thomas and Gabriel exchanged concerned looks as the Loyalists and many of the spectators broke into sudden peals of laughter at this amusing turn of phrase. But Martin was making a serious point. "An elected legislature can trample a man's rights just as easily as a King can."

"Captain Martin," Burwell said, unhappily surprised, "I understood you to be a Patriot."

"If you mean by a Patriot, am I angry about taxation without representation in the Parliament? Well, yes, I am. Should the American colonies govern themselves independently? I believe they can and I believe they should. If that makes me a Patriot, then I'm a Patriot." Then his voice became grave. "But if you're asking me whether I am willing to go to war with England, the answer is most definitely no. I have been to war and I have no desire to do so again."

His friends among the Whig party were stunned and disappointed by his words. One of them, Mr. Middleton, rose and spoke bitterly. "This from the same Captain Benjamin Martin whose fury was so famous during the Wilderness Campaign?"

It was a personal attack, but Martin answered it calmly. "I was intemperate in my youth. My departed wife, God rest her soul, dampened that intemperance with the mantle of responsibility."

"Temperance," Middleton snarled, "can be a convenient disguise for fear."

Colonel Burwell glowered at Middleton. "Assemblyman, I fought alongside Captain Martin under Washington during the French and Indian War. His bravery is beyond question. There is not a man in this room, or anywhere on this continent, for that matter, to whom I would more willingly trust my life." Middleton backed down at once under the intensity of Burwell's gaze.

"I stand corrected," he said, then quickly reoccupied his chair.

"But there are alternatives to war," Martin continued. "We take our case to the King. We *plead* before him, we *beg*, if necessary. If he will not listen, we appeal to William Pitt and the others in the Parliament who are sympathetic to our cause. If they cannot help us, we seek judicial redress."

"Yes, we've tried all that," Burwell reminded him.

"Then we try again! And again and again, in order to avoid a war."

"Benjamin," said Burwell, coming forward and speaking to him as if they were alone in the room, "I was in Boston last year at Bunker Hill. The British advanced on us three separate times and we killed over seven hundred of them at point-blank range and still they took the ground. That is the measure of their resolve. We have moved beyond negotiation and conciliation. If your principles dictate independence, then war is the only way. It has come to that." The Patriots murmured their agreement.

Gabriel and Thomas leaned forward and held their breath, hoping their father would see the logic in Burwell's words. Martin stayed quiet for a moment. He knew his words were disappointing to his sons and his colleagues, but felt the need to say more. When he spoke again, his voice had softened.

"I have seven children. My wife is dead. Who's to care for them if I go to war?"

Gabriel cringed, ashamed by his father's show of weakness. The assemblymen shifted uneasily in their chairs, unaccustomed to hearing words of such a personal nature spoken in the chamber. Burwell, who was married but had no children of his own, was stunned by Martin's words, but only for a moment.

"Wars are not fought only by childless men," he pointed out.

"Very well," Martin said, "but mark my words." He knew how the vote on the levy would go, but felt compelled to speak his piece. "This war won't be like the last one. It will be fought, not on the frontier nor on distant battlefields, but in our own backyards. Our children will learn of it from their own eyes, and the innocent will die with the rest of us." He searched the faces around him with a mournful expression. "I will not fight. And because I won't, I will not cast a vote that will send others to fight in my stead." Feeling weak, Martin turned and started back toward his seat.

"And your principles?" Burwell asked.

"I'm a parent," Martin told him. "I don't have the luxury of principles."

Burwell looked at him with more sympathy than disappointment, but Martin's fellow legislators were appalled. They began muttering to themselves, quietly at first, but then louder and louder. In a moment or two, another full-blown shouting match had erupted, and almost no one noticed when Gabriel stood suddenly and hurried from the room in red-faced humiliation.

The argument raged on for thirty minutes before the Speaker could regain control and submit the matter to a vote. Soon after, the doors of the chamber pushed outward and a page boy ran onto the landing overlooking the crowd in the courtyard. He cupped his hands to his mouth and shouted.

"Twenty-eight to twelve, the levy passed!"

"Huzzah!" A roar of approval went up and quickly spread from the courtyard to the surrounding streets. Cheering men raised their pistols and fired into the sky. Jubilant women threw themselves into the arms of equally jubilant men, and copies of the Stamp Act were tossed high in the air. The captain of the Continentals ordered his fife-and-drum corps to play a marching song and in less than a minute, fifty young men had crowded up to the recruitment table.

Wilkins and Simms were the first two assemblymen to exit. Disgusted by the celebration, they marched angrily away from the building. The other delegates began pouring out a moment later and the crowd cheered again when Peter Howard, hobbling out on his crutches, raised a victorious fist in the air. When Martin came through the door, his fellow legislators, Whigs and Tories alike, gave him a wide berth.

He spotted Gabriel where he feared he would, among the crowd of men at the recruiting table. Leaving Charlotte and Thomas to wait for him, he strode across the courtyard.

"Do you intend to enlist without my permission?" he asked.

"Yes, I do," answered the young man in a clipped tone. He kept his eyes straight ahead of him for a moment, but then turned with a pained expression on his face. "Father, I thought you were a man of principle."

Stung by the remark, Martin nearly lashed back. He wanted to explain that he was a man of exactly *seven* principles—Gabriel being one and his six siblings the others—and that he lived every moment of his life in service to them. But he could see that Gabriel's mind was made up and wouldn't be changed by a speech.

"When you have a family of your own, perhaps you'll understand."

Gabriel looked him coldly in the eye. "When I have a family of my own, I won't hide behind them." He pushed deeper into the jostling crowd, leaving Martin standing by himself. Harry Burwell was standing nearby, listening.

"He's as imprudent as his father was at his age," said the colonel, coming to stand at Martin's side. Martin nodded.

"Regrettably so."

"I'll see to it that he serves under me. I'll make him a clerk or a quartermaster, something of that sort."

"Good luck," Martin said, managing a thin smile. The two men shook hands, and after a last look at his son, Martin turned and walked away, leading Charlotte and Thomas through the courtyard.

As they snaked through the crowd, there was a commotion. The people around them turned their heads toward the rooftop of the Assembly Hall. A trio of daring, acrobatic men had climbed onto the cupola dome and lowered the South Carolina flag. In its place, they raised a white banner that showed a black rattlesnake coiled between the words of a Patriot slogan, DON'T TREAD ON ME.

Pistols and clenched fists were raised in the air. The colonists were ready for a fight if the English wanted one.

For the next six weeks, the British armada under the command of Sir Peter Parker moved closer to Charles Town while Colonel Moultrie continued to fortify his position at the mouth of the harbor. His "fort" consisted primarily of sand and palmetto logs stacked up high enough to hide his cannons. When Burwell went out to Sullivan's Island and toured the site, he called it a slaughter pen and made plans to have Moultrie replaced. But there was no time. On June 29th, a stiflingly hot day, the mighty British navy swept into Charles Town Harbor. Thousands gathered on the wharves, climbed church steeples, and hung from the windows of tall buildings to watch the engagement. What they saw was an awesome spectacle.

The first ship in position was the bomb ketch *Thunder*. Her cannons opened up and met with only a feeble reply from Moultrie and his defenders. Soon the *Active*, a twenty-eight-gun frigate, came up less than half a musket shot from the fort. Then the fifty-gun *Bristol*, and the fifty-gun *Experiment*, and the twenty-eight gun *Solebay*. General Burwell, no stranger to hard-fought battles, called it "the most furious fire I ever heard or saw." Smoke blanketed the water, and the shelling continued all day and deep into the evening, not ceasing until half past nine. During the long night that followed, Charles Town braced itself for the devastating attack certain to come the next day. But when morning broke, they saw that Moultrie's fort still stood and the British warship *Actaeon* was heeled over, run aground on a sandbar. The British had misjudged the depth of the harbor. Unable to float their ship, they set fire to her that morning and retreated. The victory had been an accidental one, but the spirits of the Patriots soared and recruitment doubled.

Private Gabriel Martin was on duty during the victory. He spent the entire time guarding the intersection of two insignificant roads a safe distance from the city. When Burwell marched his troops north to support General Washington, he took Gabriel with him.

4

It was a sunny day when Gabriel's letter arrived at Fresh Water. It was addressed to Thomas, and he read it a dozen times before sharing it with his brothers and sisters. He gathered them on the porch where they pored over it word by word. By that point, their brother had been away for almost two years.

When their father passed by on his way from his workshop to the house, Thomas invited him to read the letter. Although Benjamin desperately missed his son and was anxious for news of him, he said he would wait until after supper. Determined to set an example, he returned to the barn and worked there until Abigale called them inside to eat. Before the meal was served, however, he found the letter and could resist no longer. He excused himself and escaped down to the little yard around the oak tree, where he read by the last light of the day.

My dear brother Thomas,
It was with great sadness that I learned of the fall of Charles Town. As you must know, the British arrived with a great force of warships, determined not to fail a second time. They laid siege to the city for eleven days, keeping up a constant bombardment. It distresses me considerably to spend another winter away from you and to imagine the hated Union Jack flying over the Assembly Hall. I know of these things from several reports we have had here in the camp and through a letter I received some days back from Aunt Charlotte. She has closed up the house on Tradd Street and moved to her plantation on the Santee. I pray

she will be safe there, but the Redcoats have spread themselves across South Carolina, establishing a series of strongholds.

Their strategy is to secure South Carolina and Georgia, then to advance north, gathering Tory militia to fight with them until they meet Washington. This plan, we are told, comes directly from that tyrant, King George III, who follows the war in every detail. His Excellency General Washington is much concerned that this plan will succeed, especially now that Charles Town has fallen and the five thousand Patriots there have been made prisoners.

Here in the North, our campaign has been marked by defeat and privation. We are presently encamped for the winter and suffering bitterly, as we lack nearly every comfort. Our tents and clothing are worn, providing little shelter from the snow. Instead of good food and meat, we are fed nothing but firecakes and water. Washington has appealed to the Congress for monies and supplies and each day we pray they will arrive. Each day that they do not, we suffer more desertions. The 400 men we have here from Massachusetts plan to march home on New Year's Day when their enlistment term is expired. They are the most quarrelsome and undisciplined group of soldiers imaginable, but they make up a large part of our force, and their departure will leave the rest of us to wonder how we will manage once spring brings a resumption of hostilities. All the while, the British are comfortably settled in at Morristown. They have money that allows them to buy livestock and supplies from the farmers in the countryside, many of whom are eager to profit from the situation.

Still, our troops show a resilient spirit, finding occasions for laughter even under these difficult circumstances. Our dedication to the cause sustains us, while the Redcoats fight only for money. We have musical instruments and several fine players among us. When they play at night, my mind drifts back to happier days spent with you at Fresh Water.

Our losses during the last months have been grievous. My good friend, Peter Cuppin, was one of many who fell during the engagement at Elizabethtown. Though we stood side by side, he was cut down while I left the field without injury. His death has been difficult for me to bear. It was several days before I could compose an acceptable letter to his family in Orangeburg.

News of Charles Town's fall has compounded our misery, opening a new front against us. I have a better situation than many of the men here, General Burwell sees to that. I often bring his dispatches to other camps and sometimes go out to forage for provisions. Of late, there is talk that our company, Burwell's men, will march south with General Gates to check the north-ward advance of the Redcoats under Cornwallis. I think there is some truth to these rumors and I am hopeful that I may see all of you soon.

Dear Thomas, I hope you no longer burn with the desire for battle you once did. War is not what we imagined it would be. I envy you your youth and your distance from this cruel conflict of which I am a part. Still, I consider myself fortunate to be serv-ing the cause of American Liberty and, though I fear death, each day in prayer I reaffirm my willingness, if necessary, to give my life in its service. Pray for me, but above all, pray for our cause.

Please share the contents of this letter with our family. Offer them my greetings and tell them they are never far from my thoughts.

> *Your loving brother,*
> *Gabriel*

Martin folded the letter and put it in his pocket. He was relieved to learn that Gabriel was alive, and thankful for the way the letter had closed, warning Thomas of the hor-rors of war. Hardly a day now passed without his second-oldest son letting it be known he considered himself of soldiering age. Martin was wounded, however, to see there was no message in the letter for him and guessed that Gabriel was still disappointed and angry.

He leaned against the oak and looked up through its thick branches to the North Star. It had been more than a year since he'd set foot off of Fresh Water plantation. He knew, of course, about the British landing and fanning out across the colony. He read the broadsheets, wrote and received frequent letters, and listened to the news Abigale brought back from her visits to Wakefield, Pembroke, and other nearby towns. He knew there was no organized opposition to the powerful British army, only isolated pockets of resistance. Those who took up arms were quickly captured and executed, usually by hanging in the public squares.

Martin worried about Gabriel every day. He wished he could go up North and bring the boy back with him, hogtied if necessary, but tried to find comfort in the fact that Burwell seemed to be keeping his promise to look after the young man. He had hoped his son would tire of fighting and return to him after his term of enlistment expired. The letter made it clear that he intended to continue fighting until the war had been either won or lost.

As for Charlotte, Martin had sent food and other provisions to her place on the Santee with the promise of more to come, but did not dare to deliver them personally. Given his reputation, he knew what might happen to him if he were intercepted by a band of Tory sympathizers. He was doing everything he could to keep the war away from his farm and family. The North Star was the first to appear in the evening sky. Martin looked up and asked Elizabeth to help him if she could, then said good night and started back toward the house with a heavy heart.

• • •

His parents' room had remained unchanged for as long as Thomas could remember. As elsewhere in the house, all of the furniture had been made by his father, from the heavy-timbered bed frame to his mother's delicate dressing table. The signs of his mother's presence were stronger here than in the rest of the house. Her perfume bottles, hairbrushes, and other personal effects were arranged almost exactly as she had left them. Next to the chest of drawers, there was a tall mirror that swiveled on hinges, and hanging over the windows was a set of expensive lace curtains sent from Aunt Prudence in Rhode Island many years before. There was a brick fireplace and, hanging above it, a silk-on-silk needlepoint tapestry that showed Adam and Eve standing in the Garden of Eden, wearing only the outfits God had given them. It was the most valuable object in the entire house, not only because of its cost but because of the senti-mental meaning it held for Martin. To him, it was the very picture of his life with Elizabeth at Fresh Water.

When Thomas slipped into the room carrying a sconce with four candles, he went directly to the side of the bed, knelt down, and looked underneath the mattress, which was suspended on a web of ropes. There was a wooden storage trunk there, made especially to fit the narrow space, that bore his father's mark: "B Martin S Carolina." He pulled it out, then went across the room and climbed onto a chair, reaching up to the high place where the key was hidden. He unlocked the trunk and lifted the lid.

Inside was a trove of his father's old military gear and tro-phies. There was a buckskin jacket, a scrimshaw powder horn carved from whalebone, an assortment of knives and metal buttons, a pair of pistols with gold filigree, and about two dozen rings, some of them with French words inscribed along the insides of the bands. Thomas slipped his arms into a moth-eaten British battle coat and went to the mirror to inspect himself. Three sizes too large, the cuffs hung down past his fingertips. He went back to the box and picked up one of the strangest items of all—a Cherokee tomahawk with a wooden handle worn smooth by long use. He held it threateningly in the air and struck a menacing pose in the mirror, rehearsing the savage look he planned to give the Redcoats he would attack. He was not as handsome as his older brother, but he thought his long and angular face gave him the look of a noble young commander. He cupped his hand to his ear and practiced listening to a report from a trusted lieutenant, nodding thoughtfully.

"What are you doing?" Martin asked from the doorway.

Thomas backed away from the mirror, certain he was in for a tongue-lashing or worse. The tomahawk trembled in his hands as his father stalked into the room, but Martin seemed more sad than angry. He took the hatchet away and told the boy to turn around, then helped him out of the coat.

"Not yet, boy." He laid the coat on the bed.

"When?" Thomas asked. "When can I join?"

Martin looked him over carefully, sizing him up. Thomas felt like a new recruit standing before a commanding officer and stood at attention in an attempt to look soldierly. But Martin was using the moment to calculate how much longer he could keep Thomas at home and out of harm's way.

"Seventeen." It was a first and final offer.

"Seventeen?" the boy complained. "But that's two years away. It's already been two years. The war could be over by then."

"God willing."

Thomas thought it over and reluctantly agreed. "Fine, then, seventeen."

"Now put those things back where you found them," Martin said, "and give me the key."

Thomas fished it out of his pocket and turned it over. When he did so, Martin noticed he was wearing one of the French rings. He slipped it off the boy's finger and tossed it into the trunk, then started toward the door.

"Father, what happened at Fort Wilderness?" The question stopped Martin dead in his tracks. He paused, turning in the shadowy doorway, and looked back.

"Put it away," he said.

Less than a month later, the war paid its first visit to Fresh Water Plantation. It was barely dawn on a chilly morning and a patchy mist was creeping across the ground. A flock of sparrows had gathered around Elizabeth Martin's grave to feed on what the tree had dropped that night when a sudden sound, low and rolling, came through the trees and scared the birds away.

Within seconds, the front door of the house opened and Benjamin Martin stepped outside, pulling a shirt over his head. He came down the steps and stood barefooted in the yard, his head cocked slightly to one side, listening. It was a sound he recognized all too well—the booming report of cannon shot. Between the rumbling explosions he could hear the pattering crackle of musket fire. Bright flashes of burning gunpowder were visible in the distance.

"Father, what is it?" Margaret asked, coming to join him. Martin put an arm around her without answering. One by one, the rest of the children wandered outside and quietly gathered around him.

"Is it going to rain?" William asked.

"That's not thunder," Nathan said.

The ominous noises continued, sending vibrations through the ground and air. Susan, the last child awake, was so frightened by the shaking in the house that she came running out the door and leapt into her father's arms, burying her face in his chest.

"That's the sound of cannons, isn't it?" Thomas asked.

"Six-pounders," Martin said, "and many of them." Thomas nodded as if he were familiar with the weapons. Soon an idea came to him and he slipped away from the others, heading back into the house. Down toward the river, the freedmen came out of their cabins and stood in their yards listening to the worrisome sounds.

"Are they shooting at us, Father?"

"No, son."

"How close are they, Father?"

Martin stared upriver, in the direction of the shooting. "Four, maybe five miles." The battle was too far away to cause an immediate panic, but too close for the family to remain calm.

"We could go stay with Aunt Charlotte at her plantation," Margaret suggested quickly.

"No," Martin said firmly. "There will be skirmishes on the roads. We'll be safer to stay here." Thomas came from the house carrying three hunting rifles. He handed one to Nathan and offered another to his father.

"Thomas," said his father, "put them away."

"But they might come this way."

"Put them away." He kept his voice calm so as not to alarm them. "We'll all stay close to the house today. You're not to go further than shouting range. Is that clear?"

The children promised to obey.

The guns soon fell quiet, but not before setting everyone's nerves on edge. When the freedmen came up the hill to speak with him, Martin suspended the day's work in the fields and advised them not to wander out onto the roads. He spent the morning pacing the porch until he decided his idleness was driving him to distraction and that the only cure for it was work. He harnessed a horse to a plow and began cutting furrows for a new corn crop.

As he worked, the sun pressed down hot. Flies buzzed, and the July bugs droned in the trees. The children spent the morning inside, reading and playing quiet games, and Abigale tried to keep them occupied with tasks and treats. But Samuel and Nathan were children who could not survive a day without making some mischief. After lunch, they sneaked out to the barn and began teasing an old horse named Virgil. When the animal had had enough of them, he stormed out into the corral and kicked open the gate. The sound of cracking wood was audible for a mile in all directions. Abigale heard it and rushed to the porch.

"Samuel! Nathan!" she shouted, but the boys were already out of earshot, chasing Virgil through a field of young tobacco. The horse paid them back with some teasing of his own. He stood perfectly still as they approached and tried to take hold of the rope harness tied around his head, then bolted away before they could grab it. He ran circles around them until stopping to invite a new attempt. Abigale could see what the horse was doing.

"Margaret, go after those boys and bring them back here."

Margaret, glad for the chance to leave the house, went after them.

Martin paused and leaned against his plow to watch the pursuit. He knew the children, working together, would soon round up Virgil, and on a normal day, he would have let them do it by themselves. But it was not a normal day.

"Behave yourself!" he told Socrates, the horse helping him plow the field, as he started to walk away. After only a few steps, he doubled back, reached into the saddlebag on Socrates's back, and pulled out a loaded pistol, tucking it into his waistband before setting off again.

"Stop running," Samuel yelled. "Come here, boy!"

Virgil knew the farm as well as any human. From the tobacco field, he trotted toward the riverbank for a game of hide-and-seek among the cedars. But when he came to the water's edge, he stopped frolicking and began to neigh, kicking the air with his forelock. He made no attempt to run when the children came to the spot.

"Virgil!" Martin shouted at the horse. "What's the matter with him?" he called to the children, but none of them answered. In fact, none of them moved. They stood as still as statues, hypnotized by what they saw in the river.

The water was running a pale shade of pink and, in places, blood red as bodies floated past. First, a pair of uniformed soldiers, one Redcoat and one Bluecoat, moved by, their limbs tangled together as if they were still fighting. Blood oozed from their wounds and mingled together in the lazy current.

Next came a tall, skinny fellow in a dark suit of clothes. He could have been a civilian on his way to church except for the blue sash across his chest that identified him as a Patriot militiaman and the fact that one of his arms was missing.

A Redcoat soldier floated peacefully on his back. His long black hair had come untied, and it twisted around his half-submerged face like a nest of sinewy water snakes. He had a clean bullet hole the size of a Spanish dollar coin in his forehead that left a red string of blood in the water.

Everything was quiet. No birds sang in the trees. Martin came to the bank and stood behind his children, watching the gruesome procession for a moment before breaking the spell that had come over them.

"Back up to the house," he said gently.

It pained him to have his children witness this bloody scene. He had known the moment would come and had tried to warn the men of the Assembly that it would. Now that it was here, he felt the sting of failure for not having protected them better. At the same time, he knew the die had been cast and that there was little he, or anyone else, could do to stop the chain of events that had already been set into motion.

For the next two days, they waited.

Martin spent the time pacing the porch like a ship's captain monitoring a threatening sea. War, he knew from experience, was as unpredictable as a sea squall. When it appeared on the horizon, it might move off in another direction without causing any harm. But there was an equal chance that it would descend and tear everything to pieces. Many of the freedmen he employed came up to the house to discuss the situation and what they ought to do. They had heard reports of slaves found traveling the roads without their masters being pressed against their wills into military service, usually by the British but also sometimes by groups of American militia. The freedmen, Martin said, would be in danger if they stayed at Fresh Water but equally in jeopardy if they chose to leave. He advised them to stay but reminded them they were free to choose for themselves. When Ezra, a man who had been with Martin for several years, decided he would risk the journey up to

Virginia, Martin didn't stand in his way. He paid the man cash to settle their accounts, wished him good luck, and gave him a pair of goats to add to his personal flock. As soon as he was gone, Martin returned to pacing the porch, wishing he knew the best way to keep his children safe and cursing himself for not having the answer. Should he load them into the wagons and run? Send them away with Abigale? Take them to Charlotte's place farther down the Santee? Hide them in the woods?

Again and again, he looked into the sky and consulted with the North Star, but received no guidance he could understand. He kept the wagons loaded with food, blankets, and other provisions in case the need arose to make a quick evacuation.

Late in the afternoon, the cannons roared again, this time from a new direction. They seemed a little farther off this time, offering at least the meager hope that the battle was drifting away from Fresh Water. Several of the freedmen climbed high into the cedar trees along the river for a better view of the flashing lights on the distant battlefield. The roar of the six-pounder cannons kept up until darkness fell and it was nearly ten o'clock before Abigale called the family in for a late-night snack.

Nathan came from the barn with a bucket of warm milk and poured each person a cup. The children sat at the table, the cannons still echoing in their ears, and talked quietly. Abigale made a great show of fussing in her normal way around the kitchen, talking gaily about small matters and pretending it was an ordinary evening. Martin sat at the head of the table eating quietly until excusing himself and stepping outside to check the view from the porch.

Samuel turned to watch him go. "They're going to come."

"Quiet," Margaret said, "and eat your food."

Nathan looked around the table with a grim expression. "We're going to have to fight them off."

"Won't Father do that?" said William.

Nathan poked at his food with a fork. "They'll probably kill us men, then do Lord knows what to you women."

"Nathan!" said a flustered Abigale, "that's enough."

Susan, sitting quietly in her usual place, stopped listening to the conversation and turned toward a sound the others hadn't heard. Thomas followed her gaze and, though he saw nothing out of the ordinary, raised a hand over the table and called for quiet.

"What is it?"

"Listen," he said.

One of the floorboards on the porch groaned and they heard the front door open.

"It's only Father," whispered Margaret, even though it didn't sound like him.

Dragging footsteps came into the hallway, moving closer to the kitchen. Abigale picked up the nearest heavy object, a cast-iron skillet, and stationed herself near the door.

"Mr. Martin, is that you?"

A man's voice muttered something unintelligible from the other side of the half-closed door. Abigale motioned the children away from the table and slowly opened the door, letting the light from the kitchen spill into the hallway. Her heart began pounding like a kettle drum when she saw the silhouette of a ragged intruder. He was leaning, half-collapsed, against the wall and holding a musket in one hand. There was the sharp click of a firing pin being cocked and a second later, Benjamin Martin came up behind the man, pointing a rifle at the back of his head. He had every intention of using the weapon until he recognized the man in the hallway.

It was Gabriel.

He wore the blue jacket and white pants of a soldier in the Continental Army. There was a leather case slung over his shoulder and his uniform was stained with blood. When he turned around to face his father, he tried to speak, but his legs melted beneath him and he went down with a crash.

Martin carried him into the sitting room and laid him on the day bed. When candles were brought in, he saw that the young man had been through a painful ordeal, a fight of some sort, and then had made his escape through the forest. His boots and trousers were muddy, his face was scratched and bruised, and there were pine needles in his hair. He unbuttoned Gabriel's jacket and found a deep gash across his ribs and stomach where he'd been cut with a bayonet or large knife.

"Abigale, quickly!" he shouted, "get bandages and water. The rest of you, upstairs."

The children backed out of the way, but stayed close enough to watch.

Gabriel's eyes opened and focused slowly on his father's face. "Have you seen any Redcoats?"

"No," Martin said. "Not yet."

"Gabriel," Thomas said. "We heard a battle. Were you there?"

He nodded and closed his eyes. "It was a disaster. General Gates marched us straight at the Redcoats. Our lines broke and the Green Dragoons rode in and cut us to bits."

"Try not to talk," Martin said as Abigale arrived with a basin of water and some clean linens, but Gabriel went on.

"I was given these dispatches to deliver. As I left, I saw the Virginia Regulars surrender to the Redcoat infantry. They were stacking up their arms when the Dragoons rode into the spot and killed them all, over two hundred men."

"They had surrendered," Martin said. Gabriel nodded his head and grimaced in pain when he tried to force himself up into a sitting position.

"I have to go. I have to get these dispatches to Hillsboro."

Martin held him down. "You're in no condition to ride."

"I can't stay here," he said, "it's not safe for you. I must get to Hillsboro." He struggled weakly against his father's strong hands for a moment, but eventually subsided into the comfort of the bed and lapsed into sleep. Martin cleaned out the wound and wrapped bandages around Gabriel's middle. As he was finishing the job, gunfire erupted outside. A volley of about twenty shots, close to the house.

"Stay away from the windows," Martin said calmly. He grabbed his rifle and headed out the door, closing it behind him. It was a dark night, nearly pitch-black. He heard the horses neighing frantically in the barn, and farther off, down toward the main gate, the sounds of men shouting and running across the fields.

Then came a fresh round of shooting. Each powder flash lit up a new part of the night, allowing Martin to see that one hundred or so Redcoats were squared off against an equal number of Patriots. The battle was raging in a freshly planted field less than a hundred yards from where he stood. Each time the firing paused, the screams of the injured pierced the night, adding to the sounds of the chaotic battle. Sergeants shouted orders to their men, ramrods clattered against gun barrels, and footsteps ran from place to place. The battle lasted more than half an hour until one side—Martin couldn't tell which—chased the other one down the road and away from the house. The moaning of the injured went on for some time, but eventually the night became quiet once more—the only noises were the rustling of the trees and the distant lapping of the river. It wasn't until an hour had passed with no sign of danger that he stepped inside for a moment to check on the children. He brought a blanket outside and spent the night sitting in a chair with his rifle across his lap.

The next morning, Fresh Water Plantation was transformed into a military field hospital. Just after dawn, Martin went with Thomas and a few of the freedmen into the fields where the skirmish had taken place and found bodies everywhere on the ground. None of them were prepared for what they saw. Muskets were not particularly accurate weapons, but when they found their marks, they did a tremendous amount of damage. The dead were horribly disfigured, and blood was sprayed across the leaves of the crops. But as the men of Fresh Water waded through the carnage, what they found most disturbing was the tender age of the combatants. Many of them, especially on the Patriot side, were Thomas's age or younger.

The corpses and stray limbs were carried away and stacked in a pile near the property-line fence. The wounded survivors were put in wagons and taken up to the house for medical attention. The less seriously injured were left in the yard, while the more severe cases were brought onto the porch—Redcoats to the right, Patriots to the left.

Martin, thrust into the role of chief physician, moved from soldier to soldier without regard for the color of their uniforms and ministered to them the best he knew how. He quickly exhausted the supplies he kept on hand. When the bandages were gone, he asked his daughters to begin cutting up the family's spare bedsheets. When his store of tinctures was used up, he broke open his reserve of fine Irish whiskey and poured it on the wounds to sterilize them. Abigale and the other African women helped tend to the wounded, while Joshua and Abner searched the surrounding area for survivors and brought them in. The children also brought food and water to the soldiers and did whatever small chores were asked of them.

Martin's experience during the last war had given him a rough knowledge of medicine, but he was ill-equipped to deal with many of the wounds. There was an unconscious Patriot who had been shot in the kneecap. After examining him, Martin guessed the safest thing was to cut off the mangled remains of the leg and sent Thomas to the barn for a saw. One of the Redcoats, a giant of a man with only two teeth in his head, had been shot in his private parts, and though he continued to lose copious amounts of blood, he was too modest to allow himself to be examined. It took Thomas and eight men to hold him down while Martin extracted the bullet with a pair of tongs. One of the young Continentals had an eye gouged out on a sharp branch while trying to escape through the forest. He screamed horribly when alcohol was poured into the empty socket to cleanse it. The noise he made woke Gabriel, who was inside, still stretched out on the day bed in the sitting room.

He was groggy and disoriented as he stirred, but when he tried to sit up, the sharp stab of pain in his stomach instantly cleared the cobwebs from his head. He looked down and saw that he was naked. His body had been washed, head to toe, while he'd been sleeping, and there were clean bandages wrapped around his torso. His clothing, freshly washed, was hung up to dry over the fireplace.

He came outside buttoning his shirt and surveyed the bustling scene on the porch. Bloody rags, buckets of water, and muskets were scattered everywhere. Some of the wounded were propped up against the porch rails, while others lay flat on their backs, staring up at the porch ceiling, painted aqua blue to ward off demon spirits.

He had been standing there less than a minute when he noticed movement on the horizon. Steel bayonets were coming through the bushes and trees along the property line, glinting in the morning sun. Twenty-five Redcoats and a handful of Cherokee braves climbed over the fence and started across a corn field. A similar group emerged from the peach orchard on the opposite side of the road. The presence of the Cherokee told Gabriel that these were probably scouting parties protecting the flanks of a larger force. And soon enough, he saw that he was right. Three hundred British troops and several horse-drawn wagons rounded the last bend and marched toward the house.

Their commanding officer stayed a safe distance from the house until it was surrounded, but then came across the yard and up the steps without an escort of guards. He made an impressive sight in his lieutenant's uniform. He wore a tall bearskin hat, a stiff red jacket with crossing white sashes over his chest, and clean white gaiters buttoned over his shins. Gold epaulettes on his shoulder and gold fringe decorated his cocked, tricorn hat. He moved slowly, making a careful study of the scene. He turned down the "English side" of the porch, inspecting each person he passed. Gabriel held his breath when it was his turn to be examined. The lieutenant looked him over calmly with a pair of hard, bright eyes, noted his behavior, and moved on. He said not a word to anyone until he was standing face to face with Benjamin Martin.

"This is your farm, sir?" he asked in a surprising voice. It was soft and distinctly feminine, very much at odds with the powerful look of his uniform.

"It is," answered Martin, wiping the blood from his hands with a rag.

"Thank you, sir," the lieutenant said softly, "for the care of His Majesty's soldiers."

Martin knew he had to choose his words carefully. Under the rules of war, neutrality could only be maintained if care were given to an equal number of wounded from both sides. If the lieutenant chose to do so, he could count the number of soldiers on either side of the house and, if the Patriots outnumbered their Redcoat counterparts, he could arrest Martin as a rebel sympathizer.

"I have tried to help any and all who needed my assistance."

"So I see," said the lieutenant. "I noticed a fair number of men from the opposite camp on the other side of the house." After a moment, he added, "They appeared to be few in number."

Martin breathed easier for a moment, but only for a moment.

A menacing rumble began to shake the earth, growing louder by the second. Horses' hooves beat the ground like the skin of a drum. Everyone turned toward the road and watched as a large group of British cavalry galloped into view.

"Green Dragoons," Thomas whispered, recognizing them by their uniforms and riding caps.

In crisp formation, they thundered toward the house, leaving an enormous dust cloud in their wake. The Dragoons were the finest light cavalry in the world and, man for man, the most lethal fighting force in history. They made an impressive sight and struck fear into the hearts of everyone present that morning—including the soft-spoken British lieutenant.

"God help us," he muttered as he hurried away to meet them.

The Dragoons fanned out to surround the place without once breaking stride. Their leader and a dozen of his men trotted their horses straight into the yard and stopped near the front stairs. The lieutenant approached them to offer his reconnaissance report, but before he could say a single word, he was told to shut up and stand aside.

The commanding officer was a young aristocrat, Colonel William Tavington, who was about thirty years old and athletically built. His uniform was decorated with gold braids, and he wore a tall bearskin riding cap. Everything about him seemed to radiate power and control. He stayed on his horse, towering above the scene, and studied the situation through a pair of cold blue eyes. Without consulting anyone, he decided Fresh Water's fate in a mere ten seconds.

"Lieutenant, have a detachment take our wounded to the surgeons at Winnsboro. Use whatever horses and wagons you can find here."

"Yes, sir."

By this time Martin had come to the front of the house and stood at the top of the stairs, his children surrounding him like iron shavings on a magnet. He studied the faces of the Dragoons, all the while remembering the fate of the Virginia Regulars. Colonel Tavington noticed him and called out.

"You there, are you a doctor?"

Martin shook his head.

That wasn't good enough for Tavington. "I asked a question, and I advise you to answer it."

"I'm not a doctor," Martin said, gesturing toward the porch. "These men fought here last night and I thought it was my duty to offer them care."

Tavington turned to the half-dozen Dragoons behind him and said something to make them laugh. Then he called out to the infantrymen.

"Fire the house and barns," he told them. Raising an arm above his head, he made an official proclamation for all to hear. "Let it be known: Those who harbor the King's enemies will lose their homes."

The Dragoons nodded and said amen.

"What?" The Martin children looked at one another in disbelief.

"He can't do that," Thomas said. "Father, do something."

The soldiers broke open their packs and began to prepare their torches.

"Father, do something," Nathan and Samuel urged.

Martin wanted very badly to react, but stayed where he was. There was nothing he could do. Losing the house would be a catastrophe of the worst magnitude, but he controlled himself and remained steady. All seven of his children were within sight and as long as they were safe, he told himself, nothing else mattered.

Tavington took note of the Africans helping to tend the wounded and made a second announcement. Again, he lifted his arm and shouted in the same official style. "Let it be known: By standing order of his Majesty, King George, all slaves of the American colonies who fight for the crown shall be granted their freedom with our victory. Lieutenant, take them with you to Winnsboro. Enlist the younger ones and find some good use for the rest."

"Yes, sir."

Joshua, wearing a rag tied around his head, came sheepishly toward the colonel's horse. "We're not slaves, we're freedmen."

Tavington looked down at him, annoyed and amused at

the same moment. "How nice for you. In that case, you're *freedmen* who will have the opportunity to serve in the King's army."

Abigale beseeched Martin with her eyes. She had been at Fresh Water since the very beginning, and the thought of being taken away by these strange men terrified her. The whole world they'd built for themselves was unraveling at nightmare speed, and a moment later, the situation went from bad to worse. A Redcoat came out of the house carrying Gabriel's satchel.

"Rebel dispatches, sir."

To Martin's horror, he saw that his son had retrieved his blue uniform jacket and was putting it on.

Tavington opened the case at once and tore into the letters one after another. As he suspected, they were from General Gates's army, part of which he had already destroyed. He hoped the letters would contain information about the colonials' plans, which, in fact, they did. But as Tavington scanned through them, he saw nothing more interesting than letters from the enlisted men to their sweethearts and families. He didn't realize that Gates and his staff had written their messages in invisible ink, a mixture of ferrous sulfate and water, between the lines of the innocent letters. If he had heated the pages over a flame, Tavington could have learned every detail of the Continental plan.

"Who carried this?" he demanded.

When no one answered, the cold fury that was always just below Tavington's surface erupted. "WHO CARRIED THIS?" he screamed.

"I did, sir," Gabriel stepped forward. "I was wounded. These people gave me care. They have nothing to do with the dispatches."

"Seize him," Tavington ordered. He handed the dispatch case down to the lieutenant of the infantry as evidence. "Take that man to Camden. He's a spy. He will be hanged and his body put on display."

"Yes, sir."

Martin could tolerate losing the house, but not one of his children. At first he tried to believe it was only a misunderstanding. When a pair of burly Redcoats took hold of Gabriel and started to take him across the yard, Martin stepped into the path and stopped them. Then he turned urgently to Tavington.

"Colonel, he's a dispatch rider and that's a marked dispatch case."

"Take the horses, kill the rest of the livestock," Tavington said to the lieutenant, ignoring the farmer.

Martin strode directly to the feet of Tavington's mount and looked up at him. "A uniformed dispatch rider," he explained sharply, "with a marked case can*not* be held for spying!"

The colonel spoke to Martin as he might speak to a child, enunciating carefully to help him understand. "We're not going to *hold* him, we're going to *hang* him."

"But you know as well as I—" Martin began to lose his temper.

Gabriel saw what was happening. "Father, don't!"

"Oh, I see!" Tavington said. "He's your son." He looked at both of them, noting the family resemblance, then leaned forward in the saddle and clicked his tongue like a displeased schoolmaster. "You really should have taught him something about loyalty."

Martin felt the rage flare inside of him. He was close enough to put his hands on Tavington's throat, but steadied himself and tried again. "Colonel, I beg you," he said quietly, almost choking on the words, "I beg you to reconsider. By the rules of war, a uniformed dispatch rider with a marked case—"

With his horse shifting below him, Tavington drew his pistol and took careful aim at the bridge of Martin's nose. "Would you like a lesson, sir, in the rules of war?" Martin stared at the gun without flinching. Instinctively, Tavington began searching for his weak spot and found it almost instantly. He shifted his aim toward the front steps of the house. "Or perhaps your children would." Terrified, they squealed and ducked away from the weapon, all except Thomas, who stood his ground and glared. Martin ran toward the steps and spread his arms to protect them.

"No lesson will be necessary," he said.

Tavington lowered the pistol, and the Redcoats pulled Gabriel away to the far side of the yard.

The soft-spoken lieutenant cleared his throat. "Excuse me, sir, what of the Rebel wounded?"

Tavington squinted in the direction of the battered Patriots and made another quick decision. "Kill them."

The lieutenant's head snapped back, shocked by the order. He was not alone. The Redcoat infantrymen exchanged alarmed glances, and even the mounted Dragoons behind Tavington murmured in surprise.

"Do it quickly," Tavington advised, "or they'll put up a fight."

"Yes, sir," the man said meekly.

Martin, hopelessly outnumbered, could only stand and watch the horrific scene unfold around him. The soldiers sparked their torches, then went off toward the farm's wooden structures. Gabriel's hands were bound and the end of the rope was tied to a wagon. Farther away, the freedmen were being forced out of their cabins at the point of British bayonets. All the while, Tavington sat on his horse, chatting easily with his men and issuing instructions as they occurred to him. Martin kept his mind focused on only one goal—to keep the children safe until the Dragoons were gone. He sensed Thomas growing more agitated by the moment beside him.

"Father, do something," the boy demanded.

"Quiet," Martin ordered, gesturing with his hand for the boy to stay the course.

Thomas tried to rein himself in, but failed. He took his father's inaction as a sign of weakness and decided he wouldn't allow the Redcoats to take Gabriel, not without a fight. He gauged the distance between Gabriel and the cover of the nearest trees, then, without warning, pushed past his father and broke into a dead sprint. He aimed himself like a cannonball at the men holding Gabriel and his trajectory took him past Tavington, still holding his pistol. Gathering speed, he lowered his shoulder and battered into one of the burly Redcoats, blindsiding him and knocking him to the ground.

"Run!" he yelled. "Gabriel, run!"

But Gabriel didn't run. Tied and surrounded as he was, he knew escape was impossible. He appreciated Thomas's attempt, but realized it was futile.

As the cursing Redcoat and Thomas both lifted themselves off the ground, Tavington took aim and fired. The shot hit Thomas in the back, squarely between the shoulders, and knocked him forward to his knees. With a bewildered expression, he looked up at his brother and then down at the massive exit wound in his chest. Slowly, he toppled forward and fell face first on the ground.

"NO!" Martin tore across the yard with his children following hard on his heels. They threw themselves on the ground and clustered protectively around the fallen boy. He looked up at them, blinking and confused, unsure of what was happening to him. He moved his lips to speak, but no sound would come.

"Oh, Thomas, please!" Margaret wailed.

Martin cradled the boy in his arms and whispered words of encouragement. "You did well, Thomas. That's my man, you did very well." He could feel the boy dying, his energy slipping away. The bullet had torn a hole the size of a man's fist through his chest, and his blood was pooling quickly on the hard-packed earth. Half in shock and half in agony, Martin looked up at Tavington, his face twisted in pain.

The colonel sat on his horse, obscured by the wisp of lingering smoke from his gun. He showed no remorse for the killing, because he felt none. Maybe the boy had got what he deserved and maybe shooting him had been too harsh a punishment for a moment of poor judgment. In either case, Tavington didn't care. The killing of a colonist meant nothing to him, and he had already moved on to the next order of business.

Martin felt a powerful anger boil up inside him, an all-consuming fury the likes of which he had not felt since the Wilderness Campaign twenty years before. He laid Thomas down and stalked toward Tavington, intending to rip him apart with his bare hands. He didn't get far before dozens of pistols and muskets were raised and pointed at him from every direction. He stopped short, flaming with hatred, and realized he would die if he took another step.

Tavington made a show of putting his pistol away and folding his hands calmly across his lap, inviting an attack. Then he leaned forward in his saddle and studied Martin's anguished face as if he were examining an angry hornet trapped under a glass.

Martin kept his feet planted where they were as Tavington's horse shifted under him, bringing him closer and farther away. Margaret sensed that her father was only waiting for an opportunity and called to him in the same firm voice her mother had often used. When Martin heard it, he slowly backed away.

"Stupid boy," Tavington said. He glanced once more at where Thomas had fallen before turning his horse and riding out of the yard. His Dragoons filed in behind him and thundered away down the road, disappearing in another column of dust.

Glass shattered as Redcoats began breaking open the house's windows and lobbing their torches inside. From the barns came the sounds of gunshots and the squealing of the livestock. Then more gunshots came from the side of the house as the executions began. The Patriot wounded shouted and tried to run when they realized what fate lay ahead of them, but by that point it was too late, and the Redcoats had slaughtered all of them in a minute or two.

Gabriel struggled against his captors, but when the wagon began to roll and pulled the rope taut, his choices were to cooperate or be dragged across the ground. He walked away with a detachment of twenty soldiers. Soon flames were climbing the sides of the house and began to lick out of the interior through the broken windows.

Stunned and helpless, Martin returned to Thomas and held him once more. Abigale stood behind him, comforting the other children until the lieutenant of the infantry arrived with a handful of soldiers. They showed the points of their bayonets to Joshua and Abner, who were standing nearby. The other freedmen were already marching away in a group, half a mile down the road.

"Take these Africans," said the officer, "and catch them up to the others."

"I am not leaving these children," Abigale declared.

Abner held his hands in the air to show he would cooperate and hissed at his daughter to do likewise.

"No, Father! They can shoot me, but I'm not leaving."

The Redcoats leveled their guns at her, perfectly willing to oblige. Still, she stood her ground. She had no children of her own and had never married. Along with Abner, this was her family.

"Abigale," Martin said, "go." It was both an order and a plea. He understood what the children meant to her, and he promised her with a look that he would do everything humanly possible to keep them safe until she could see them again. With tears rolling down her cheeks, she let herself be led away.

A few minutes later, less than an hour after his arrival, the soft-spoken lieutenant left with the last of his men. It had been an ugly beginning to the day and he was anxious to leave Fresh Water behind him as quickly as possible. He led his men away at a brisk march, hurrying to catch up with the main body of his troops.

5

Tears streamed down Nathan's face as he watched the detachment of soldiers lead Gabriel away and disappear around a bend in the road. "Father, you can't let them take him."

"Quiet," Martin ordered him. He remained motionless, continuing to hold Thomas's body in his arms until the last of the Redcoats were out of view. Then he flew into action.

"Don't move," he said to the children, "stay exactly as you are." He stood and ran toward the burning house.

"Father, don't! It's too late."

The fire had been well set. The house was burning front to back, inside and out. Everything Martin had worked so hard to build—the precisely turned balusters of the porch rail, the flawless box beam ceilings, the hand-made furniture— all of it was burning. The house was his masterpiece, the three-pound rocking chair of rural homes. Martin realized it was already lost, but he needed to get in and out one last time. The main entrance was fully engulfed, impassable. He sprinted around to the kitchen entrance, kicked open the door, and crashed through the flames without hesitation.

The children did as they'd been told and remained where they were standing, staring fearfully at the house. The flames roared out the windows and spread along the underside of the broad blue porch ceiling. Black smoke began leaking from the attic windows. Each moment their father stayed inside was a torment to the children, who began to fear something had happened to him.

"We've got to go help him," Nathan said.

"What if he dies, too?" William asked.

Martin stumbled outside a moment later, gasping for breath, his eyes teary and bloodshot from the smoke. He was carrying guns. There were four rifles, three pistols, a supply of balls and powder, and, protruding from his waistband, the handle of a Cherokee tomahawk. With a fierce look on his face, he turned in the direction the soldiers had gone with Gabriel. He spoke abruptly, as he would to troops in action.

"Margaret, if we're not back by dawn, take William and Susan to your Aunt Charlotte's place." He tossed a rifle to Nathan and another to Samuel.

"I don't know how to get there," Margaret protested urgently.

He pointed southeast as he turned to leave. "Santee River. You'll find it."

Tears rolled down Margaret's cheeks. "What about Thomas?"

"Leave him." He broke into a run and shouted over his shoulder. "Nathan! Samuel!"

The boys hesitated for a moment, reluctant to leave the younger ones behind, but soon obeyed the command and ran off after their father.

Margaret called after them, begging not to be left behind, but the men crossed the fields and disappeared from view. She turned to William and Susan, both of them more frightened than she, and took them under her arms. They watched the house burn for a few minutes until she decided it would be safer to go and hide along the river.

Martin crashed through the low brush and leapt over fallen logs, moving as fast as he could. He was already short of breath and there was still a long way left to go. He could hear the boys behind him, keeping up. He plowed straight ahead, weaving around trees and ducking under branches, keeping up a punishing pace. He was no longer as agile as he had been years before, but he was still strong and made up in cold fury what he lacked in youth. There was a trail not far to the north, but it wasn't the most direct route to where Martin needed to go, so he took the harder path. Nathan and Samuel, more accustomed to running long distances, weren't nearly as winded as their father, but they struggled with the rifles, which were as long as they were tall.

The boys knew the area close to Fresh Water almost as well as their father did, well enough to realize they were moving roughly parallel with the road toward Camden. There was a glen ahead of them and they didn't want to think about what might happen once they got there. They put their heads down and concentrated on their running.

In time, Martin slowed the pace and began to move quietly around fallen branches and piles of leaves. He ran the same way he did while hunting deer, choosing each step quickly and carefully. He led the boys down into the glen and came to the road well ahead of the British.

It was a place where trees and tall brush grew especially dense, fed by the creek that ran nearby. Beads of sweat rolled down Martin's face and dripped from his chin. He pulled one of the pistols from his waistband and set it in a hiding place in the bushes, then did the same with the two others. He led the boys to a place on the slope where they hid themselves behind the trunk of a fallen tree.

"Nathan, there," he said, pointing. "Samuel, there."

The boys put themselves in position.

"Now, pay attention. We'll kill the officers first and work our way down. Do you know how to tell the difference?"

The boys nodded. "Good. Wait for me to fire. Then, Nathan, you kill the officer closest to Gabriel. And Samuel, you look for an officer at the back of the line." The boys' mouths dropped open under the weight of the order. Samuel made a small whimpering sound, but Martin pressed on.

"After that first round, Samuel, you load for Nathan. Now, if something happens to me, you put down your weapons and run as fast as you can. Make your way back to the house and take the others to Aunt Charlotte's. You know which direction she lives?"

They both pointed southeast.

"Good. Now, what have I taught you boys about shooting?"

"Aim small, miss small," they recited in unison.

"That's right. Aim small, miss small." He turned to go, but had one last thought for them. "And boys . . . steady."

Martin turned and moved downhill, wading into the underbrush until he disappeared completely. For the next several minutes, they waited. The singing of the birds and the quiet lapping of the creek suddenly seemed to take on a sinister quality, as if they were part of the deadly trap. Eventually, they heard the squeak and groan of the wagon wheels rounding the bend.

With trembling hands, the boys peered out of the trees and inspected the Redcoats coming into view. They were normal-looking men except for their impressive uniforms and long guns with bayonets affixed. They walked along in a relaxed way, talking amongst themselves, completely unaware of the danger that lay ahead.

"I count twenty of them," Nathan whispered.

"Too many," Samuel whispered back.

They saw Gabriel near the rear of the march, his hands

leashed to the wagon. They took aim at a pair of officers and waited for their father to begin.

Martin, hidden behind a tree only a few feet above the road, forced himself to be patient. He waited until the lead wagon had rolled well past him before edging into the open and taking careful aim at the only man on horseback, a captain.

He fired and hit the man in the head, killing him before he fell off his horse. The sound of the explosion ripped through the trees in a disorienting echo. As the soldiers looked around in confusion, Martin was already reloading. Nathan and Samuel quickly killed the only other officers, one of them only a few feet from Gabriel.

The Redcoats flew into a panic. Shouting to one another, they raised their guns and pointed in all directions, searching for the source of the attack. As the horses screamed and bucked, a sergeant stepped up to assume command.

"Form by twos!" he shouted, but neither he nor his men were certain which direction to face. "Back-to-back lines for—" Martin fired again and his bullet pierced the sergeant's throat before he could finish the command.

"There he is!" screamed the one of the men, pointing at the smoke from Martin's gun. Some of them fired at once, while others ran along the road for a better angle. They took aim at the spot.

"Ready! Take aim!" shouted a Redcoat.

Martin fired again, this time from a new location, killing another man with a shot through the heart. The victim staggered backwards off the road and fell into the muddy creek bed. The Redcoats fired immediately into the fresh rifle smoke, but Martin dove out of the way and rolled across the ground to safety.

From that point on, he never stopped moving. Instead of running, he took quick, long strides and stayed just inside the brush line, moving closer to and then farther from the road to offer the Redcoats occasional glimpses of himself. He changed his pace and direction frequently, ducking and weaving, reloading and firing on the move. He never gave them a stationary target, especially one marked by a billow of smoke. It was a tactic he'd learned from the Catawba Indians, and it worked.

"Where is he?"

"Here!"

"No, over there!" The Redcoats hurried to a new spot and tracked Martin as he moved through a stand of young pin oaks. Just as they squeezed back on their triggers, he stopped and reversed his direction. Their shots flew astray and they lost sight of him again. As they hurried to reload, a rustling came from the bushes close to the road. Martin used one of his hidden pistols to kill another man at nearly point-blank range.

With Samuel loading, Nathan continued to fire from his sniper's nest, killing three men and hitting another in the hip. The wounded man crawled into the grass and kept up a constant, horrible screaming. Their brother Gabriel used the confusion to duck under the wagon and begin working on the rope binding his wrists. There was only one Redcoat left guarding him, a brute with hunched shoulders and a flattened nose.

In a matter of moments, nearly half the detachment had lost their lives, but they stayed on the road, exposed. None of them had experienced an attack of this sort. They were too frightened to chase the enemy into the trees and too angry to turn and run.

Moving in the same unpredictable fashion, Martin circled back to another of his waiting pistols. He stepped onto the road not far from the rear wagon, where a Redcoat was reloading his musket. Both Gabriel and the flat-nosed soldier were astonished to see him, especially so near to them. Martin didn't look at them. He shot the reloading soldier in the head, and started back into the foliage. The flat-nosed Redcoat raised his Brown Bess and aimed into the middle of Martin's back. Before he could fire, Gabriel bulled into him, knocking him sideways and sending the shot astray. The angry man, seeing that Gabriel had freed himself, slammed him across the jaw with the stock of his musket, knocking him to the ground. As he began reloading, a bullet grazed the side of his head and bit off a chunk of his ear. Cursing and holding the side of his head, the man looked into the trees and saw the puff of smoke hanging in front of Nathan and Samuel's nest. He whistled through his teeth and pointed a thick finger to the spot.

His fellows understood the signal and took aim. Before they had a chance to fire, however, Martin came out of the trees, making a whooping noise that drew the attention away from his sons. Boldly, he walked down the middle of the road, a pistol in either hand. In quick succession, he killed two more men with close-range shots.

Another pair of Redcoats, seeing that Martin had emptied his guns, rushed at him, one a few strides ahead of the other. Instead of retreating, Martin snatched up a fallen British musket and charged forward. This was not the Benjamin Martin who had dedicated himself to mastering the wildness within him and raising his children on Fresh Water Plantation. It was the savage and brutal Benjamin Martin of the French and Indian War, flaring to life after a long sleep.

The first Redcoat pulled to an abrupt stop and tried to aim his weapon, but he'd misjudged his enemy's speed and dexterity. Martin used the bayonet to slash open the soldier's face, then shattered his chin with the blunt end of the weapon. As the man toppled backwards, Martin pulled the musket out of his hands and fired into the gut of the second charging Redcoat.

With a demented cry, another soldier rushed forward with his bayonet lowered. Before he could attack, his head was snapped to the side by one of Nathan's bullets.

"Over here, farmer," called the flat-nosed man.

Martin turned and saw that the man had a long knife pressed against Gabriel's throat, holding him like a human shield. Without hesitation, he began marching in that direction, drawing the Cherokee tomahawk from his belt. Two of the last Redcoats stood in his path, neither of them reloaded. As Martin approached, they prepared to defend themselves with their bayonets.

Martin batted one of the blades aside, but felt the other stab into his shoulder. Lightning-fast, he hacked one man in the chest and the other across the neck. Both of them were dead and Martin had hardly broken stride. He continued relentlessly toward the man holding Gabriel.

But he stopped when the flat-nosed brute pressed the blade hard against Gabriel's throat. He threatened to do worse unless Martin dropped his weapon. They stared at one another about ten paces apart, but only for a brief moment.

Martin raised the hatchet to his shoulder and threw it with a quick, smooth motion. The blade flashed through the air, brushed past Gabriel's head, and buried itself in the Redcoat's forehead. He dropped his knife, staggered backwards, and slumped to the ground with a stunned expression permanently frozen on his face.

That left just one Redcoat standing on his feet, an athletic young man with a plump, boyish face. His musket was loaded and primed, but he was too unnerved by what he'd seen to use it. He threw it down on the road and started to run.

By that point, Martin was deep inside his killing frenzy. He pulled his tomahawk out of the dead man's face and chased after the one who was running. When he was close enough, he threw the hatchet again and hit the soldier in the back. Howling in pain, the man veered off the road and stumbled in the waist-high grass. Martin leapt on him, pulling the tomahawk out of him. The soldier rolled onto his back and raised his hands, begging for his life. Martin didn't hear him.

He swung down hard, planting the blade deep in the man's chest, then worked it free and chopped again. Clearly the man was dead, but Martin swung down at him again. And again, and again, and again, hacking the body into a pulp and covering himself completely in blood.

When he was finished, everything was quiet except for the gentle splashing of the water running through the creek and the sound of Nathan and Samuel sobbing behind the trees.

Slowly, like a repetitive sound that eventually penetrates the stronghold of a dream, the sound of his sons' crying caught his attention. Coming slowly out of his trance, he turned to see the boys coming out of the trees. Gabriel stood farther off, clearly stunned by what he'd seen his father do.

As if waking up, Martin surveyed the carnage—the red clay of the earth, the red coats of the soldiers, the puddles of red blood. He drew a quick breath of air into his lungs and realized it was over. He had done what he came to do. Gabriel had been rescued.

Covered in sweat, blood, and mud, he looked at Gabriel and saw the expression of disgust and alarm on the young man's face. He never imagined that his father was capable of the things he'd just seen. And Martin had never imagined that he would show this dark side of himself to his children.

"Get those wagons turned around," he said quietly. "We can use them."

The boys silently complied, while Martin stepped over and around the dead to go wash himself in the creek.

Somewhere in the scatter of bodies, a pair of eyelids fluttered open. A disoriented Redcoat private looked out through blood-clogged slits at the aftermath of the nightmare. As he lay there, an apparition appeared to him, moving through the lingering smoke of the muskets. It took the shape of a muddy, blood-soaked man silhouetted from behind by the bright sun. It was a ghostlike figure carrying a Cherokee tomahawk, and it was moving directly toward him. Before it arrived at the spot where he had fallen, the disoriented soldier blacked out.

The sky had gone slate gray and cloudy by late afternoon when they returned to Fresh Water in the British wagons. The place was almost unrecognizable. Both barns had burned to the ground and collapsed. The house was still standing, but it was only a charred and smoking skeleton, a framework of blackened beams under the gloomy sky. The crops in the fields had been trampled during the engagement of the previous night, and the entire place was eerily silent. No field hands were there to wave and shout a greeting; no animals were fussing for attention in their pens. Even the crows that usually flocked to the cedar trees along the river were absent.

Martin drove the lead wagon while Gabriel and the boys followed in the other. They found Margaret near the house tending to her withdrawn younger siblings, William and Susan. The family was too devastated to celebrate their reunion.

"We have to leave here as soon as possible," Martin announced. But there was some important business to be done before they could go.

Martin dug the boy a perfectly rectangular grave under the oak tree next to his mother's. The children found a large sheet of cloth in one of the freedmen's cabins to wrap around him. As they were doing so, a number of Thomas's lead soldiers spilled from his pocket. Martin reached down and picked up the little men. He decided at once on a good use for the hand-painted toys and whispered it to the boy as he carried him to his final resting place.

The family assembled inside the picket fence and listened to the breeze move through the branches of the oak as Martin covered Thomas's body with earth. Margaret had collected a few wildflowers, which she shared out to the others. They stepped forward one by one to lay the flowers down and say good-bye. When Martin had pushed a rough cross into the ground to mark the spot, he indicated that it was time to leave.

But the children lingered sadly, expecting their father to say a eulogy. Martin felt there were no words left inside him, but did what he could.

"Lord, we pray that You accept this child, Thomas Martin, and give him a place at Your side with his mother. We ask that You embrace him and help us to understand the manner in which Your mercy works and forgiveth our sins. This we ask in Your name. Amen."

"Amen."

The Martin family filed out of the yard and went directly to the wagons. It was time to leave Fresh Water Plantation, possibly for the last time.

6

Under the command of Lord Cornwallis, the Redcoat army established a massive field encampment near Moncks Corner, a strategically important site that acted as a natural gateway between Charles Town and the upcountry. Laid out on a grid, the camp was a model of European military orderliness. Everything from the distance between tents to the manner in which the cannon balls were stacked for display was done strictly according to procedure. It was a show of England's overwhelming power that was meant to frighten the local population into submission. Cornwallis invited men from the better classes of society to come and tour the place, and once he had them there, used the opportunity to recruit them to the service of the crown. During these occasions, his officers played a crucial role. They circulated among the civilians, making small talk and veiled threats and generally guiding them into the proper frame of mind to enlist.

Colonel Tavington was not asked to attend. Although he was one of Cornwallis's most effective soldiers, he was far from being a diplomat. He was in the bad habit of saying whatever came to mind and made no effort to conceal the simmering contempt he felt for the Americans. During one of these recruiting sessions, Tavington, finding himself with time on his hands, wandered out beyond the perimeter of the camp and walked up a grassy hillside to take in the sunset. Much to his delight, he came upon a swarm of fireflies flitting through the tall grass. He chased one down, cupped it in his hands, and turned with an excited grin to show Bordon, his second-in-command, who stood by, patiently attending his commander.

Colonel William Tavington had grown up in Liverpool, the only son of a semi-aristocratic family. Though extremely close with his mother, he despised his father. In this he was not alone. Garrick Tavington, a petty nobleman who inherited the family's profitable flour mills, was well liked in his youth but grew to become a drunk and a bully. He ruined the family's name and squandered their fortune. Eventually, he lost his son as well.

At twenty-four, the younger Tavington took all the money he had and moved to London, where he cut a dashing figure. He set himself up in a lavish apartment on the Thames River, frequented the most fashionable drinking establishments, and pursued young women with the instincts and tenacity of a hunting dog. When his money was spent, he lived another year on credit and a silver tongue. During this time, he followed the political news coming from America and grew increasingly outraged by the lack of respect and gratitude the colonists showed for the mother country. One evening, he surprised his drinking chums by announcing that he would join the army, sail off to North America, and teach the colonials their proper place. None of them believed he would actually do it, but he did. He scraped together a large sum of money, enough to buy himself an officer's commission, then left London, and his many debts, behind.

Soon after his arrival in America, he discovered his natural talent for warfare. He was fearless, quick to strike, and, most important, showed a knack for winning battles. During the Northern Campaign, General Cornwallis quickly recognized his contributions and promoted him to lead the Green Dragoons, a turn of fortune that only whetted Tavington's appetite for further advancement.

He crushed the firefly between his fingertips and smeared its glowing fluid across his skin. Then he caught another and repeated the operation. There was so much about this new continent that fascinated him.

Tavington loved America. He loved its vast size, the mystery of its haunting forests, the clarity and depths of its rivers. There was spectacular weather, exotic plant life, and a strange mix of people from many nations. It was an untamed continent, full of dangers and opportunities. It was, as he liked to say, as fierce as he was. And although he disliked the colonists, there was one quality of their character that he found absolutely infectious—their belief that almost anything was possible. From the first moment he'd set foot in the New World, he knew he had found a home.

A Redcoat infantryman came up the hill and spoke to Bordon, who then interrupted his commander's experiments.

"Sir, there is news," he called.

"What is it?" Tavington asked testily. "I'm thinking."

"We have that private you wanted. The one the Cherokee scouts brought in."

"Very well, let's have a word with him." He wiped his hand on the grass and followed Bordon to the field hospital.

The surgeon's tent was fifteen paces wide and was lit by an extravagant number of candles. A bright glow came through its fabric walls, bright enough to attract a large number of flying insects. Tavington lifted the curtain and stepped inside, pausing at the entrance until his eyes adjusted to the glare. The tent was well-stocked with supplies—surgical implements, clean linens, ointments, purgatives, and tinctures.

At the center of the room was the lone survivor of the attack in the glen. The man lay motionless in a long basin, a solid slab of wood that had been carved into the shape of a shallow coffin to serve as a catch pan for blood and other fluids. The young, dark-haired man looked as though he might have been handsome before the attack, but it was impossible to say now because of the injuries to his face.

"They don't hold out much hope for him," Bordon reported after a word with one of the doctors.

"I should say not," said Tavington, coming closer to admire the work the attackers had done. The soldier had been shot in the chest just above the heart. The wound, although cleaned and dressed, continued to ooze. The bridge of his nose had been shattered by a blow of some sort, causing a great deal of swelling and discoloration. The bruises formed black-purple rings around his eyes, making him look like a raccoon. The pillow under his head was brownish red, having soaked up a quantity of the blood in the basin. Tavington spoke to him roughly. "Private, wake up. Can you hear me?"

The man's eyes shot open and he made a feeble attempt to sit up. He seemed coherent, but afraid.

"Private, I am Colonel William Tavington of the Green Dragoons. Tell me what happened. Who did this to you?"

The soldier's body went rigid when he remembered the nightmare he'd lived through, and he began to rave. "I don't know! I don't, I, I don't know what it was. It was mad. All in one moment . . . we couldn't see into the trees, then I couldn't . . . it was mad."

Tavington leaned forward and stroked the man's forehead soothingly. "Calm down, calm down. Now, listen to me. Twenty of His Majesty's men are dead. I want you to tell me how it happened."

Bordon came to Tavington's shoulder. "He told the scouts that—"

"Were you there!?" Tavington growled. "Let the man speak!"

Bordon retreated and allowed the colonel to continue the interview.

"Take your time, Private. Concentrate. And now tell me, how many were they? Were they militia or regulars?" The man looked up at him in confusion.

"I can't say for certain. Maybe only one."

"One man!?"

"I saw only one. He was hidden in the brush, then on our flank . . . among us, all around us. I barely could see him. He was there and then he was gone."

"One man?" the colonel repeated. "And then he simply vanished?"

The man nodded earnestly.

"Sounds more like a *ghost* than a man," Tavington said with a smirk.

At the mention of the word, the man on the table gasped, recalling the sight of the muddy, blood-spattered figure moving between him and the sun. "A *ghost*, that's right! He fell on us like a *GHOST!*"

"Enough!" said Tavington. He was not a superstitious man and did not believe in ghosts, but the fear in the private's voice gave the word a chilling power that seemed to hang in the air. The description unsettled Tavington more than he was willing to admit. He tried to dismiss the feeling by making a joke. "Captain Bordon, it seems these rebels have realized the hopelessness of their situation and have begun recruiting the dead to do their fighting for them."

Bordon chuckled dutifully.

On his way to the exit, Tavington continued speaking to his second-in-command. "Take a patrol back to the area and see if you can't track down this *ghost* before word of his exploits has a chance to spread." Then, in the same breath, he asked, "Who's this?"

A stranger stood just inside the entrance dressed in the uniform of a Green Dragoon and holding a riding cap under his arm. He was a few years older and a few inches taller than Tavington, an impressive figure.

"This is Captain Wilkins, sir," Bordon explained, "a leader of the Loyalist militia. He is a well-respected local gentleman who is familiar with the area. I understand he owns a plantation of considerable size not far from here."

Wilkins smiled, expecting the same warm welcome he'd received in other parts of the camp, but Tavington only stared at him sourly, inspecting him from toe to tip.

Bordon, sensing trouble, tried quickly to warn his commander against saying the wrong thing. "Captain Wilkins, sir, was a member of the Provincial Assembly before that body was disbanded and he has been sent to us by Lord Cornwallis, who *personally* recruited him based on his fine reputation."

Tavington understood the warning, but wasn't the sort of man to back down. "So you're a colonial, then? Tell me, Captain Wilkinson, exactly where do your loyalties lie?"

"The name is Wilkins," said the man, returning Tavington's hard look, "and my loyalties lie where they always have—squarely with King and country."

"I see. And why should I trust a man who betrays his neighbors, rebels though they may be?"

"Those neighbors of mine who stand against England deserve to die a traitor's death." They were strong words, but Tavington remained unconvinced.

"We shall see." With a quick nod, he indicated that Wilkins had been admitted into his Dragoons. He turned around and gave a last, thoughtful glance at the wounded private before he left.

That night Benjamin Martin and his children stole through the night, driving the captured British wagons along the Santee River. It was nearly midnight when they arrived at Drakespar, the Selton family plantation Charlotte had inherited from her husband. Set in a wealthy area, it had less than half the acreage of Fresh Water, but its gracious manor house was almost twice as large. Surrounded by mature trees, the house contained a music conservatory, a basement kitchen, and marble columns that supported a semicircular upstairs balcony. Though grand in style, there were many minor flaws in its construction. Whenever Martin had come in the past, he'd always brought his tools along with him and stayed busy making small repairs. This time he came with only the clothes on his back and six devastated children. Leaving behind the only life they'd known, they arrived at Drakespar facing an uncertain future.

Matthew, Charlotte's longtime butler, was still awake, sitting around a nearly dead campfire talking with some of the field hands. He greeted the family in his usual formal manner, but quickly softened his tone when he noticed Mr. Martin's bloodstained shirt and saw how badly shaken the children were. He led them into the main house and hurried upstairs to wake his mistress.

Exhausted, Gabriel and the children soon went to bed. Charlotte sat with the girls while they fell asleep, then came downstairs and joined Martin in the parlor. After listening to the children's scattershot description of the day's events, she was anxious to hear Martin's version. He was extremely weary and before telling the story, he asked for a drink. By the time Charlotte returned with it, he was sound asleep. She covered him with a blanket, kissed him on the forehead, and returned to her room.

When the first birds began to sing, she went downstairs and found Martin still in the same chair. He was awake, sitting in front of the fire he'd built and holding a necklace that had once belonged to her sister, a purple ribbon with a medallion that showed the North Star. He was working it between his fingers like a set of Catholic prayer beads. The sun was not up yet and he stared at the inside of the darkened windowpanes, lost in thought. She sat down in a chair facing his.

"Benjamin, what happened yesterday?"

"They killed Thomas," he said in a hoarse whisper, "then they tried to take Gabriel. I stopped them, but the boys had to help me." He grimaced in pain as he remembered. "Last night, putting Samuel to bed, he pulled away from me like I was some sort of monster."

"You've done nothing for which you should be ashamed," Charlotte said.

Martin studied the necklace in his fingers. "I've done nothing," he said with self-loathing, "and for that I am ashamed."

A door squeaked open and Gabriel came in from outside, dressed in his Continental uniform. He looked as if he were making ready to ride away. His father pretended not to notice this and invited him into the parlor, motioning for him to take a seat. Gabriel did so reluctantly, expecting a conflict.

"I've been thinking," Martin said. "I think it's best we try to get to Saint Helena, one of the freed slave islands north of Charles Town."

Gabriel sighed impatiently, realizing his father didn't understand.

"It's the perfect place to hide," Martin said with enthusiasm. "It's right under the British noses. They'll never think to look for us there. In fact, if—"

"Gates and the Continental Army are at Hillsboro," Gabriel interrupted. "I'll be joining up with them."

"What?" Martin raised his voice. "Your place is here now."

"I'm going back. I'm a soldier, it's my duty."

"Your *duty* now is to your family!"

Gabriel threw his haversack over his shoulder, nodded to his Aunt Charlotte, and started toward the door. Martin shot to his feet and followed.

"Don't you walk away from me, boy!" he shouted, loud enough to shake the house.

Gabriel found his musket in a corner beside the door. "I'm sorry, Father. I'll find you when this is all over."

"No! You're *not* going. I *forbid* you to go!"

"I'm not a child!" Gabriel shouted back.

"You're my child!" Martin cried desperately.

There was a dead silence. The two men stood almost toe to toe, looking into one another's eyes. Martin tensed himself in preparation for a scuffle if that became necessary, but Gabriel only shook his head in disappointment. For the first time in his life, he looked at his father with pity. The other children, drawn by the shouting, started coming down the stairs. Martin frightened them by shouting harshly, "Back upstairs, all of you!"

"Good-bye, Father." The decision was final. He slipped through the door. Martin made one last attempt to stop him from going.

"Gabriel," he pleaded, "Thomas is dead. Who else must die before you'll heed my word?"

He didn't intend to blame the boy for his brother's death, but that's how Gabriel heard the words. He stopped suddenly in the middle of the porch, reeling as if he'd been hit with a brick. He had known that troops were concentrating in the area on that night he'd stumbled into Fresh Water, and the thought had occurred to him that he might be putting his family in danger by going to see them. Looking back on it now, the decision seemed selfish and stupid. If he had stayed the course and continued on to Hillsboro, Thomas might still be alive.

Matthew was waiting for him at the bottom of the steps, holding the reins of Gabriel's horse. The young man climbed into the saddle and rode away without a backwards glance. Martin went out onto the porch to watch him go, and continued standing in the same spot long after horse and rider had disappeared from view.

When, at length, he turned back toward the house, Charlotte was standing in the doorway waiting for him.

"I'm losing my family," he said. "I don't know what to do."

She studied him for a moment before slipping her arm under his. Like her level-headed sister, she always seemed to know what the situation called for. "Walk with me," she said.

Martin allowed her to guide him down the steps and into the yard. From there, they took a long stroll along the road that wound through the oak trees. They were gone almost an hour, and when they returned, Martin had come to a decision.

He was going to join the war, and he was going to leave immediately.

The children were going to stay at Drakespar with their Aunt Charlotte while their father went to find Gabriel. Within minutes, he had changed into fresh clothes and was tying his gear to a horse.

"When will you come back?" asked William, clinging to his aunt's skirt.

"I don't know, son."

"Tomorrow?" he asked.

"No, not tomorrow. This is going to take a while. I might not be back for a long time. But I have great confidence in all of you."

He bent to give William a last hug, then did the same with Margaret, whispering some secret words of advice in her ear. She smiled broadly when she heard them and kissed him on the nose.

He bent low and looked Nathan and Samuel in the eyes, man to man. "I'll be needing help from you two," he said quietly. "I want you to take care of the others. Can I count on you boys?"

They nodded solemnly, accepting the responsibility. Nathan offered him a handshake to seal the deal, a gesture Samuel quickly copied.

And finally there was Susan. As usual, she stood apart, looking on in silence. The hem of her dress was still stained with the blood of the soldiers she'd been helping care for the previous day. While the other children sobbed and wiped their noses on their sleeves, Susan tried to hide her feelings, but her big dark eyes gave her away. They were confused and perhaps angry, trying to understand why Martin was abandoning them.

"Good-bye?" he asked, trying to coax a word out of her. "Just give me one word. That's all I want, just one word."

Susan shook her head. She wasn't ready.

Defeated, Martin gave her a kiss and climbed onto his horse. As he galloped away, Susan whispered to him unnoticed and unheard.

"Good-bye."

7

Gabriel walked his horse along a deserted road, keeping watch ahead and behind. He knew he was not far from the town of Camden, but there was a suspicious absence of traffic. On his right, there was a large plantation with tall fields of winter corn. As he approached the main gates, he spotted the first person he'd seen in an hour. A middle-aged white man driving a carriage piled high with belongings hurried away from an opulent manor house. The carriage had been hastily packed and as it turned onto the main road, the wheels dipped into the ditch, throwing a chair and a pair of framed paintings over the side. The driver looked back over his shoulder and kept going.

Curious, Gabriel led his horse cautiously toward the house, a white building two stories tall with bright green shutters. The yard was littered with objects the man couldn't carry: a mattress, a stack of old books, and many items of clothing. The front door was open. Gabriel tied his horse to the porch rail and went inside.

Many of the possessions were gone, and some were scattered on the floor. The cabinet doors were open. The wall over the mantle, stained gray by smoke from the fireplace, had a clean white rectangle in the center of it where a painting had been hanging. But there were no other signs of trouble, no clue as to why the place had been abandoned.

There was a noise on the second floor, the sound of someone moving in a hurry. Gabriel decided to investigate, but the moment he set foot on the bottom stair, the sound of nearby cannon fire shook the house. Objects rattled off the shelves and crashed to the ground. A window in some distant part of the house shattered, and suddenly a shrieking slave woman came running down the stairs holding two bolts of silk fabric in her arms. She screamed all the way down the stairs, brushed past Gabriel, and ran out the front door.

"Wait!" Gabriel called, wanting to question her. But she was gone.

Outside, the terrified woman screamed as she ran down the steps and across the yard, attracting the attention of a man who was galloping along the road. He slowed down when he saw her in the yard and when he did, he noticed something he would otherwise have missed—Gabriel's unattended horse.

Gabriel went up the staircase to the second floor, hoping for a view of the cannons. Even without seeing them, there was no doubt in his mind that they were British. There were too many of them to belong to the Patriot side. He wandered into a large parlor with windows that offered an excellent view of the action.

The Battle of Camden, as it would come to be called, was in full swing only a few hundred yards from the house in an open grain field. In size, it was equal to any engagement Gabriel had seen during his time in the North. More than a thousand Patriots were facing an even greater number of British. A massive slash of red was moving forward to confront a massive slash of blue, each side flying dozens of flags and regimental banners. Gabriel stood in awe of the spectacle for a moment until he slowly became aware of someone standing behind him. He spun around to defend himself and came face to face with his father.

"How did you . . . ?" he began. "I'm not going back."

"I know," said Martin, moving to the window. He studied

the action on the grain field for only a brief moment before shaking his head in disgust. "Damn you, Gates."

Gabriel looked at him.

"He doesn't understand," Martin said. "He's spent too many years in the British Army. A large part of his force is militia, but he's going muzzle to muzzle against Redcoats in the open field. You've faced them?"

Gabriel nodded. "They're fearless."

"They're well trained," Martin corrected him. "They spend three years—sometimes longer—practicing for exactly this type of warfare. Most of them are hard, stupid men who join the army to get out of prison or because they owe money they can't repay. If Gates knew how to fight them, they'd be plenty afraid."

Gabriel watched the British cannons fire a volley into the Patriot lines and cringed when he saw the carnage. Each six-pound steel ball cut its own insane path through the wall of American men. Skittering over the ground, bouncing unpredictably, they tore some men in half while shearing off the legs and arms of others.

When the Redcoat infantry came to within fifty yards of the Patriots, they stopped suddenly. In perfect unison, exactly half of them raised their muskets and fired. Dozens on the American side fell to the ground as smoke from the guns filled the space between the two armies. Before the Patriots could organize a return volley, the Redcoat front line was smoothly replaced by the fresh second line. They leveled their muskets and fired, inflicting the same heavy damage.

When the Patriot response finally came, it was sporadic and weak. A few Redcoats fell, but in a moment they had reloaded and were advancing once again.

"This is madness," said Martin.

"We've got to do something," Gabriel said.

Martin shook his head. "It's not for us. This battle was over before it began."

The Patriot lines began to disintegrate as the Redcoats bore down on them. All of the uniformed soldiers, or Regulars, stood and fired, but the militia turned and deserted the field. They broke one or two men at a time, but soon whole companies abandoned their positions, many of them tossing their weapons away as they went.

"HUZZAH!" With a thunderous cry, the Redcoats broke into a running charge. Before they'd closed half the distance between themselves and their enemy, the ground rumbled as the British cavalry galloped onto the field. The fast-moving Green Dragoons stormed through the hanging smoke in pursuit of the outmatched Patriots. The leader of the Dragoons rode far ahead of his men, madly leading the charge. They quickly overtook the retreating Patriots and hacked them around the heads and shoulders with their long swords. Gabriel turned away, unable to watch the horrible spectacle. But Martin continued studying the scene, paying particular attention to the leader of the Dragoons.

"Too early," he noted quietly. "He's coming in too early."

The few pockets of blue that held along the front line were quickly overrun by the wave of advancing Redcoats, and those in retreat made no attempt to oppose the onslaught of the Dragoons. Every man for himself, they ran pell-mell for the trees as Tavington's horsemen continued to brutally hack them down.

Martin and Gabriel left the house and mounted their horses. They rode quickly and without a word.

The British command position was situated on a hilltop that overlooked the battlefield from a safe distance. Lord

General Cornwallis was not entirely displeased with what he saw. Dressed in full battle regalia, he and a dozen of his staff officers sat on horseback directing the action. One hundred of his best troops were arrayed in a long, open line in front of him, while another hundred remained hidden from view behind the hill. To his immediate left, a fife-and-drum corps stood ready to relay his signals to the officers on the field.

He and his officers began the battle in grim silence, but as the engagement quickly developed into another easy victory, the mood lightened. Cornwallis and Brigadier General O'Hara broke into relaxed smiles and began exchanging amusing remarks. The Lord General's battle plan had been executed to perfection, with one infuriating exception. To no one's surprise, that single exception came from the Green Dragoons under Tavington's command. The impetuous young officer had bolted onto the field without waiting for his signal.

Before turning to go, Cornwallis surveyed the four corners of the blue sky and the battlefield spread before him. Everywhere he looked, the rebel survivors were giving themselves up for surrender and being marched away. With a mock sigh of disappointment, he lamented to O'Hara, "These American rustics are so craven and inept, they nearly take the honor out of victory." Then, with a sly smile, he added, "Nearly."

Immediately following the battle, several of Cornwallis's key officers were asked to visit his tent for a modest victory celebration. Tavington, sometimes in and sometimes out of His Lordship's favor, was elated to find himself invited, especially after leading his Dragoons to such an overwhelming victory.

A buffet table had been set up in the center of the tent's main room to hold the food and drink. The serving trays and candlesticks were made of the finest silver. Fluted goblets filled with sparkling wine stood in a row, waiting to be raised in a toast.

As Tavington rode toward the tent, Bordon, his second-in-command, alerted him to the fact that he had sustained a cut over his right ear that was leaking blood down the side of his face. Tavington decided not to wipe it clean before going inside. It would serve as a small reminder that he and Bordon risked themselves in battle while the others watched from a safe distance. When they entered, Cornwallis was visible in another part of the tent, inspecting his appearance in a full-length mirror.

"My Lord General, gentlemen," Tavington said, "a glorious day to His Majesty." The officers greeted the two Dragoons with awkward silence, glancing at them only furtively.

Tavington and Bordon were the youngest members of the staff and the only two not wearing the powdered wigs favored by their superiors. With their arrival, the total number of guests reached eleven.

"Ah, Colonel Tavington," said the Lord General, swaggering into the reception area, "always too early, always too eager for glory."

"For *victory*, my Lord. I believe we took the field."

Cornwallis's dogs followed him over to the buffet table. They were a pair of Great Danes, each one nearly the size of a Shetland pony. There was a silver platter set especially for them with thin slices of fresh red meat. He allowed the animals to eat from his hand.

"Next time, you will wait for my command."

"It appears that the colonel prefers to follow his *own* commands," said General O'Hara in a smug tone. He was constantly trying to poison Cornwallis's opinion of the headstrong Tavington.

The reception was not going at all as Tavington had hoped it would. Rather than being toasted and congratulated for his contributions, he was receiving nothing but criticism.

"By the way," Cornwallis went on, "General O'Hara tells me you've earned the nickname 'the Butcher' among the local populace." Tavington moved his lips to speak, but Cornwallis silenced him with a finger. "We'll discuss the matter tomorrow."

Then Cornwallis raised one of the goblets in the air to his men. "Gentlemen, my compliments." Intentionally or not, he turned his back on Tavington when he made the toast.

"To victory!" O'Hara called.

That afternoon, the sun, as if stained by the blood of the Camden battlefield, turned various deepening shades of red as it sank through the treetops toward the horizon. Benjamin and Gabriel steered a safe, circuitous path around the battlefield before looping back and picking their way through a dense pine forest. It wasn't difficult to find the remnants of the American forces. They followed the screams.

In the gloom of the lengthening shadows, they came upon a small farm where some four hundred men had gathered in the aftermath of the slaughter. Sentries had been posted on the outskirts of the camp, but none of them challenged the Martins as they passed. When they arrived at the center of the gathering place, they found a group of two dozen horses tied to the trees. They dismounted and tied their horses in the same way. Sullen men milled about the trees aimlessly, while others sat and stared at the air in front of their faces.

Gabriel noticed a patch of color on the ground and realized it was a tattered flag, an Old Glory. It was encrusted with mud and torn to shreds. He stooped down and began to gather up the pieces, shaking them out and stuffing them into his haversack. A wounded Continental limped past, using a cut branch to help steady himself. When he saw what the young man was doing, he gave a quick, bitter laugh.

"Don't bother with that," he said. "It's a lost cause."

Gabriel found a last bit of gold fringe, tucked it away, and followed his father deeper into the camp. They soon came to the source of the screaming. The field surgeons had established an emergency work site to do what they could for the many wounded survivors. At least three score of moaning, battered men lay in the dirt, using tree roots as pillows, waiting for attention. One of them glanced up at the Martins as they walked past. A medical case lay open, revealing various saws and other rough tools.

"Give him the rum," said the doctor as he reached into the case and withdrew a serrated blade a foot long. His patient had been hit in the shin with a cannonball, and the shattered flesh below the knee looked like a tangle of red rope. The scream that came from the wounded soldier when the surgeon went to work was so shrill and high-pitched, it sounded like the cry of a wounded bird. With this sound ringing through the camp, Martin led the way to the command tent. Worried, nervous men stood outside arguing over the best way to reorganize and retreat before the British could find them and finish them off completely.

Inside the tent, surrounded by a handful of men who were hidden in the shadows, a solitary figure sat at a folding campaign table, leaning on his elbows, his head hanging forward. Martin went inside and told the man exactly what he thought.

"This Gates is a damn fool."

The man's head snapped up in surprise. It was Colonel Harry Burwell, and he looked like hell. He seemed smaller than when Martin had seen him last, standing cocksure and stalwart at the podium in the Assembly Hall. He had the same rock-hard face, but his skin and eyes had turned a bit gray and his whole body radiated a deep exhaustion. He was too harassed and worried to offer his old friend much of a welcome.

"Benjamin Martin, if you've come here to give me a lecture, I'm not in the mood to hear it."

He shook his head and explained. "I lost my son Thomas."

Burwell was sorry to hear it.

"Where is Gates now?" asked Martin, looking around the camp, prepared to give the general an earful.

"Last anyone saw," Burwell said, pointing into the distance, "he was riding hard to the northeast, his staff a hundred yards behind trying to catch up. It's a strange situation—a general deserting his army. We've lost more than four hundred and fifty men. We figure the British lost about twenty."

"So, who's in command?"

Burwell looked around and shrugged his shoulders. "I am. At least, I think so."

Martin stood at attention. "What are my orders, General?"

Burwell and Gabriel were both surprised. After a quick glance around, the general confided in a low voice, "Ben, we're a breath away from losing this war." When Martin didn't react, Burwell pushed himself onto his feet and came around to the front of the table. He turned one of the maps he'd been studying and used it to explain the situation. "In the North, Washington is reeling from Morristown and a winter worse than Valley Forge. He's down to maybe two thousand men, running and hiding from twelve thousand Redcoats. Here in the South, Cornwallis has pretty well broken our backs. He captured over five thousand of our troops when he took Charles Town."

"And today," Martin added, "he destroyed the only army that stood between him and New York."

"I'm afraid so. And they've established a series of strongholds here in South Carolina. At Beaufort, at Moncks Corner, at Ninety Six, at King's Mountain, at Columbia . . ."

"So now Cornwallis can head north and finish off Washington."

Burwell sucked in a deep breath and rubbed his face wearily in his hands. "Unless we can find a way to keep Cornwallis occupied in the South until the French arrive, I'm afraid that's exactly what's going to happen. They've promised a fleet and ten thousand troops."

"When?"

"Fall. Six months at the earliest."

Martin studied the map in silence for a moment. He hadn't realized the situation was quite so desperate. It didn't take a military genius to understand the implications of what Burwell was telling him: For all practical purposes, the outcome of the war had already been decided. Another moment of tense silence passed before Martin spoke again.

"Keeping Cornwallis here in South Carolina is our only hope," he said. "And you trust the French will keep their word?"

"*Absolument!*" came a voice from one of the dark corners

of the tent. A stout, belligerent Frenchman came out of the shadows. About Martin's age, he had unruly blond hair flecked with silver, mutton-chop sideburns, and wore the uniform of a major in the French infantry. He looked every inch a soldier as he stepped crisply to the table and stabbed a finger at the map, pointing to the coast of Virginia.

"There is only one problem," he said in a thick accent. "Our Admiral de Grasse will not sail beyond your Chesapeake Bay for fear of early storms." Then he shrugged his shoulders disdainfully. "What do you expect from the navy!"

Martin was quite surprised to find himself standing next to the man. He hadn't met a Frenchman face to face in over twenty years, since the war. And in those days, every one he met, he tried to kill.

"Benjamin Martin," Burwell said, doing the honors, "allow me to present Major Jean Villeneuve, French Seventh Light Foot. He's here as a volunteer, come to help train the militia."

Now it was the Frenchman's turn to be surprised. "Ah, so *you* are Benjamin Martin," he said, looking him up and down. "Your reputation precedes you," he said sarcastically, "the hero of Fort Wilderness."

Gabriel noted the comment and the sudden bristling tension that passed between the two men. He angled himself to see the expression on his father's face, but Martin ignored the remark and turned back to Burwell.

"Do you seriously expect to hold Cornwallis here with only militia?"

"Not me," Burwell said. "You."

Martin frowned. "But these men aren't soldiers, they're farmers. They'd be better off letting the British move on."

"*They'd* be better off," Burwell agreed, "but the *cause* wouldn't."

Martin looked from Burwell to Gabriel to Villeneuve, searching for an answer to this impossible problem. "How many men does Cornwallis have under his command?"

"In the entire colony," Burwell replied, "approximately eight thousand infantry and about six hundred cavalry, including the Green Dragoons under that butcher Tavington."

Tavington. It was the first time Martin had heard the name. He didn't know how he was going to do it, but he knew he had to keep Cornwallis pinned down in South Carolina. Every day he succeeded would represent another day of hope for Washington in the North, and another chance to settle accounts with the man who had senselessly killed his son.

Burwell used a quill to scrawl some words in ink onto a square scrap of parchment. He blew on the paper, then handed it to Martin.

"I'm giving you a field commission as a colonel."

Without a moment's hesitation, Martin began recruiting. There was one man he wanted above all others. "I'd like you to transfer my son Gabriel into my command."

"Sir, no!" Gabriel said with a start. "I'd like to continue in your—"

"Done!" Burwell said immediately. "And I'll give you Major Villeneuve as a drill sergeant to help you train your men. Good luck, Benjamin."

After shaking Burwell's hand, Benjamin left the tent and stepped into the gathering darkness to contemplate his first move. Gabriel was at his shoulder in a flash.

"Colonel Martin," he said formally, "I'd like for you to reconsider. I've been a soldier now for two years. I don't believe I belong with the militia. I've acted as a scout, a horseman, a courier, a scavenger, a marksman, a—"

Martin cut him off, starting back toward the horses as Villeneuve followed. "Is that so?"

"Yes, sir. In my opinion, I could be of better service with the Regulars."

"Where'd you learn all of those things? The riding, the shooting, the scouting?"

Gabriel paused awkwardly. "My father taught me."

Martin stopped long enough to stare into the young man's face. "And your father, did he teach you humility?"

Gabriel worked hard not to smile. "He tried. It didn't take."

"Well, he did teach you every deer path and swamp trail between here and Charles Town, which is why he asked for your transfer." Martin untied his horse and lifted himself into the saddle. "As good as you are, we won't be able to do much by ourselves. We've got to put out the word and start gathering men. We'll start on the south side of the Santee and . . ."

"We'd cover more ground if we split up," Gabriel interrupted. Martin barely held his temper, but quickly realized his son was right. He sighed and reluctantly agreed as Villeneuve found his horse and mounted up.

"Very well, Corporal, you take Wakefield, Pembroke, and Harrisville. I'll take our new friend here," he said, indicating Villeneuve, "and head up the north side of the river. We'll meet at the old Spanish mission in Black Swamp." As Gabriel climbed onto his horse and turned to leave, Martin couldn't resist giving him another order. "And one more thing, Corporal. Be careful."

"Yes, sir." Gabriel spurred his horse and disappeared into the trees. When he was gone, Martin turned to Major Villeneuve. The Frenchman was not happy to find himself in the middle of a nonprofessional, family situation.

"You have children?" Martin asked.

Villeneuve only scoffed. He didn't consider it an appropriate question. The two men, strangers and uneasy allies, rode away from the camp in an awkward silence.

8

For several days after the Battle of Camden, Lord Cornwallis remained at Fort Carolina, waiting for his supply trains and troop reinforcements to complete their movements. Although anxious to begin moving north, his stay was surprisingly pleasant. The chief reason for this was the fact that South Carolina was falling into his hands almost as fast as he could reach out and take it. In addition, the quarters he had selected were comfortably furnished and included an extensive library of illustrated books. Musicians culled from among the ranks played for him and his officers most evenings.

The fort, situated on an isolated hill, offered commanding views of the surrounding green valleys. The headquarters building was a stout, three-story brick mansion—one of the largest structures in the upcountry—that towered above the ten-foot-high perimeter wall. Until recently, it had been the winter home of the Darden family. Samuel Darden, who owned a fleet of cargo ships, had never openly expressed sympathy for the Patriot cause, but neither had he signed any of the circulating loyalty petitions, though he was invited more than once. When Cornwallis learned that Darden was related by marriage to the rebel leader Charles Sumner, he ordered the property seized and fortified.

By April, the mansion was unrecognizable. The outbuildings had been converted to serve as barracks, and there were hundreds of white canvas tents scattered about the hilltop. A perimeter wall, ten feet high, had been constructed using five thousand white pines from the surrounding area.

On a bright, chilly Wednesday afternoon, a stiff breeze blew up the hill, flapping the walls of the tent city and fluttering the Union Jack that flew above the headquarters building. Two hundred troops, fresh from Charles Town, were marching up the road. Tavington and his Dragoons thundered past them, kicking up a long column of terra cotta dust.

Flanked by Bordon and Wilkins, he was returning from one of his daily forays into the surrounding area to search for resistance. As Cornwallis had predicted, Wilkins was proving to be an invaluable asset. The British, being strangers to the land, had no way of telling the American Loyalists from the American Patriots. Whigs and Tories looked alike unless they were wearing uniforms, which they rarely were. So they relied on Wilkins and his long memory to tell them who stood with whom. Sometimes only a stern warning was issued, and sometimes men were shot or hanged. The outcome depended as much on Tavington's mood as on anything Wilkins had told him.

As the Dragoons entered the fort, Tavington, already late for his appointment with Cornwallis, peeled out of formation and rode directly to the front steps of the headquarters mansion. He left his horse with a foot soldier and swatted some of the dust out of his clothes as he hurried up the fifteen stone steps to the entrance.

Everyone inside knew where Tavington needed to go. They stepped out of his way as he strode into the west wing, where he found Cornwallis in the map room, leaning on a giant hand-carved teak table. His lordship was dressed in his battle uniform and was analyzing a large chart that showed the colonies, western Canada, and the unclaimed interior. General O'Hara was in the room with him, listening to Cornwallis go over the particulars of the land grant he'd been promised by the King upon the successful conclusion of the war: a vast tract of land in the Ohio River Valley. In Cornwallis's mind, it was already his. He spent a great deal of time daydreaming about the many ways he might profit from owning such an immense piece of real estate, most of it virgin forest.

As a member of Parliament, Cornwallis had opposed the series of taxes and punitive laws that had incited the current trouble. Nevertheless, he took his duty to England and the Crown very seriously and thus volunteered to serve. Like many of England's elite, he had first learned to fight on the playing fields of Eton Academy, and he had a scar from a field hockey stick over his left eye to prove it. Upon graduating, most youth of his social standing went directly to Oxford to study law, physics, or literature, but Cornwallis decided on a military career. And he did something about it that none of his contemporaries even considered doing—he studied. England at that time did not have a single military academy, so he enrolled himself at the highly regarded Turin School in northern Italy. He was not a belligerent or violent person, but knew that war was a useful and necessary thing, so he became very good at it.

"And then it extends from the headwaters, here," Cornwallis was saying, "to the far bank of the Ohio River, one hundred thousand acres."

"An imposing land grant, my lord," O'Hara said, suitably impressed. "You will be a country unto yourself."

A country unto himself. Cornwallis liked the sound of that. He smiled broadly as he imagined it, then frowned just as suddenly when Tavington entered. O'Hara bowed, excusing himself from the room.

Tavington had already heard Cornwallis wax poetic about the beauty of the Ohio Valley and its vast potential. Like the rest of the staff, he had suffered through lectures about the colonial population's gradual westward migration and its effect on land values.

Still breathing hard from his ride, he moved close to the general—close enough to let him smell the dust and perspiration of a day's work—and joined him in leaning over the table. He looked at the map, studying the huge windfall he was helping Cornwallis earn. Tavington was bitterly jealous of Cornwallis's good fortune and made little attempt to hide it.

"His Majesty King George is a generous man," Tavington said. "But then your service in this war warrants such a gift, my lord."

"Yes, this is how His Majesty rewards those who fight for him." Then he added, with emphasis, "Those who fight *as gentlemen*."

Tavington smiled impatiently. "I dare to presume that my own meager contributions will be rewarded one day."

Cornwallis stared at him. "You may presume too much."

"And why is that, my lord?"

Cornwallis crossed the room to sit behind his desk. "Because the King of England, like history itself, judges us not merely by the *outcome* of a war, but also by the *manner* in which it is fought. Whether it is done honorably."

Tavington cocked his head. "Honorably, my lord?"

"We serve the Crown, Colonel. We are his agents here in North America and we must conduct ourselves accordingly. From this point forward, surrendering troops will be given quarter. The use of these brutal tactics will cease."

Tavington bristled. "Is it not enough, my lord, that I have never lost a battle?"

"No, it is not," Cornwallis said. "You serve under me, and the manner in which you conduct yourself among the population here reflects on me. For pity's sake, man, I personally appointed you to lead the Dragoons. You have become a threat to my good reputation. I should think that one from a family as esteemed as yours would understand that." By mentioning the younger man's embarrassing family situation, Cornwallis hoped to shame him into obedience. But Tavington surprised him by speaking openly about the subject.

"My late father squandered away any esteem in which we were held, along with my inheritance. I advance myself only through victory."

"No," Cornwallis said emphatically, "you advance yourself, sir, *only* through my good graces." He let that idea sink in, and after a tense silence, Tavington acknowledged the truth of it. Nodding deferentially, he adopted the bearing of a willing subordinate. Cornwallis, satisfied with what he saw, paced back to the map on the table. "Remember, Colonel, these colonials are our brethren and when this conflict is over, we will be reestablishing commerce with them. Do you understand that?"

Tavington looked at the map of Ohio and nodded his head. "I understand, my lord."

Pembroke was a typical upcountry settlement. Surrounded by vegetable gardens and small cornfields, it was a collection of houses clustered within reach of the church steeple's shadow. Most of the homes were two stories tall and built of wood, but afforded very little living space, since they also served as storefronts catering to the local farmers. The enterprising merchants there offered ready-made clothing, ribbon, soaps, candles, hand tools, nails, seed, string, stationery, and books in three languages. Wagons and plows were brought to the blacksmith for repair, and the local minister, Reverend Oliver, offered instruction in the tiny schoolroom next to his house.

Gabriel knew most of the people who lived there, but there was one family in particular he was anxious to call on—the Howards. Although it had been two years since he'd seen her in Charles Town, the picture of Anne was fresh in his mind. He had remembered her often during his long months in the North, hoping they would meet again. On more than one occasion, he had invented imaginary conversations between them, full of clever, flirtatious dialogue. It had been a dark night when he'd seen her, but her image had grown luminous in his memory, as if lit by a sun that fell only on her.

Coming around the last bend in the road, all such pleasant thoughts were wiped out of his mind. He saw the horrible evidence that the British had been already been to Pembroke.

Three uniformed Continentals and a pair of civilians had been hung from a tree near the side of the road, their hands tied behind their backs. The bodies, having begun to rot, were discolored and bloated with gas. Their tongues, stiff and black, protruded past the teeth. Gabriel held his breath against the stench as he hurried past them.

Horses and carriages were crowded around the church, where a special service was underway, but the town was otherwise deserted. A flock of white chickens and a few dogs patrolled the road. As he came closer, Gabriel could hear the people inside the church singing a hymn. He tied up his horse and went to the side entrance, staying a step away from the doorway.

Reverend Oliver, a tall, frail man about sixty years old,

stood in his pulpit at the top of a curving staircase and looked down on his flock, conducting their voices with quick jabs of his index finger. He wore a coarse wool vestment and a powdered wig. When he noticed Gabriel's blue uniform jacket, he quickly looked away. Dan Scott, a burly young man about Gabriel's age, sat with his wife singing loudly and slightly off-key. Dan stopped in mid-note when he spotted Gabriel, then quickly turned away and rejoined the other voices. Mr. Peter Hardwick, a well-off tradesman, slipped a protective arm around his young son's shoulder. Although most of Pembroke knew and liked the Martin family, no one was glad to see another soldier.

The worshippers were separated by a series of partitions with private boxes toward the front and open pews at the back. The Howards, the congregation's most prestigious family, occupied a stall in the front row to Reverend Oliver's immediate right. Anne was seated between her parents, and the sight of her sent a sudden tingle up Gabriel's spine. She sat very straight at the edge of her bench, wearing a simple yellow dress, her hair tucked up in a bonnet. She was singing along with the others, but without much enthusiasm. Her eyes were fixed on the floor near her feet, and she didn't notice Gabriel standing in the doorway.

As the hymn ended, the reverend opened his Bible to begin the sermon. Gabriel cleared his throat and stepped into the church.

"Reverend, with your permission, I'd like to make an announcement."

Every head in the place turned at the same time. There was a good deal of rustling and whispering.

"Young man, this is a house of God."

"I understand that, Reverend, and I apologize. But this is a matter of the utmost importance." Gabriel looked at the congregation and took a moment to gather himself. He'd spent the previous day in Wakefield without convincing a single soul to join him, and knew he needed to do a better job here in Pembroke. But with the dead men hanging from the trees nearby, he had a difficult task ahead of him. The parishioners were badly shaken by the hangings and intimidated by the British.

"The South Carolina militia is being called up. I'm here to enlist every man who is willing and able to fight," Gabriel announced.

Silence.

A few of the townspeople exchanged glances, but none of them spoke. During this uncomfortable moment, Gabriel's eyes met Anne's. He offered her a stiffly formal nod.

"Young man," Reverend Oliver said in a kind voice, "this is a sad occasion. We are here today to pray for the souls of those men outside."

"Yes, pray for them," Gabriel answered, "but honor them also. Honor them by taking up arms with us."

Peter Hardwick clucked his tongue. "Go ahead and call away. I'm not joining nothing."

"Neither am I," said a man from the back row. "If we're smart, we'll join the British side and curry favor for the future."

Mr. Howard stood and held the railing to keep his balance. "Gabriel Martin, do you understand what you're asking of these men?"

Anne, in a state of agitation, wanted to respond to her father's question. She went to stand up, but didn't. She opened her mouth to speak, but Dan Scott beat her to the punch. The slow-moving young man wore a jacket of rough, homespun cotton. He looked at the ground as he worried his hat in a pair of big hands.

"If old King George can hang those men, he can hang any one of us."

He was right, of course, and Gabriel knew it. He stood tongue-tied before the congregation until Anne Howard boldly got to her feet and began to say everything he wanted to say.

"Dan Scott, shame on you! Barely a week ago, you stood at the counter of our store and talked for two hours about independence and how we shouldn't submit to British tyranny."

The townspeople were shocked to hear these fiery words coming from a woman, especially one so young. Both Reverend Oliver and her father tried to coax Anne into her seat, but it was too late. She had broken her silence, and now she intended to speak her mind. She spun around and pointed a finger.

"And you, Mr. Hardwick, how many times have I heard you speak of freedom at my father's table? The last time you came, as I recall, you brought along a copy of Tom Paine's pamphlet and read a selection from it. But now, when this soldier asks for your help, you mock him." She swept the room with a gesture. "Why, half the men in this church, including you, Father, and you, Reverend Oliver, are as ardent Patriots as I. Will you now, when you are needed most, stop at only words?"

The men found it difficult to look her in the eyes.

"I ask only that you act upon the convictions of which you have so eloquently spoken and in which you so strongly believe."

With her speech concluded, she relinquished the floor back to Gabriel with a small curtsy and sat down between her parents. They looked at her with a mixture of astonishment and pride.

"I can't say it any better than that," said Gabriel. He sensed that Anne had convinced at least a few of the men, so he wasted no time with further discussion. "Who's with us?"

There was a long moment of soul-searching silence. Some of the men turned to confer with their families.

A man in the back row raised his hand. Then, one after another, exactly half the men stood and signaled that they would volunteer, Dan Scott among them. It was a tense and solemn event, and as it unfolded, Gabriel's eyes remained glued to Anne. She smiled at him so brightly, he could feel the warmth of it on his face.

Colonel Benjamin Martin and Major Jean Villeneuve tried several times during the long hours of riding to make conversation but quickly came to the conclusion that they worked better without words. The problem was not that the two men had nothing in common, but that they had both fought in the last war—on opposing sides. It hung over their conversation like a ghost, always lurking. Martin couldn't quite get used to riding beside a Frenchman, or worse, letting him get behind where he couldn't keep an eye on him. It didn't help when Villeneuve told him that his name was well known in French military circles and that "*comme Ben-jah-MEEN Mar-TAN*" was synonymous with "uncivilized" and "brutally violent." Martin trusted him a little more for being honest about how he felt, but that didn't make it a whole lot easier for him to relax when the major and his sword were riding only a pace or two behind him.

On the other hand, they developed a tense rapport as they moved silently beneath the canopy of oaks along the Santee, ever alert to the danger of British and Cherokee scouting parties. At Martin's insistence, they soon turned away from the river and climbed into the hilly backcountry where, he promised, they would find a number of experienced soldiers.

They came to the village of Bradford Crossroad shortly after dark. It was a dingy, run-down settlement with a trading post, an inn, and not much else. In other villages, the houses were built up to the road, but here they were set unsociably far back in the trees. Many of them were not proper houses at all, but mere shacks without windows or fireplaces. Rough-looking men, loggers and trappers, stood in the road speaking in hushed voices and stared at the strangers as they rode past. Bradford Crossroad was only a few hours' ride from the Santee River and polite society, but it had the bleak and dangerous atmosphere of a frontier town. Neither the Crown nor the colony had ever attempted to establish law enforcement in the area, and there was not even a church.

Martin steered toward the inn, an ancient-looking building covered with moldy black shingles. A sign over the door proclaimed the name of the establishment: BOAR'S HEAD TAVERN.

Candlelight and raucous conversation wafted from inside the building. As Martin tied the horses to a hitching post, Villeneuve peeked through the wavy lead-glass window and didn't like what he saw. The crowd inside looked to him like a convention of outlaws. Nevertheless, when Martin pulled the front door open and stepped inside, Villeneuve followed.

The interior was bright, crowded, noisy, and absolutely filthy. Coarse, grizzled men had packed themselves around rough-hewn tables under an open-timbered ceiling that sagged visibly at the center. They sat feasting on freshly killed meat and cups of hard cider. The walls were stained brown with smoke, and the plaster was flaking. The innkeeper, a fat old man with his arm in a sling, did not skimp on candles. He kept scores of them burning in wall sconces, on tabletops, and in the wagon-wheel chandeliers that hung from the ceiling. But they were made of tallow, the cheapest material available, and filled the air with smoke and the rancid odor of burning animal flesh. None of the Boar's Head patrons seemed to mind. One of the few women in the place fixed her eyes on the dashing and handsome French major. She was about fifty years old, and her face was painted pale white with makeup. When she caught his eye, she gave him a toothless smile, lifted her petticoats off her lap, and made a lewd, inviting gesture. Villeneuve, repulsed, leaned toward Martin with an urgent question.

"Are you certain this is a good place to recruit for the militia?"

Martin shrugged. "There's only one way to find out." He cleared his throat and shouted at the top of his lungs, "GOD SAVE KING GEORGE!"

The roar of conversation immediately gave way to a menacing silence and a scuffling of chairs. Men on all sides rose to their feet, glaring viciously. Pistols were pulled and cocked into the firing position. Martin nodded to his companion.

"I'd say we're in the right place."

A ceramic mug streaked through the air and shattered against the wall only inches from Martin's head. In a flash, the newcomers retreated out the door and pulled it closed behind them. Villeneuve started for his horse.

"No! Over here!" Martin called. "Help me hold the door."

The major was beginning to have serious doubts about his new partner's sanity, but raced back and helped resist the strength of the angry men trying to pull the door open from within. Tugging on the handle, he cursed a blue streak in French.

"Don't worry," Martin said with a grin. "They're good men. Friends of mine."

Villeneuve stared back at him, trying to decide who was more dangerous, the ruffians inside the tavern or the smiling madman at his side.

Two hours, three rounds of drinks, and a long explanation later, the two men were seated behind a recruiting table with a quill pen and a book of blank pages for writing down names. The tavern's owner, reduced to tears by the speech Martin gave, sent over a jug of his best rum and half a roasted turkey. The line of men waiting to volunteer was fifteen deep and stretched to the far side of the room.

The first to join was Dickey Ludwell, an olive-skinned man no more than five feet tall. His face was puckered with deep, fleshy wrinkles acquired by years spent in the sun. His black hair and beard were flecked with gray. Concentrating mightily, he bent over the enlistment book and carefully signed his name.

"How's that?" he asked when he had finished, blowing the ink dry.

Martin regarded the man's penmanship. "Very well done. Since when did you learn to write, Ludwell?"

The little man smiled at his accomplishment. "I got me a wife since you seen me last. She taught me." A dark thought passed through his mind, wrinkling his already wrinkled forehead. "I guess I ought to tell her I'm leaving."

"You probably should. See you here tomorrow morning, early."

Next up was Rollins, who looked half human and half Scandinavian wolfhound. He had blond whiskers, short blond hair he'd cut himself, an angular face, and a pair of ice-blue eyes that never rested in one place for long. Mistrustful of others, he carried most of his earthly possessions with him at all times, stuffed into his saddlebags or carried on his shoulders in a pair of large haversacks. He prowled up to the table with a lump of tobacco under his cheek and nodded when Martin greeted him by name.

"What sort of fighting you got in mind?" the man asked.

"Partisan warfare, harassment," Martin told him without hesitation. "We'll make the English miserable any way we can, then keep moving."

Rollins chewed his tobacco and thought it over. "I'll wager those bastards have some pretty rich supply trains."

"I'll wager they do."

"Any bounty?"

"No. There's no scalp money this time, Rollins, but you can keep or sell back to me the muskets and gear of any Redcoat you kill at twenty shillings a kit."

"I won't make much at that rate," Rollins told him.

Villeneuve leaned forward. "It all depends on how many you can kill."

Rollins smiled, spat a hocker of brown juice on the floor, and rapped his knuckles on the tabletop. "I'll try it for a while."

Villeneuve, handing him the pen, reminded him that the minimum term of enlistment was one year. Rollins only smirked in reply as he scratched his name onto the paper, then made his way toward the bar.

Danvers was a long, lean, rawboned man about fifty years old who suffered from bad nerves. He parted his long hair down the middle, but there wasn't enough of it to hide his oily scalp, which glistened in the candlelight. His clothing was tailor-made, and he kept an expensive pair of eyeglasses perched at the end of his nose. He looked over the top of them as he spoke.

"I can't say how glad I am to see you men. It's past time we done something about this situation." The smell of liquor on his breath was overpowering. "I hate them British. My brother got hanged down at Acworth, the only family I had. Every damned one of them Redcoats deserves to die the same way, or worse."

Martin nodded sympathetically and pushed the enlistment book across the table.

"Sign on up."

Danvers looked surprised by the suggestion. "What? With my ailments? I wouldn't last through my first skirmish, but you can have my Negro to fight in my stead." He pointed across the room at a tall African. "Occam, get over here," he snapped. "He been with me twenty years. Ain't real smart, but strong as a bull. Should do you some good." Danvers took up the pen and signed the book.

Occam was very dark-skinned and just as strong as Danvers had described him. He had square, muscular shoulders and a pair of hands that looked like they could bend iron. He shuffled to the recruiting table with little confidence. Withdrawal and silence were his way of shielding himself against his master, and he made it a habit to keep his expression as blank as possible. But Martin could see the nervousness in the man's dark, watery eyes.

"Can you write?" Martin asked.

"Course he can't," Danvers answered. "But I just signed for him."

Martin ignored the comment and looked at Occam. "Make your mark if you're with us."

Occam took a long look at Martin, wondering what kind of a new master he was getting. He couldn't remember the last time a white man had given him a choice on an important decision, and he guessed it could only mean Martin would be leading him into an especially tough situation. Still, he reached dutifully for the pen and held it awkwardly between his fingers.

"Only if you're willing," Villeneuve spoke up.

Occam made a shaky X on the paper, and before the ink was dry, Danvers was heading for the door. Occam watched him go, uncertain of what was expected of him. He stood waiting for an order, but Martin and Villeneuve only thanked him and motioned him aside so the next person in line could come to the table. Occam decided to go back to his table and finish eating his dinner.

"I want to kill me some Redcoats," said the next eager recruit, whose chin barely reached the top of the table.

"I'm sure you do," Martin said. "How old are you, son?"

The dirty six-year-old boy laughed and shrugged his shoulders. He had bright red hair and a splash of freckles across the bridge of his nose. Unable to answer the question, he raised a toy musket instead and pretended to shoot Martin in the head.

"A beautiful child," Villeneuve remarked dryly.

"Thank you," said the boy's father. "He's not quite old enough for this war, but his time will come."

"John Billings," Martin said with obvious affection. "I was hoping you'd turn up somewhere."

"And so I have." Billings stood six feet tall, had greasy hair that fell to his shoulders and a smile full of sharp, crooked teeth. "I'm glad to see you've kept pace with the changing fashions of the day, Ben." When Martin didn't understand, Billings pointed toward Villeneuve with his chin. "Never thought I'd see the day when Benjamin Martin would ride with a damned Frenchman!"

It was his idea of a joke. He threw his head back and broke into a high-pitched, gibbering laugh that sounded like someone was tickling a goat.

Like many of the backwoodsmen in the Boar's Head that evening, John Billings was a veteran of the French and Indian Campaign, part of a remarkable generation of men who had learned the arts of war from two very different teachers, the British Army and their allies, the Catawba Indians. Although he was a sturdy, mean-looking man, Martin remembered him primarily for his trickiness, a soldier more likely to rely on cunning than brute force. He'd put on weight over the years and his nose had turned lumpy and red from too much drink.

"I suspected I'd see you before long," Billings told him, reaching for the jug of rum and raising it to his lips.

"Why is that?"

"Well, there's a story going around about some twenty Redcoats, maybe more, were marching along a road down near the Santee River and got themselves killed by a ghost or some damn thing. They said this *ghost* carried a Cherokee tomahawk. I found it very interesting."

"Aren't you a little old to believe in ghost stories?" Martin asked.

Billings broke into another goatlike laugh. He made a quick, illegible scrawl in the book and treated himself to another long swig of Martin's rum.

The next morning, Gabriel and the men who had volunteered to join the militia gathered in the courtyard of the Pembroke church and made ready to leave. As they saddled their horses and tied up their gear, they were surrounded by their families, who had come to see them off. Most of the village had come out for the somber occasion, including those like Mr. Hardwick who thought resisting the British was a grave mistake. Still, there were a few conspicuous absences. One of the volunteers, Dan Scott, was missing, and so was Reverend Oliver, who had promised to come out and say a few words. But most of all, Gabriel was aware that the Howard family was nowhere to be seen. He glanced down the road at their house every few seconds, waiting for them to come outside.

Dan Scott finally made his appearance. He came to the church with his crying wife, Jessica, who was holding their small daughter in her arms. With his arrival, it was time to go. The men said their final good-byes and climbed onto their horses. Just then, Mr. Howard finally hobbled out the door of the dry goods store that occupied the lower floor of his home. Anne was with him, carrying a bolt of fabric.

Gabriel asked his men to wait and spurred his horse down the road. He dismounted near the Howards' front gate and held his hat over his heart. The one-legged merchant looked him over suspiciously, already guessing what he wanted. Gabriel came directly to the point.

"Mr. Howard, may I have your permission to write to Anne?"

The gray-haired gentlemen stared back as if he didn't understand. He raised his ear trumpet to the side of his head and shouted, "Ay?"

A little louder, Gabriel repeated himself. "May I have permission to *write to Anne*?"

"*My right hand*?" Howard asked, perplexed. "No, boy, it's my left leg."

"Oh, Father, stop it," Anne interrupted, swatting him playfully on the arm. Her smile was brighter than a lighthouse beacon. "Yes, Gabriel Martin, you have permission to write me."

"Oh, to *write* her?" said her father. "Very well."

"Thank you, sir." Grinning like a happy idiot, Gabriel climbed onto his horse and started away, riding half turned in his saddle so he could keep his eyes on the lovely young woman as long as possible. As he returned to the church, he saw Reverend Oliver come out of his small house. With his powdered wig on his head, it appeared that he was going to say a prayer for the departing soldiers, but he was leading a horse with an old musket poking out of the saddlebag. The confused townspeople asked what he was doing.

"A shepherd must tend to his flock," he explained, "and at times, that means fighting off the wolves!" He tore off his wig in a revolutionary gesture and tossed it to a child standing nearby. Then he climbed onto his horse and followed Gabriel out of town.

9

Over the next two days, Gabriel tripled the size of his force. Having the group from Pembroke behind him when he entered a new town made recruiting easier. Reverend Oliver helped by delivering some of the speeches. Soon they were nearly forty strong. They were moral, upstanding men, respected members of their communities, and Gabriel was proud to ride with them, but couldn't help becoming frustrated by the slow pace of their progress toward Black Swamp.

Complaining that they were too old to ride at a gallop, they walked their horses through the lush forests, stopping occasionally to admire the views. Stirred by patriotic feelings, they took turns making speeches on the subject of American liberty. They stopped often for meals and even more frequently to relieve their bladders. None of them had fought in the previous war. They were farmers, tanners, coopers, brightsmiths and blacksmiths—peace-loving and educated. Corporal Gabriel Martin did what he could to keep them moving forward.

On the night they entered Black Swamp, the men found themselves wishing they'd made better time during the daylight hours. The watery forest of the swamp, teeming with life, could be an eerie place when the sun was down. Giant cypress trees towered out of the water to impossible heights, their limbs reaching out to form a leafy cathedral ceiling that obliterated the moon. Bladderwort and lily pads jostled one another on the surface of the black pools as frogs croaked ominously from their hiding places. Mosquitoes licked at their faces while cattail reeds and soft rushes brushed against their legs. Each time a fishtail slapped against the water or a raccoon moved through the bushes, the men reacted with a start, certain it was the sound of an alligator coming out of the water to make a meal of them.

Gabriel led them slowly along a trail that was nearly invisible even in the light of day, moving as fast as he dared. The danger was not alligators but cypress knees, tiny stumps that poked out of the ground and grew in clusters. They could break a horse's leg and impale a rider who fell on them.

About an hour after they entered the swamp, Gabriel stopped suddenly when he heard something out of the ordinary. Dan Scott cocked his rifle, but Gabriel waved him off. He turned his head to the side and listened to the swamp's nocturnal melody, attuned to some sound the other men couldn't hear. Then he cupped his hands over his mouth and made a bird call.

"*Quack.*"

A moment later, he received an answered. "*Quack, quack.*"

"We're here," he told them. He led them a little way into the shallow water, found a barely submerged land bridge, and followed it to a wooded island where his father had set up camp near the remains of a decaying mission. The Spanish, eager to convert the local Catawba, had built a small mission outpost on the spot nearly a hundred years before. The Indians, rather than resist them, simply moved away. All that remained of the building now was a moss-covered wall with an arched doorway. A cross and a hand-ful of gravestones stood nearby in the water.

The moment the churchgoing men from Pembroke came face to face with the dirty, ill-mannered men from the Boar's Head Tavern, everyone realized there would be problems. Martin's recruits sat around their campfires drinking and playing dice. They were poorly dressed, unshaven, and heavily armed. They welcomed the new-comers with threatening stares and mocking laughter.

Gabriel led them a small distance from the others before going to find his father. Colonel Martin was knelt down at a campfire making bullets while John Billings looked on. He was melting down a handful of Thomas's toy soldiers in a cast-iron pan and pouring the hot lead into a bullet mold.

"How many did you get?" he asked when his son came to the spot.

"Thirty-seven."

When Gabriel saw the toy soldiers, his first reaction was that it was a nice tribute to his slain brother, but he quickly began to have doubts. He could guess how Martin was planning to use the bullets and hoped his father hadn't joined the war only to seek revenge. As he stood by watching, Billings took a swig off a bottle, then offered Gabriel a drink.

The young corporal refused. He looked over at the trap-pers, drifters, and backwoodsmen from the Boar's Head. "Those aren't the sort of men we need," he said, chastising his father.

Martin looked up only briefly from his work. "That's *precisely* the sort of men we need. They've fought this kind of war before." The hot mold hissed when he plunged it into a bucket of water to cool.

Gabriel gave him a disappointed look before turning his back and walking away. Billings watched him go.

"What about me?" he asked Martin. "Am I one of *that sort*?"

"No, you're the sort that gives that sort a bad name."

Later that night, when it came time to bed down, Gabriel and his recruits spread their blankets as far as they could from the rougher men. It had been a long day of riding, but they found it difficult to sleep in this strange new environment. Their ears were alert to every rustling of leaves, every gurgle of water, and every small pocket of silence. Long after the Boar's Head men were snoring, Gabriel's gentlemen lay rigidly awake, imagining jaguars creeping through the branches overhead and alligators slithering between the reeds along the water's edge.

Morning arrived like unexpected cannon fire when the sun topped the nearest ridge and sent cold yellow rays slicing between the trees. Ten thousand birds broke into shrill song and swooped low across the water. Sleep quickly became an impossibility, even for those who had gone to bed stone drunk. Cursing and rubbing their eyes, the men threw back their covers and stumbled to the banks of the water to urinate and collect water for their tea.

Martin was the first to notice Gabriel was missing. He questioned the Pembroke men about it, but none of them had seen him go.

"Dan Scott must have gone with him," Reverend Oliver observed, "and taken most of his gear with him. I hope they haven't deserted."

Martin was sure they hadn't. For one thing, he spotted the neatly folded pieces of Gabriel's flag, the Old Glory he'd picked up from the mud after the disaster at Camden, something he wouldn't have left behind. Besides, he knew Gabriel was far too dedicated to the Glorious Cause to abandon his post, even under the duress of having his father as his commanding officer. Martin bent down to examine the flag and saw that it had been partially stitched back together with an iron sewing needle and thread taken from a rag. He assured the worried men that Gabriel would return soon and moved on.

Shortly after the breakfast fires were lit, the two absent soldiers came back to the small island in dramatic fashion. They emerged from the thickly overgrown vegetation, splashed over the land bridge, and dismounted on the fly. They hurried to where Martin was frying up his corncakes and offered him a breathless salute.

"Where have you been, Corporal?" the colonel asked, clearly displeased.

"Scouting expedition, sir," Gabriel said stiffly.

Martin gave him a sharp look, but held back from saying more. The other men were gathering around them, and he didn't want another confrontation. Dan Scott was so worked up, so eager to make his report, that he looked like he had redbugs crawling in his pants. "Well then, let's have it," Martin said. "What did you find?"

"Redcoats!" Scott shouted, pointing through the trees with his hat in his hand.

"A supply train, sir," Gabriel reported with greater self-restraint. "About twenty wagons defended by three dozen men."

The eyes of the rougher men went wide with anticipation. It sounded like a chance to kill some Redcoats and capture valuable supplies at the same time. They made it clear they favored an attack. No one was more anxious to engage the enemy than Villeneuve. Nevertheless, he stepped forward to dampen the mood with his assessment of the situation. He looked at Martin and gestured at the ragtag group around him.

"These men need training. They are not ready to face the British."

The veterans in the crowd grumbled. They were suspicious of the Frenchman to begin with and didn't like what he was saying. Martin saw Villeneuve's point, but continued to think it through. He lifted his corncakes out of the pan and looked up at Gabriel.

"Only three dozen soldiers, you say?"

"If that."

There was a moment of silence before Martin came to a decision. He turned to Villeneuve and said, "Major, have the men ready to ride in thirty minutes."

Rollins was so happy he clasped his hands together over his chest and dropped to his knees. "Oh, thank you, Lord above!" he shouted, only half in jest. He was in it for the money, after all, and finding a British supply train so quickly was a magnificent stroke of luck.

A few of the men laughed at his joke, including Billings, who broke into his squeaky billygoat cackle. The sound that came out of him was so odd, so ludicrous, that it started all the others laughing as well. Even Villeneuve had to crack a smile. It was a moment that helped smooth over the differences between the village tradesmen and the coarse backwoodsmen, at least temporarily. As the gathering broke up, the men had the sense of coming together as a unified force.

The supply shipment was under the command of a promising young officer, Lieutenant Quartermaster A. J. Dristen. It consisted of twenty-three wagons, forty-seven horses, two howitzer field guns, and two dogs, all under the protection of thirty-four of the King's soldiers. Most of the wagons contained supplies and ammunition that had been brought to Charles Town Harbor by ship and were now being transferred upcountry to Fort Carolina and the other strongholds Cornwallis had established.

The convoy was headed northeast, following a route that led through an especially scenic corner of the swamp. The road was empty, wide, and well maintained, which left Lieutenant Dristen free to marvel at the beauty of the environment. Every so often, he spurred his horse away from the road for a better view of the ancient trees reflected in the mirror-smooth water or to pinch off a sample of some interesting plant. A man of letters, Dristen planned to write a sprawling romantic novel set in North America once he returned home, and these forays into the woods were part of his research. He made notes of everything he saw in a small journal.

Shortly after returning from one of these side excursions, Dristen looked up suddenly from his journal, sensing that something was out of place. The wagons were rolling past a place where an earthen embankment ran parallel to the road. He shouted to his second-in-command.

"Send someone to check the other side of that berm."

After relaying the order, the officer brought his horse alongside Dristen's for a conference. They were soon distracted by the sight of a man stepping from behind a tree and pointing a Kentucky hunting rifle at them. The first shot hit Dristen in the heart and killed him instantly. The other officer died only a second later.

A sudden hailstorm of bullets came out of the trees. With their officers dead, the Redcoats were slow to form their lines. They massed themselves in the middle of the road and pointed their guns at the unseen enemy.

"Present arms! Aim and fire when ready!"

With pounding hearts and fingers quivering against their triggers, the Redcoats waited to catch a glimpse of their attackers. From somewhere deep in the trees, someone lobbed a section of tree branch through the air, and when it cracked loudly against the ground, most of the nervous soldiers fired by mistake.

"Quick-time load!" one of them shouted.

Those words were the cue for the Pembroke men to enter the fray. Martin had stationed them behind the embankment. They crept to the top of the small hill, sent a well-aimed volley into the enemy's backs, then immediately scattered. Realizing that they were surrounded, many of the soldiers panicked and ran. As they did, another round of shots came out of the trees and picked them off.

Despite their losses, the soldiers stayed on the road, exposing themselves, having been thoroughly conditioned by their training to stand and fight in a certain way. They shouted for the men in the trees to show themselves, calling them cowards. But the militiamen stayed where they were, and the British caught only fleeting glimpses of them as they darted from tree to tree, or rustled the high grass on the crest of the berm. It was a fluid and chaotic style of fighting that the Redcoats didn't understand. It was a battle with ghosts.

In time, they realized their position was hopeless and called on one another to abandon the wagons and escape. They took off down the road, but soon discovered their path was blocked.

Martin stood in the center of the road, backed by a phalanx of his roughest men. He pulled one of two pistols from his belt and ran at them, leading the assault with Villeneuve and Billings hard on his heels. Some of the Redcoats reversed field and fled in the opposite direction, while the others lowered their bayonets and prepared to accept the charge.

Screaming like a banshee, Martin raced forward and shot one man with a pistol before using his tomahawk to kill another. The men behind him quickly joined the fray, engaging the Redcoats in hand-to-hand combat. Villeneuve showed himself to be an expert swordsman and a blood-thirsty warrior. He made quick work of his opponents and chopped at them when they fell to make certain they were dead. Billings used a sneakier method. He stayed back until the Redcoats engaged the other militiamen, then came up from behind and stabbed them with his enormous hunting knife. In a matter of moments, the road was soaked with blood and nearly all the British were dead.

The handful of survivors, realizing surrender was their only hope, began throwing down their weapons. But it was too late even for that.

By that point, Martin had worked himself into the same frenzied trance state he'd been in when he had rescued Gabriel in the glen. As the good men of Pembroke watched in horror, Martin, Villeneuve, and Billings advanced on the unarmed survivors without breaking stride and butchered them. They hacked and slashed their victims to death with furious efficiency—Martin with his tomahawk, Villeneuve with his sword, and Billings with his massive knife.

"STOP!" Reverend Oliver cried. "For the sake of God, stop!"

They didn't stop until the last soldier was dead.

Gabriel and his group of decent men were stunned to silence. Thirty-four dead bodies were scattered up and down the road, and everything smelled of gunpowder. Slowly, Occam and a few others started coming out of the trees. Rollins bent down and started searching one of the dead men, going through his pockets for loot.

"Have you no decency?" the reverend demanded.

Rollins eyed the gray-haired preacher as coldly as a vulture eyes a next meal, then returned to his business. If the men from Pembroke hadn't fully understood the differences between themselves and their backcountry allies before, it all became chillingly clear in that moment. Gabriel was horrified by what he'd witnessed.

"Father, those men were about to surrender."

Martin, standing over one of the mutilated corpses, looked at the tomahawk in his hand, then at his bloodied shirt and then at his son's face. He reacted strangely to Gabriel's words, as if hearing them from a great distance.

"They were trying to surrender!" Gabriel said again, anger rising in his voice.

"Perhaps," Villeneuve said sarcastically, "but now we will never know."

"That was murder," Reverend Oliver added hotly.

"Hell, Reverend, they're Redcoats," Billings explained. "They earned it." Some of the others grunted in agreement.

"No," said Gabriel loudly. "Father, don't you see? This is no better than what Tavington and his Dragoons did at our home." The words drew Martin, still half-dazed, farther out of his killing place. "It's not right," Gabriel went on. "We're better men than that!"

The rough men reacted to these high-minded words with sneering laughter and grumbles. They didn't consider themselves honorable men, and the evidence of their depravity lay on the ground before them.

"We're a regular bunch of angels," Billings sniggered.

"Quiet!" Martin shouted. "He's right. In the future, we give quarter to wounded British soldiers and any who surrender."

"To hell with you," said Villeneuve. "The British man-of-war *Tamar* offered no such quarter when it fired on the ship carrying my wife and daughters! They raised the white flag, but no matter. I watched from a few hundred yards away as they burned alive. I'm going to kill as many as I can."

Martin heard the Frenchman out, finally understanding his motivation for fighting a war so far from home. "You have my sympathy," he said, "but the order stands."

"Damn your sympathy," Villeneuve spat back, his face red with anger. "And who are you to give such an order? I know who you are, Benjamin Martin. I know what you did to my countrymen at Fort Wilderness. Did you offer *them* quarter?"

Martin was steady.

"This is the militia," he explained, "not the regular army. Every man here comes and goes as he pleases. But while he is here, he follows my orders. Any man who doesn't, I'll have shot." Still holding his tomahawk, Martin locked eyes with the boiling Frenchman, and for a moment it looked as if they might come to blows. But Villeneuve blinked first and stepped away, wiping his sword clean on the trousers of a dead Redcoat.

"Very well," he said, "it is my *pleasure* to give quarter to wounded and surrendering British soldiers," but then he added, "for the time being."

Martin accepted the answer. He might not like Villeneuve personally, but he was beginning to recognize his value. He was smart, independent, and had just proven he could fight as well as any man in the unit. Moreover, the men needed the drills and training he could give them. Not every battle, after all, would be an ambush against smaller numbers.

"What about the rest of you?" Martin asked. "Do I have your word?"

The men answered in the affirmative, promising to abide by the rules of war and accept the enemy's surrender. Once that issue was settled, at least temporarily, the men turned their attention to the wagons to see what spoils had come into their possession.

Jack Moore, a man with a few black teeth and thin, greasy hair, threw back the canvas covering on the hindmost wagon and hooted when he saw that it contained eighteen kegs of what they needed most—gunpowder. He ran to the next wagon and found eighteen more.

"We could fight for ten years on this!"

Moving wagon by wagon, they found almost everything an army might need to fight a war. There were chests of white biscuit and corn flour, crates of sugar, cured hams and tongues, jugs of maple syrup, bricks of Gloucester cheese and chocolate. There were sacks of green tea, bohea tea, and coffee beans—the first coffee they'd seen since the beginning of the British embargo. There were fishing nets, fishing hooks, iron skillets, saucepans, spoons, forks, and ladles. There were medical supplies such as bullet extractors, trephines and saws, oils, balms, laxatives, and fine cotton bandages. One wagon contained overcoats, socks, leather boots, haversacks, and cartridge boxes with clever wooden blocks for keeping the bullets separated. They found wool blankets, picks and shovels, two hogsheads full of cheap rum, and one copy of *Poor Richard's* almanac open to the page listing Benjamin Franklin's 10 Rules for Moral Perfection.

A commotion of barking dogs drew the attention of the men to one of the farthest wagons. Martin strode to the spot and found Billings gnawing on a piece of dried meat he'd found in one of the crates. A pair of enormous Great Danes stood guard over one of the wagons, barking and snarling whenever one of the men tried to approach.

"Shoot them!" Billings called out. "Shoot the damn things."

Rollins, eager to begin rifling through the contents of the wagon, raised a gun and took aim.

"Put that pistol down!" Martin commanded.

Dan Scott pointed to the horse-sized dogs. "They won't let anyone near that wagon."

Martin looked the animals over for a moment before grabbing the meat from Billings's mouth and waving it in front of them. When he tossed it on the ground, the dogs pounced for it. He ordered Moore and Ludwell to bring more food for the starving beasts, then began exploring the contents of the wagon. It only took a minute for the men to realize it had not come from Charles Town with the rest of the shipment. It was loaded with valuable objects, and the crates were all made of teak and other expensive woods. Dan Scott broke open a trunk filled with bottles and read the labels.

"Rum, French champagne, and Madeira."

"No wonder they were guarding it," said Billings, quickly moving to that side of the wagon and helping himself to one of the bottles. In the trunk Gabriel opened there were powdered wigs, all perfectly coifed and stored on head-shaped wig stands.

"What do you think all this is worth?" asked Rollins as he greedily forced the lock on the first of several identical cases, hoping to find valuables inside. To his disappointment, there were only papers and books. He flung them aside as he dug deeper into the case, looking for something he could sell for cash. Reverend Oliver, standing behind him, picked up a handful of the pages and began to read.

"The personal correspondence of Lord Cornwallis," he announced.

Astonished, Martin grabbed a handful of pages and looked them over. He exchanged an excited look with the reverend, who understood the importance of the find. They quickly broke open the matching cases.

"These are his journals, letters, maps and books," said Reverend Oliver. Billings brought his bottle over to where the two men were reading.

"I say we drink the wine, eat the dogs, and use the papers for musket wadding."

The reverend, who had already seen too much barbaric behavior that day, was mortified. He didn't realize Billings was only joking. "Eat the dogs?"

"Oh yes," Martin joined in, "a dog is a very fine meal."

"Good heavens!"

10

After hauling the captured English supplies back to Black Swamp, the exhausted but victorious troops spent a quiet evening around their fires. Gabriel sat near the archway of the ruined Spanish mission, stitching his tattered Old Glory back together little by little. His father used Cornwallis's folding camp furniture to set up an open-air office. He sat in a padded chair with his boots up on a table reading the Lord General's papers by the light of a lantern. He was surrounded by a music box, a few oil paintings, and an elaborate folding commode. The Great Danes had taken a liking to him and sat patiently at his feet, waiting for him to finish reading. Rollins retreated into the shadows to take inventory of his personal stash of loot, making neat stacks of the coins and other valuables he had taken that day.

Near where Gabriel was sitting, Villeneuve was organizing the crates of newly captured weapons. Although nearly all of the men had brought some sort of firearm with them from their homes, many of them were old and in need of repairs. Villeneuve began calling the men over to him, inspecting their weapons and issuing a Brown Bess, as the British muskets were called, to the men who needed one. Occam was one of the few who had no gun. His contribution during that morning's ambush had been limited to tossing a heavy branch through the trees and getting several of the Redcoats to waste a shot when it hit the ground with a crack. Villeneuve paused before handing over the weapon.

"Do you know how to use this?" he asked. When Occam

didn't answer, Villeneuve began to explain. "You pull the hammer back like this and—"

"I know how to use it," Occam said in his deep baritone voice. "I hunt for my master and now I'm expected to die for him."

The major, a bit chastened, put the musket in the man's hands. He also began to outfit him with the other gear he would need, such as a powder horn and cartridge box. Dan Scott saw what was happening and offered his opinion.

"I sure as hell don't like the idea of giving muskets to slaves."

Some of the other men expressed their agreement in grunts and nods. Villeneuve coldly noted their disapproval.

"Your sense of freedom," he said, "is as pale as your skin."

Occam, the only black man among them, took his gear and started toward the place he'd made for himself a little apart from the rest of the men, but Gabriel called to him and invited him to have a place at his campfire. Occam accepted and came to sit down.

"Don't listen to them," Gabriel told him. "If we win this war, a great many things will change."

Occam stared into the fire for a moment before he spoke. "What will change?"

The question caught Gabriel off guard, and he had to dig deep for an answer. "Well, they call this the New World," he began, "but it's not. It's the same as the old. But we'll have a chance to build a new world here, one with freedom and justice. A world where all men are created equal under God."

"Equal," said Occam, listening to the sound of the word. "Sounds good."

For the next hour, the two of them sat by the fire discussing the changes they expected the war would bring. Gabriel did nearly all the talking, mentioning the philosophers he had studied and discussing the strengths and weaknesses of the colonial economy. Occam only understood half of what was said but was glad to listen. It was the longest conversation the silent man had had in years and the more Gabriel said, the more clearly Occam began to imagine what America had the chance to become.

It was late in the evening before Martin put down his reading. With the dogs following at his heels, he walked to a campfire and sat down with several of his men.

"Well?" Billings asked. Martin took the bottle out of Billings's hands and took a drink. Then he let out a long, contemplative sigh.

"Cornwallis is a military genius," he announced. "He knows more about war than we ever will."

"Cheerful news," said Billings.

"His victories at Charles Town and Camden were perfect, strategically, tactically, and logistically. But he has a weakness." He paused to take another drink from the bottle as his men waited impatiently to hear what he would say next. "Lord Cornwallis is brilliant. His weakness is that he knows it."

"How so?" asked Gabriel

"Pride," said Martin. "Pride is his weakness." The men looked into the fire and considered the idea. Villeneuve was less than thrilled.

"Personally," he said, "I would prefer stupidity."

Martin smiled. "Pride will do."

Over the next few months, Martin's humble army of citizen soldiers maintained their secret camp in Black Swamp, emerging frequently to conduct actions against the powerful British, each one a bit more daring than the last. They used Martin's Indian-style tactics of sneaking up on the enemy, striking quickly, and then melting back into the landscape. News of their exploits spread quickly, and their reputation grew. Soon, rumors and gossip about the Ghost and his men were being whispered in every village market and country tavern in the region. Ordinary folks were surprised when they heard about a band of upcountry fools who were daring to oppose the King's professional army. And they were absolutely shocked to learn that the fools seemed to be winning. For the first time since the fall of Charles Town, Patriots began to feel hopeful again.

They burned bridges, they raided British jails and freed the Patriot prisoners, they sent sniper fire into the English fortresses and harassed the Redcoats in any way they could. But primarily, they disrupted the enemy supply lines. They captured or destroyed enough of these shipments to cause major logistical problems for Cornwallis, who was forced to abandon some of his more remote strongholds. Little by little, the English began to scale back their goals. Instead of sweeping north to engage General Washington, they concentrated their efforts on being able to feed and arm their troops in South Carolina.

Handbills and posters began to appear throughout the colony promising reward money to anyone who would betray the militia.

By order of The Royal Land,
REWARD OFFERED
for the Capture Or Death of the REBEL known as
THE GHOST
signed, Lord General Cornwallis by order
of King George the III.

These notices did not have the effect the British hoped they would. They only served to confirm the fact that the South Carolina militia was achieving some success, and thus acted as recruitment posters for the Patriot cause. The number of men riding with Martin grew steadily until he had four hundred men under his command and was forced to stop bringing new members into the camp at Black Swamp.

Since much of the raiding was done in darkness, the mornings belonged largely to Villeneuve. Working in an open field two miles from their island hideout, he endeavored to train the men and turn them into a credible fighting force. It was no easy task. On the first day, it took half an hour just to have them stand in a straight line. The Americans were not nearly as obedient as the Europeans he had trained in the past. They disliked taking orders and asked questions constantly. Villeneuve, like General von Steuben in the North, soon concluded that his Old World methods would need some alterations if they were to hang properly on the headstrong colonials. He adjusted his style and became less dictatorial. He conferred with the men more often and forced himself to listen when they expressed their opinions, but he never let them forget he was in charge. He was a talented drill sergeant and within a month, he had taught them a simplified, "democratized" version of the British Thirty-five Count military drill. The men, to their surprise, came to enjoy it. Learning to fight as the British did built the morale and confidence of greenhorns and grizzled veterans alike.

By early spring, the militiamen felt that they were ready to meet the British in the open field, but Martin wouldn't hear of it. He sensed that before the war was over, there would be a day when they would have to confront Cornwallis's army head to head, but he hoped he was wrong.

During these months, he made a practice of paying random, unannounced visits to the towns and villages surrounding the swamp. Accompanied by a handful of his men, he would descend on a local tavern and buy several bottles of the finest grog on offer. He always paid in hard English coin and kept the innkeepers happy by leaving a generous gratuity. These visits were not lighthearted amusement but part of the serious business of fighting the war. Armed with the bottles Martin had bought, his men fanned out and mingled with the locals, offering to share the liquor. For an hour or two, the tavern would overflow with laughter, rough jokes, and feelings of camaraderie. But the militiamen were busy spreading more than good cheer. Along with the free drinks, they poured out stories of how a "Ghost" had risen in South Carolina and was moving through the colony giving the Redcoats hell.

Dear Miss Howard,

Do you now regret permitting me to write you? By my count, this is my tenth letter and I fear I am becoming a pest. I pray any exasperation on your part will be soothed by the good news I have today for all who yearn to see America standing independently. The English continue to hold South Carolina but two days ago we took another lot of their supplies. It is much smaller than the first I described, but it was a another solid blow and was cleverly done. We delayed their six wagons by felling a tree across the road and made our preparations. We were much concerned that the ground where we would meet them offered no Obstacles or Hiding places, but our Commander bid us cut many bushes and vines with which to cover ourselves. We gave the English a nasty surprise when we rose out of the ground on all sides of them like Demons from Below and began to fire. We took many prisoners, but set them free again, instructing them to deliver a message to Cornwallis. They were told to say that the Ghost and his men thank him for his continuing contributions.

Most Sundays I go to a church to hear the sermon and to persuade the men there to join us. Yesterday, I paid such a visit to a town I cannot name in this letter and came away with Three new soldiers. We now count fifteen men for every one who was here when we began.

I hope this report finds you in good health and good spirits. My dedication to the cause of liberty, which we both love so well, makes me bold. I fear not for my life, and only pray it lasts long enough for me to visit Pembroke again.

Your friend,
G. M.

"Finished, my lord!" the tailor announced, scurrying into the opulent drawing room.

"Thank Goodness!" said Cornwallis, half-dressed and impatient. "Let's have a look at it."

They were standing in the west wing of the manor house at Middleton Place, northwest of Charles Town. Considered the grandest plantation in the Carolinas, Middleton Place bordered the Ashley River and featured an enormous brick mansion three stories tall, surrounded by elegantly landscaped gardens. It rivaled the finest homes in England, and when Henry Middleton offered to hold a ball in honor of Cornwallis's arrival, the Lord General accepted immediately and enthusiastically, ignoring the fact that Middleton was known as a Whig sympathizer. To ensure his comfort, Cornwallis was given three large rooms for himself and a dozen more for his top staff.

Smiling meekly, the tailor held the coat up for inspection. "I've taken it in at the back and added the wider epaulettes, as you requested. I even found a bit of gold braiding for the cuffs." Plainly, it was not the finest dress coat an English officer might wear, but under the rushed circumstances, it was a rather remarkable achievement. Cornwallis tested the coat's fabric with his fingers.

"A horse blanket," he declared.

The tailor shuddered visibly.

To Tavington, the situation was highly amusing. Waving his finger like a conductor's baton in time to the music already playing in the main hall, he stepped closer to examine the jacket for himself. Dressed in his smartest formal uniform, he was the very picture of a dashing and well-put-together military gentleman. An apple pomade rubbed into his hair kept it perfectly in place.

"It's really quite nice, my lord."

"It's a nice horse blanket," said Cornwallis, anguished by the idea of having to wear the thing in good company. He turned and sneered at the tailor. "Where did you get that braiding? It's all wrong."

The man stuttered and stumbled over his answer until the general was distracted by one of his valets coming to repowder his wig.

Charles Cornwallis was the eldest son of a titled and respected family. His grandfather had been a baron, his father an earl, and his uncle the Archbishop of Canterbury. His family was not especially wealthy, but their social connections were better than gold. He had grown up attending all the most important balls and social functions. He enjoyed these affairs immensely and made it a point of honor to always arrive on time and to be perfectly dressed. That evening at Middleton Place was a humiliating exception.

His anger swelled as he recalled the precise reason his own garments were not available to him. They had fallen, along with many other valuables, into the hands of the insurgents—no doubt a horde of unwashed, uncultured heathens who would have no good use for them. In fact, his spies in the country taverns informed him that the uniforms were in the possession of the rebel leader known as "the Ghost." He stared at the horse blanket with dread and loathing.

"Colonel Tavington," he asked through clenched teeth, "why am I here?"

"For a ball, my lord. I believe you find them amusing."

"You misunderstand me, sir. I am asking you why, after all this time, I am at Middleton Place to attend a ball in *South* Carolina. By now, I should be attending balls in *North* Carolina." He made it clear that he expected an answer to this question.

Tavington pursed his lips. "Our supply line, my lord."

"Excellent guess, Colonel!" he said in a mocking tone before suddenly turning cold and serious. "First the theft of my personal baggage, including my memoirs, on which I have sacrificed countless hours of work. Then we find half the bridges and ferries between here and Charles Town burned and broken. Colonel, if you are incapable of securing our supply line against these militia, how in the world do you expect to do so against the colonial regulars? Or against the French, if and when they arrive?"

Tavington bristled. "My lord, they're not like regulars. We can't find them. They melt away after they attack and we have found no way of predicting when or where they will strike next."

"*Militia*, Colonel, they're *militia*," he said with utter contempt. "Farmers with pitchforks!"

"They are more than that, my lord. Made so by their commander, this so-called Ghost."

A different valet came forward with a pair of brandies on a silver tray. Cornwallis drank one of them in a single gulp, then waved the man away.

"This *Ghost* was created by you."

Tavington was puzzled. "How so, my lord?"

"By *your* lack of restraint. Your brutality has swelled his ranks, without which this Ghost would simply disappear and I would be in *North* Carolina, if not Virginia, by now."

"My lord, I . . ."

"Enough!" Cornwallis cut him off with a dismissive flick of the hand. "A fine officer you are, bested by a bedtime story!" Enunciating each word carefully, he gave Tavington an emphatic order. "Colonel, secure my supply line."

Tavington, choking on embarrassment and anger, tried to strike a deferential posture. "Yes, my lord."

Cornwallis turned imperiously away and studied his half-dressed reflection in a mirror. "Oh, very well," he sighed, "give me the horse blanket."

A valet snatched the coat from the tailor and helped Cornwallis into it. His Lordship kept his eyes away from the mirror, choosing not to view the full extent of his misery, and made directly for the door. Instead of opening it immediately, he lingered for a moment with his hand on the knob. He looked down at the braiding on his cuff and then at the gold-trimmed curtain on the wall, which matched exactly. A foot-long section of the curtain's trim was missing, and it was obvious where it had ended up. He gave the tailor a last scowling look before stepping into the adjoining hallway.

There was nothing to do but make the best of a bad situation. Cornwallis decided he would compensate for the deficiencies of his costume by making his best display of wit and charm. Gathering himself, he stepped into the lively ballroom. English officers and Tory gentlemen were engaged in spirited conversation, entertaining the lovely colonial women who had dressed themselves in sumptuous gowns. A small orchestra played as liveried servants moved through the room offering hors d'oeuvres and refreshments. A number of the guests had wandered outside through the tall glass doors that opened onto a grassy hillside overlooking the Ashley River. Since the ballroom was ablaze with candles, Cornwallis decided to venture outdoors, where the dim light would mask the imperfections of his uniform. As he started toward the doors, he saw a pair of English cargo ships, the *Bristol* and the *York,* outlined by moonlight, sitting at anchor in the river.

"O'Hara!"

Cornwallis's second-in-command excused himself from his company and hurried over. "My lord, the coat turned out splendidly."

Cornwallis ignored his insincere flattery. "It looks as though our supply ships have arrived."

"Indeed they have, my lord."

"Then why in God's name am I wearing these rags?"

"My lord," O'Hara explained, "your replacement wardrobe is aboard the *York,* but Colonel Tavington thought it best to secure our arms and munitions first from the *Bristol.* They're being unloaded at this very moment."

"Tavington thought it best, you say?" Cornwallis asked, narrowing his eyes at the dashing colonel, who was just then making his entrance.

"Yes, my lord."

At that same moment, a dozen small boats were plying the Ashley, most of them carrying oil lanterns hung from their prows, moving between the *Bristol* and the shore. Middleton Place mansion, a few hundred yards away and perched majestically atop a terraced hillside, was overflowing with light like a vision of Zeus's palace in a mythological painting. It was an enchanting view, but the mood on the water was anything but serene. With the officers all attending the ball, the Redcoat soldiers were left to supervise themselves, and no two of them could agree on the smallest matter. The *Bristol*'s decks were loud with arguments and foul language.

In the confusion, the *York* was left almost completely unattended. No one noticed when a boat full of men in Redcoat uniforms, their hats cocked low over their brows to hide their faces, boarded the ship, loaded up several crates of supplies, and then rowed away in the wrong direction. Before leaving, they left a surprise package in the belly of the ship, taking care that the fuse was lit.

When the "Redcoats" were a safe distance away, they lit a lantern to help them navigate and began to laugh.

"You see?" Martin said, pushing the hat back on his head, "with the proper attire, you can get anything." He leaned on his elbow, relaxing in the prow as he watched Villeneuve and Gabriel pull the oars. He took a good long look at Villeneuve.

"That uniform looks good on you, Major," he said with a grin. "You should wear red more often."

Villeneuve raised his arm to his nose and sniffed at the garment. "It stinks."

"I'm not surprised," Martin said, "since it came off a dead man."

Lord Cornwallis found the outdoor section of the party more to his liking. The light was dim, and the gaiety of his fellow guests slowly began to soften and improve his mood. His host for the evening, Mr. Middleton, greeted him warmly and introduced him to Mr. Simms, the wealthy, heavyset merchant from Beaufort who had been one of the Tory leaders in the Provincial Assembly. Cornwallis had been looking forward to meeting Simms for some time, but now that they were face to face, he found it difficult to concentrate on the man's conversation. The reason was Mrs. Simms, who was, to the Lord General's eye, a spectacular beauty. She wore a beautifully coifed wig and a lavish gown that rode daringly low on the crest of her ample bosom. Her face was powdered white in the style then popular in Europe, and she had used a pencil to draw a dainty beauty mark just above her lip. His erotic imagination was aroused by the idea of discovering the woman under so many layers of tasteful disguise.

To win her sympathy, he began relating some of the many hardships he had suffered since arriving to quash the rebellion. The lady empathized with him fully and was especially moved by the tragic loss of his Great Danes.

"No!" she exclaimed, fanning herself. "The beasts took your dogs as well?"

Cornwallis sighed in heartfelt pain. "Fine animals, a gift from His Majesty. Dead now, for all I know."

"Is there no decency?" Mr. Simms interjected.

Their conversation was soon interrupted by a thunderous bang. The ballgoers all turned to face the river and watched as a massive set of explosions lit up the night. The *York* burst into flame as the kegs of gunpowder stored in her hold sent great blasts of fiery debris high into the air.

"Oh, fireworks!" Mrs. Simms said gleefully. "How lovely!"

11

It was a warm spring day when Martin led about a quarter of his brigade into Pembroke. It had been almost six months to the day since Gabriel had come to recruit, and the town showed the signs of having lost half its adult males. Many of the fields had returned to seed, the ruts worn in the road by the winter rains hadn't been filled, and Reverend Oliver's small house was half swallowed up by creeping vines. The doors to the church stood wide open, and there were a number of people inside who didn't live in Pembroke.

The trip had been planned for some time, and Martin had allowed the men to send word to their families to come and meet them. John Billings's wife, Sara, and their boy, the redheaded six-year-old, were among those who had come. Jessica Scott was so excited to see her husband riding back into town that she ran up and hugged his horse until she could get her arms around him. Mr. Howard, able to hear the commotion from a distance, hurried out of this house and down the road at a brisk clip. Dogs were barking and the children ran back and forth cheering as Pembroke welcomed its returning heroes.

That evening, after the excitement of the men's return had settled a bit, Gabriel returned from a walk through the fields holding a bouquet of wildflowers. The sign in the front window of the Howards' house said the dry goods store was closed, but he saw the glow of candles through the curtains, so he walked quietly to the front door and listened for a second or two before knocking. The door snapped open almost at once, and Gabriel found himself once more face to face with Mr. Peter Howard, who didn't seem surprised by the visit, nor especially happy about it. He took note of the bouquet in Gabriel's hands, the shined-up boots on his feet, and his carefully combed hair. The purpose of the young man's arrival was painfully clear.

Gabriel could see Anne sitting at a desk, figuring the accounts of the family business in a ledger. She looked a little embarrassed, but very pleased to see him and began closing up her work at once.

Her father stood in the doorway and stared, waiting for an explanation.

"Mr. Howard, I've come to call on Anne."

The man raised his ear trumpet to his head. "Ay?"

Gabriel repeated himself, a bit louder. "I've come to *call on Anne*?"

The gentleman looked perplexed. "Well, of course you *call yourself a man!*"

Anne came to the door laughing. "Father, stop! You heard him perfectly well." She asked Gabriel to come inside, saying they'd been expecting him all along and that they'd set a place for him at the dinner table.

Mr. Howard held his ground, blocking the doorway and keeping Gabriel on the spit for another moment. Then he stepped aside and let Gabriel in with a small smile.

"Of course you can call on her."

That evening's meal was simple by the Howards' standards, consisting of roast venison, corn on the cob, and a few sliced turnips. But to Gabriel, who had not enjoyed a home-cooked meal for quite some time, it was an extraordinary treat. Though Mrs. Howard hadn't spoken to Gabriel since he was a boy, she took an immediate liking to the adult version of him and made him feel very much at home. Mr.

Howard tried to remain stern but he was, by nature, a jolly character and soon had everyone at the table laughing as he recounted stories from the days when Gabriel and Anne had played together as children. After a fruit cobbler for dessert, they retired to the sitting room, where the subject turned to the war and the Glorious Cause of American Liberty. Anne and Gabriel spoke with such passion and at such a terrific rate of speed that even Peter Howard, an accomplished speaker on the topic, could hardly keep up. When the clock struck nine, Mrs. Howard interrupted them and asked if Gabriel would care to spend the night with Anne. Suddenly bashful, he grinned and said he would. When Mr. Howard grunted his reluctant approval of the idea, his wife excused herself and went upstairs to prepare the bed.

When Gabriel and Anne came into the bedroom a few minutes later, Mrs. Howard already had the bundling bag laid out on the bed and her sewing kit open on the night table. As soon as Gabriel had climbed inside the heavy canvas bag, Mrs. Howard went to work sewing it closed around him so that only his head still showed. Originally a German practice, bundling had spread to become a fairly common part of courtship in the colonies. It gave young couples a chance to be intimate while presenting an obvious barrier to pregnancy.

As her mother sewed, Anne changed into her sleeping dress and came to lay on the bed beside Gabriel, and they continued their discussion. She was eager to hear everything she could about the war, including how the actual fighting took place.

". . . but if it was you who attacked the Redcoats at Singer's Ferry, who raided the supply house at Starksboro? It couldn't have been your men, since it happened on the same night."

"I assure you, it was us," Gabriel said proudly.

"So you split your force into different brigades?"

"No, we post fresh horses several miles apart, ride hard, and sometimes we can strike three Redcoat posts in a single night."

She thought for a moment, then nodded in approval of the strategy. "The British must think you have more men than you actually do. It must confuse them."

Anne's mother took extra care with the finishing stitches around Gabriel's neck. When she was done, she tested them with a tug, then began gathering up her sewing kit. Mr. Howard leaned on his crutches in the doorway, looking highly uncomfortable with the situation.

"You needn't worry, Father," Anne said.

"I know," Mr. Howard answered gruffly, arching an eyebrow and staring directly at Gabriel.

Anne looked at Gabriel sympathetically and apologized for the awkward situation he was in.

"Oh, I think bundling bags are a wonderful tradition," he lied, largely for the benefit of her parents. "I don't mind in the least."

Mr. Howard made a skeptical sound.

"Now, Peter," his wife chided, shooing him out of the room. She picked up one of the candles burning on the table and smiled at the young people sweetly. "Don't keep him awake all night, Anne, he's got to ride in the morning. If you two need anything, your father and I will be *right next door*." With that gentle warning, she pulled the door closed behind her. She went down the hall and found her husband in their bedroom, his ear trumpet pressed to the wall. He turned to her and let out a quiet, miserable moan.

"She's so young!"

"Oh, posh! She's well past the usual age," she whispered.

"Older than I was when you wore the bag." Mr. Howard's eyes went wide as he remembered. "But don't worry," she added quickly, "I sew better than my mother did."

"I certainly hope so," he said.

"Tea?" asked Anne.

"Please," replied Gabriel.

He lay stiffly on his back, wishing for all the world that his hands were free as she turned and reached for the tea tray. As she poured, a thought occurred to him.

"I nearly forgot! I brought a copy of *Common Sense,* hoping we might read a bit of it together."

"Splendid. I'll go and fetch it."

"No, I mean I brought it to bed with me. It's in my pocket."

"Conveniently forgotten until now?"

Gabriel looked at her questioningly for a moment, waiting to see how she would respond. When she only stared back at him, he began rustling inside the bag and eventually managed to force the paper out through the gap near his throat. "I've marked some of my favorite passages," he said, doing his best to point with his nose. Anne held the well-worn pages close to the candle and read the underlined words aloud. Gabriel spoke the words in unison with her, reciting them from memory.

"'We have it in our power to begin the world over again. A situation, similar to the present, hath not happened since the days of Noah until now. The birthday of a new world is at hand, and a race of men perhaps as numerous as all Europe contains, are to receive their portion of freedom from the event of a few months.'" She looked up and nodded approvingly. "Starting a new world. I hadn't thought of it quite like that before, but that's exactly what you're doing, isn't it?"

Mel Gibson stars as Benjamin Martin, a loving father and reluctant hero of the American Revolution.

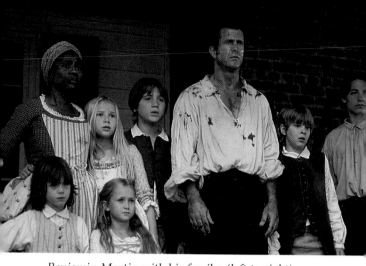

Benjamin Martin with his family: (left to right)
William (Logan Lerman), the housekeeper, Abigale
(Beatrice Bush), Margaret (Mika Boorem), Susan (Skye
McCole Bartusiak), Nathan (Trevor Morgan), Samuel
(Bryan Chafin), and Thomas (Gregory Smith).

Jason Isaacs
plays Colonel
William
Tavington of
the Green
Dragoons, a
vicious soldier
prepared to go to
any length to
defeat the rebels.

Benjamin's eldest son, Gabriel (Heath Ledger), enlists with the American army against his father's will—only to be captured by the British.

The American colonists are poorly prepared to fight the British. Early battles end in bloody defeats for the Patriots.

Charlotte Selton (Joely Richardson) is Benjamin's beautiful sister-in-law, who must watch over the younger children while Benjamin and Gabriel are at war.

Gabriel exchanges love letters with Anne Howard (Lisa Brenner).

Tchéky Karyo plays French volunteer Major Jean Villeneuve.

Benjamin Martin trains a new army of Patriots along with Major Villeneuve.

General Charles Cornwallis (Tom Wilkinson) commands the British army in the Southern colonies.

Gabriel struggles to understand his father's mysterious past.

Gabriel proves himself an able soldier in the pursuit of freedom.

Benjamin's youngest daughter, Susan, waits for her father to return home.

Benjamin bids farewell to his family before entering the war.

Benjamin uses the new American flag to rally the Patriots in a climactic battle.

"That's what *we're* doing," he said affectionately.

"A toast, then!" she said, lifting the teacup carefully to his lips. "To the new world!"

Gabriel lifted his head and sipped, savoring the flavor. "It's very good."

"I'm so pleased that you like it," she said warmly.

He let his head fall back on the pillow and gazed up at the bright angel hovering over him. When he smiled, Anne noted with a certain amount of satisfaction that his teeth were all stained black by the ink she'd added to his tea.

During his months of service in the militia, Reverend Oliver had missed nothing so much as the comfort of his own bed. Many a morning in the swamp, he woke up with a stiff neck or a sore back. A man of his age, he sometimes complained, was entitled to better than sleeping on the cold hard ground. But now his mattress seemed too soft, as if it were trying to swallow him. Besides, he'd offered his home to several of his fellow militiamen who hailed from other towns. Nearly a dozen of them were spread out on the floor or slumped in chairs with their hats over their faces, all of them snoring at once, which made his little cottage sound like the inside of a sawmill. It was still well before dawn when he gave up trying to fall back to sleep. He tiptoed past the sleeping men, carrying his boots in one arm and his coat in the other. He wandered across the road to the church, looking for a quiet place to relax, but was surprised to notice a figure kneeling at the pews inside.

He stood at the door, squinting into the darkness until he realized the figure was Benjamin Martin, a man who had for years been very lax about attending Sunday services and who had stopped coming altogether after his wife died. The reverend thought about going inside, but decided to leave the sanctuary to Benjamin, who probably needed it more. After all, Colonel Martin carried an enormous weight of responsibility on his shoulders. Despite his accomplishments over the last months, very few informed observers expected him to succeed against the British much longer. But unless he managed to keep them occupied in the South, Washington faced almost certain defeat, and the war for American independence would be lost. The reverend knew it must be a difficult cross to bear, especially for a man already loaded with emotional burdens that would have crushed lesser men.

He decided it would do him good to take a meditative pre-dawn stroll and set out along the road, but within a hundred yards he came upon an inviting patch of tall grass, where he lay down and fell fast asleep.

A few hours later, as Pembroke stirred awake, Dan Scott stepped out of his front door and started toward the church, where the wagons were being loaded for the trip back to camp. He hadn't gone far when he noticed Occam standing outside the blacksmith's shed staring at a bulletin nailed to the wall. Ludwell and some of the other men lingered nearby. Scott was certain Occam couldn't read and decided to have a little fun.

"If you're going to stand there," he called, "why don't you read it to us?" Scott, a barrel cooper by profession, hadn't had much traffic with Africans, but disliked them as a group. He sniggered at his own joke, coaxing the other white men to laugh with him.

"I can't read," Occam replied.

"Me neither," Ludwell said.

Scott, his meaty face nicked up from being freshly shaved, strode up to the spot, scoffing at the other men's ignorance. He was not a great reader himself, but could at least sound out the words he saw. In a halting style, he read the poster to the others.

"By the order of his Excellency General George Washington and the Continental Congress, it is hereby decreed that all bound slaves who shall give a minimum of one year service in the Continental Army or its allied militias will be granted their legal freedom and paid a bounty of five shillings for each month of service."

"Say, you read pretty good," Ludwell remarked.

Scott put his hands on his hips. "You understand what it says? They're going to free 'em. Not only that, they're gonna pay 'em, too. Seems to me George Washington's either desperate for soldiers or he's gone soft in the head." He searched the faces around him for agreement, but found none.

"Only another six more months," Occam said.

Disgusted, Scott started away, but turned after only a few steps. "What in hell are you Negroes going to do with freedom?"

Occam looked at him evenly. He seemed to have an answer in mind, but he kept it to himself.

Billings dug through one of the wagons, retrieved a sack of souvenirs he'd been collecting, and brought them to where his wife and son were waiting. She was a plain-looking Irishwoman with cherry red hair that spilled from a white cotton bonnet. She spoke little and smiled only rarely, making her seem standoffish to outsiders, but it was obvious to all that she dearly loved her big, brutish husband.

His brief visit with her seemed to have done Billings good. He had a bounce in his step and a smile on his face. For the first time in weeks, all the buttons on his clothes were done up properly, his boots were laced, and he'd even put a comb through his long, unruly hair. He knelt down beside the boy and pulled a toy pistol out of the sack. It was made of wood, and Billings had carved it himself.

The red-haired boy was delighted with the gift and immediately pointed it between his father's eyes. "Bang!"

Billings laughed.

Mr. Howard, limping past the spot on his crutches, stopped and stared when he heard Billings's distinctive and rather disturbing laugh, which at first he thought to be the pained cry of a small farm animal. As he continued on his way, he noticed Benjamin Martin walking toward him, flanked by the heavily jowled Great Danes.

"Good morning, Colonel."

"Good morning, Assemblyman."

"Did you get the supplies I sent with your men?"

"Yes, I did," Martin said. "In fact, I was just on my way to see you about that. I'm afraid I can't pay you for . . ."

Howard interrupted him with a sweeping gesture and a booming voice. "You pay me what you can, when you can. In the meantime, consider it my small contribution to the cause."

Martin thanked him with a handshake. "You're a good man, Peter."

"Above average, perhaps," he said with a wink. He leaned on his crutches and gestured across the churchyard toward Gabriel. "That one over there spent the night with us, sewed up in a bundling bag."

Martin saw Gabriel talking intimately with Anne apart from the others.

"Next time you come through town," Howard said with a chuckle, "we might be having a conversation about a dowry. She's very taken with him. Gets so excited when his letters reach us." He watched them for a minute, smiling fondly, then snorted a rough laugh out his nose. "He reminds me greatly of you . . . before you got old and ugly!"

Martin was watching them, too, as if from some distant place. "No, he's not like me," Martin said gently, almost whispering. "He takes after his mother." The great tenderness in his voice surprised both men. "My younger children barely remember her, of course, but Gabriel . . . she taught him well. He's already a better man than I could ever hope to be."

Howard squirmed, uncomfortable with the open display of emotion. When Martin saw this, he quickly shook the moment off in favor of a coarse and joking tone.

"What do you mean, old and ugly? I wouldn't go pointing fingers if I looked like you."

Howard put up his fists, ready to defend his honor. He took a playful swipe at Martin, which missed by a foot. The two men laughed and shook hands again before Martin saddled up. He put his fingers to his mouth and whistled loudly, telling his troops that it was time to go.

As the men climbed into their saddles, Gabriel was still staring into Anne's eyes. He slipped his hand around her waist and pulled her closer for a good-bye kiss. When she didn't resist, he leaned toward her and pressed his lips briefly to hers. He took his hand away, expecting her to retreat, but she stayed where she was, the tip of her nose touching the tip of his, and looked into his eyes. They kissed again and this time it was a real kiss, deep and sustained.

Gabriel broke it off suddenly, leaving Anne breathless, and dashed for his horse, mounting with a dramatic leap. He galloped away and soon took his place at his father's side. Overjoyed, Gabriel broke into a giant smile that revealed a set of ink-stained teeth. As his father examined him curiously, Gabriel turned and waved to Anne. He saw her waving in return, but was already too far away to see that he'd blackened her smile with his kiss.

12

The day after returning to their swamp island camp, two of Martin's scouts spotted a small shipment of British supplies, lightly armed, making its way south along a seldom-used road. After questioning the two men closely, Martin decided to ride out and investigate.

If the train of supply wagons they had captured on their very first morning of action was a great whale, the present shipment was no more than a four-inch trout, consisting of only two covered wagons. Cornwallis had learned, as the partisan attacks against him multiplied, to be more conservative. Each new shipment seemed smaller than the last and better defended. In that regard, this one was an exception, since it was under the protection of just six infantry and their sergeant. Martin spotted it from the top of a rise and studied it for a while in the lens of a collapsing telescope. It had turned into a baking hot day and the Redcoats were coming through an open sunny field, unwittingly headed toward an encounter with the Ghost. The sergeant marching along at the head of the file was a corpulent, ruddy-faced fellow who fanned himself as he walked. There were large sweat rings under both arms of his jacket, and a kerchief over his head as a sun shield. He looked like a boiled goose.

Martin studied them for a long time, perhaps debating whether it was worth the trouble on such an uncomfortable day. But the Redcoats made the decision easy for him, marching straight toward the spot where he waited in the comfort of the shade. When the sergeant came round a soft curve in the road, he was singing to himself even as he panted for air.

> *In the spring of the year when the blood is too thick,*
> *There is nothing so rare as a sassafras stick.*
> *It cleans up the liver, it strengthens the heart,*
> *And to the whole system new life doth impart.*
> *Sassafras, O, Sassafras! Thou are the stuff for me!*
> *And in the spring I love to sing sweet sassafras of thee.*

When the sergeant looked up and noticed that a band of hardened, heavily armed colonials had materialized, seemingly out of nowhere, he let out a startled cry and pulled his sword out of its scabbard. The wagons came to a sudden halt behind him.

Benjamin Martin stood in the center of the road, an immovable object, backed by Gabriel, Villeneuve, and a dozen others, all of them pointing their weapons at the ample target provided by the sergeant's chest.

"Sergeant, this road is closed," Martin announced. "Those wagons are now the property of the Continental Army."

The sergeant responded by striking an unusual pose. He spread his feet wide apart and held his sword high above his head in a way that made him look like a ballet dancer preparing for a fencing match. "This is the King's highway," he shouted back, "and I advise you and your men to make way."

The Americans glanced at one another, surprised by the officer's decision to resist. He didn't seem to care that his men were outnumbered two to one.

"Ready arms! Form by twos!" shouted the sergeant. He kept his knees bent, his back arched, and his sword in the air. The infantrymen hurried forward with their muskets and lined up. Martin waited patiently while they made themselves into a single, compact target, then raised his fingers to his mouth and whistled loudly. All at once, the bushes and tall grass around the road came to life. Fifty-five American militiamen came out of their hiding places and showed themselves, each one leveling a loaded weapon at the tiny British detachment. Now they were outnumbered eleven to one. Sweat poured freely from the officer's face and his eyes darted fearfully from side to side. The sword above his head began to tremble.

"Sergeant, there's no reason for you and your men to die," Martin said calmly. "We'll be satisfied to take the wagons. Just lay down your weapons and go."

Incredibly, the man refused. Despite the overwhelming hopelessness of his situation, he was prepared to defend the wagons.

Villeneuve spoke for the militiamen when he called the Redcoat sergeant crazy.

Martin realized there was something out of place, but couldn't quite put his finger on it until he heard the rumbling. Barely detectable at first, it quickly grew louder and the militiamen soon recognized the sound of horses' hooves pounding the earth. A column of Green Dragoons came thundering up behind the supply wagons. More cavalry came out of the trees on either side of them, rushing toward the road like water from a bursting damn. Redcoat foot soldiers who had until that moment remained hidden in the backs of the wagons began spilling outside. It was a well-set trap, and it closed on the Americans swiftly from three sides.

"Fire!" Martin shouted. His men responded and cut down more than half of the Redcoat infantry before turning to run for their horses.

The onrush of the Dragoons, two hundred strong, made

a frightening spectacle, but Martin stayed where he was, firing his pistol at the surviving infantrymen, trying to keep them pinned down while his men made their escape. He finally turned and ran when the Dragoons raced in with their swords drawn and began to swing at the fleeing American rebels. He climbed onto his horse and looked back at the mayhem in the field. Reverend Oliver and John Billings were standing near one another, their hands raised in surrender. Dan Scott nearly made it to the trees, but fell when a bullet hit him in the back. There was no chance of organizing a retreat, nothing to do but turn and flee.

Martin spurred his horse and led ten of his men away. They hadn't gone far when Gabriel called out and pointed over his shoulder. Martin looked back and saw that Tavington was chasing them, leading a column of fifty Dragoons.

"Faster!"

The Americans rode toward their hideout as fast as the horses would carry them, firing pistols over their shoulders to slow the British. It was twenty minutes of hard riding before they came to the first cypress trees and black-bottomed ponds. Galloping full speed ahead, they plunged into the thickly overgrown environment that they knew so well, but which was confusing to newcomers.

Tavington chased them with reckless abandon, urging his horse to ever greater effort with his spurs. But as the watery forest closed around him, he lost sight of his prey in the dense vegetation and had to track them by sound alone. The road beneath him dwindled to a poorly marked trail and more than one of his men were thrown when the horses began to stumble on the cypress knees jutting out of the ground. His men became separated and lost their sense of direction, but still he pressed on, following the ever-fainter sound of the retreating Patriot riders and looking for the ripples they left in the still water. He did everything in his power not to let them escape, but soon realized he had lost the trail and had no clues to follow. He stopped and listened, but could hear nothing over the sound of the birds. The ghost had disappeared without a trace, swallowed up utterly into the endless green tangle of the swamp.

Martin sat alone at his fire, staring into the flames. He busied himself with the task of turning more of Thomas's toy soldiers into bullets, but he worked absentmindedly. A distressing silence had fallen over the camp. Those who had managed to reach their horses and escape were having their wounds quietly tended to. Martin's upstart army, which had begun the day with swaggering optimism, had been shattered by a single, devastating blow. Gabriel came and sat beside the fire, watching his father pour the hot lead carefully into the mold.

"I didn't know Thomas had so many of those little fellows," Gabriel said, trying to lighten the mood.

Martin didn't look up. "Did you get a count?"

"Twenty-two dead, eighteen wounded, and twenty missing."

The mold hissed loudly when Martin dipped it into the water, and neither man spoke until it had completely cooled. They listened to the frogs croaking while that afternoon's disaster continued to resonate. When some of the men began exchanging angry words, Martin walked over to investigate.

Rollins and a handful of the coarse militiamen were making ready to leave, stuffing their gear roughly into their haversacks as they argued with Villeneuve and some of the others. When he saw Martin approaching,

Rollins made himself the spokesman of his group.

"I'm through," he yelled. "I don't know what I was thinking coming out here." Rollins lifted several packs onto his shoulder and went to his horse. When he was gone, Villeneuve tried to find something encouraging to say. The small force of battered, despondent Americans who remained was a pitiful sight indeed.

"Soon we will have help. My countrymen will arrive. The French army in Canada and New England—"

A slovenly militiaman cut him off. "To hell with you and to hell with your damned French army."

Another man, one of the recruits from the Boar's Head with a wicked sense of humor, mockingly agreed. "That's right. We don't need your French army, *monsieur*. We got Benjamin Martin on our side, and we all know what he done to your French!"

Villeneuve bristled for a moment, but walked away before he could be provoked into losing his temper. Martin did the same, going back to his campfire, where there were a few bullets left to make. He hadn't been there long when Gabriel approached and stood over him.

"Father, tell me about Fort Wilderness."

Benjamin Martin was a steady man under pressure, and he didn't scare easily. But he tensed visibly when he heard Gabriel's question, and put the pan back on the fire. It was a question he'd spent nearly half his life trying to bury and avoid. And although he hadn't spoken two words on the subject of Fort Wilderness in all that time, rarely a day went by when it didn't come into his mind to torment him. It was a curse he'd put on himself.

"Your mother asked me the same question around the time you were born. I was drunk at the time and I was foolish enough to answer her." He shook his head, remembering the scene. "If you ever wondered why it was four years between you and Thomas, there's your answer. It took me that long to regain her respect."

Gabriel reasoned with him quietly. "I'm your son. Wherever you go, men recognize you and buy you drinks because of what happened at Fort Wilderness. Strangers know more about you than I do." Martin was quiet for a long time, looking for a place to begin. The light of the fire played over the lines in his face, making him look older than he was.

"You have to understand that we considered ourselves Englishmen back in those days. I was young, about your age. The French had built a line of forts from Canada all the way down to Louisiana to hem us in, and when they started attacking our villages, we went out to stop them."

Martin broke off and wiped his lips with his sleeve, wishing there was a bottle of liquor handy. Gabriel urged him to go on.

"The French and the Cherokee had raided all along the Blue Ridge. English settlers were being scalped and killed, so they all took refuge at Fort Charles, but the French captured it. When we got there the fort was abandoned. Not a French soldier or a Cherokee anywhere. They had left a week earlier. What we found was . . . bad."

"Tell me."

Martin's eyes made quick small movements as he saw the scene again in vivid detail. "There were only a few English soldiers, and they were the lucky ones. They'd all died quickly. But the settlers . . . the men and women . . . bodies everywhere, some of them burned alive. And they put the children on . . ." He broke off and waved the memory away with a hand. "It took two days to bury them, and then we went to track. It was a cold trail and the French were moving fast. But we moved faster and caught up to them at Fort Wilderness.

"We took our time. We wanted to give them worse than they gave those settlers. We dealt with them one at a time and made the others watch. It was two weeks before they were all dead, all but two. It was hardest with the young ones. Some were younger than I was, younger than you are now. But we took them apart just the same.

"When that was done, we stacked the heads up on a big pallet and made the two we let live carry it into the French at Fort Ambercon. We put the eyes, fingers, and tongues into baskets and floated them down the Asheulot for the Cherokee to find. Soon after, the Cherokee broke their treaty with the French, which is how we justified it." He raised his eyes to meet his son's. "And not a day passes when I don't fear God's vengeance for what I did."

Gabriel studied his father closely for a moment, then shook his head.

"And men bought you *drinks*?"

Martin nodded, ashamed. He knew Gabriel was his mother's son, so he didn't expect pity or easy forgiveness. He reached for the bullet mold and pried it open, spilling the still-warm lead into the dirt. Gabriel knew the special purpose his father intended for the bullets, and he didn't like it. He'd held his tongue before, but now he stepped closer and grabbed some of them off the ground.

"Thomas was my brother, not just your son. You may not believe this, but I want satisfaction as much as you do, but not at the expense of our cause. This conflict is larger than our personal injuries. There will be a time for revenge, but until that time comes, stay the course."

Martin couldn't help but smile at receiving such parental-sounding advice from his child. He heard Elizabeth's voice loud and clear behind the words.

"*Stay the course,*" he repeated, glancing around the

nearly deserted camp. "Your mother used to say that to me often, especially when I'd get drunk or lose my temper."

"She'd say it to me when I picked on Thomas. *Stay the course.*" Martin reached out a hand to him, asking for the bullets. Gabriel turned them over.

"I miss him."

"So do I."

Both men blamed themselves for Thomas's death. The image of him falling to his knees in the yard haunted them both. But for a moment, they looked beyond it and remembered what he had been like growing up, how he had built elaborate forts with sticks and old blankets near the river, how he had nearly died at three from a sickness the doctors couldn't identify, how he had earned the nickname "the General" by ordering the smaller children around as if they were his personal army. For the first time in months, they remembered Thomas without immediately thinking also of Tavington.

The sound of sloshing water came out of the darkness. Fearing the camp was under attack, the militiamen sprang to their feet and grabbed their guns. Martin quickly doused his fire before hurrying toward the source of the trouble.

It turned out to be Occam. Battered and exhausted, he came stumbling through the waist-deep water with a wounded man draped over his shoulder. The half conscious man turned out to be Dan Scott, who had been shot in the shoulder. The men lifted Scott's heavy frame off of Occam's shoulder and carried him away for treatment. Occam, who had an ugly pink lump on his forehead, was wrapped in a blanket and brought to one of the fires, where he threw back a few slugs of rum before telling his story.

When the English had descended and surrounded them, he had tried to surrender, but had been knocked unconscious by a blow from the stock of a musket. When he'd come to, he'd made a break for the trees, pausing along the way to pick up Scott. From a hiding place, he had eavesdropped on the Redcoats until Tavington had returned from his unsuccessful pursuit.

"They've got eighteen of our men prisoner," he told Martin. "When the Colonel of the Dragoons came back, he tried to make them say where our camp is, but our boys wouldn't talk. He said he was taking them to Fort Carolina and was going to hang them one at a time until they gave up the rest of us."

This news sat heavily on the chests of the already disheartened men. Clearly, they couldn't sit by and do nothing while eighteen of their fellow soldiers were put to death, but what chance did they stand against the thousands of Redcoats guarding the fort? Martin drew a deep breath and looked up into the canopy of cypress limbs overhead, wondering what to do. He searched for the North Star—the action was a reflex when he was in need of council—but the dense forest obliterated all view of the sky. It was a dark night, the darkest he had seen for quite some time.

13

Jack Moore, John Billings, Reverend Oliver, Dickey Ludwell, and fourteen other men who had volunteered as South Carolina militiamen sat bent and cramped in their wooden cages watching with grim fascination as a crew of Redcoat soldiers and Tory civilians put the finishing touches on a handsome gallows they'd built. A heavy sack of rice was tied with a noose and set on the trapdoor. On a signal from the sergeant in charge, one of the civilian men yanked back on a lever, and the rice dropped five feet before bouncing back with a snap.

"Well done, lads," said the sergeant. "She works perfectly."

A few of the doomed prisoners applauded in sarcasm.

The cages were made of straight branches lashed together with twine, and after many hours of holding their captives, they were smeared with the blood of the wounded and rank with human waste. Billings rolled his stiff neck and looked over at Reverend Oliver.

"Mr. Preacher, have you got pen and paper with you?"

"I have a pencil," said the reverend, "and my Bible, of course."

"Can you write a letter for me? I'd like to say good-bye to my wife and boy. Maybe there's a page in there without any famous words on it. "

The reverend smiled. "I'll be happy to write it for you," he said, thumbing through the book. "But first, let us pray." He opened to Psalm 23 and began to recite, knowing full well it was probably the last sermon he would ever deliver.

The other men listened to him preach and were unaware of the commotion taking place among the soldiers manning the elevated plankway along the perimeter wall.

Heading directly toward Fort Carolina's front gates was a figure in civilian clothing who carried a large white flag. He trotted along at an easy pace, and was accompanied by a pair of monstrously large dogs. Two hundred yards behind him, a younger man was leading a small herd of saddled horses. Within minutes, General O'Hara was hurrying down a long hallway, the sound of his boots echoing off the walls. He rapped once on the door to Cornwallis's private quarters before throwing it open and entering without waiting for permission.

"Good God, man, are you trying to cut my throat!" The general was leaned back in a chair while a valet stood over him with a straight razor, shaving his face.

"I beg pardon, my lord, but there is a rider, a civilian, at the gates. He requests an immediate audience with you."

Cornwallis leaned back and closed his eye, signaling the valet to continue. "I am occupied."

"My lord, I think you might want to see him. He has a pair of dogs with him, Great Danes." Cornwallis sat up immediately, batting the razor away.

"How very interesting. Show him in."

O'Hara saluted, turned on his heels, and hurried outside. On his signal, the gates were unbarred and pulled open. Some of the caged militiamen turned to see what was happening and Reverend Oliver, sensing he had lost their attention, brought his sermon to a quick close.

"And lastly, Lord, we ask that you protect us in this, our hour of great need, and that you might judge us mercifully and allow us a place at your side. This we ask in the name of the Father, the Son . . ."

When Billings saw who was coming through the gates, he finished the prayer.

"And the Holy Ghost!"

Reverend Oliver lowered his Bible in astonishment as Martin was led up the stairs of the headquarters building.

"Amen."

Martin and the dogs followed General O'Hara through a grand foyer, and up a wide, beautifully crafted staircase that curved its way to the second story. Even under the circumstances, Martin couldn't resist tugging on the banister rail to test for squeaks and bending to run an admiring hand over the balusters. It was fine workmanship indeed. O'Hara led him to a large, richly appointed room and pointed to a chair.

"Lord General Cornwallis will be with you presently," he said with chilly disdain. He curled his lip and glared at Martin with unrestrained contempt before closing the doors behind him.

Finding himself alone with the dogs, Martin allowed himself a fleeting smile. He looked around the lavishly appointed room, which looked like an office where no actual work was done. There were no papers or tools of any sort on the huge desk at the center of the space, and only a few sheets of blank paper on the secretary desks that surrounded it. Lace curtains and heavy velvet drapes adorned the windows, and the chandelier overhead appeared to be made of silver. There were floor-to-ceiling bookcases with glass doors and shelves of expensive display objects, but the item that drew Martin's attention was also one of the simplest. A rocking chair sat near the stone fireplace. Curious, he went to examine it. He scowled when he lifted it off the ground. "Too heavy." Still, it was a handsome piece of furniture. He sat down and began to rock. The dogs came and laid their heads in Martin's lap a moment before Cornwallis, O'Hara, and a handful of junior officers entered.

The Lord General stopped short when he saw the scene. He was overjoyed to have the animals returned to him, but disturbed at the great affection they seemed to have for the ruffian who had brought them. He spread his arms wide and called to them.

"Jupiter! Mars!"

The dogs looked at Cornwallis, then at each other, and finally to Martin. "Go," he told them, at which point they dutifully trotted across the room and into the general's waiting arms.

"My boys! My boys!" he said with emotion, petting and patting with a bruising enthusiasm that was in contrast to the lukewarm feelings the animals seemed to have for him. "You look well. Did you miss me? Yes, I missed you, too. Oh, welcome back, boys!" He stood up and wiped his hands on his coat. "They seem to have been well fed. I thank you for that, Mister . . . I'm afraid I don't know your name, sir."

"I'm a colonel in the Continental Army," Martin told him. "My rank will do."

"As you wish." Cornwallis advanced to within a few feet, his retinue keeping pace behind him. "It is appropriate to the situation that our conversation should be conducted as a formal parley, which is to say it should be governed by the well-established rules professional military men use. Naturally, we needn't bother ourselves with all the nicer details, but I do feel the need to explain a—"

Martin surprised him. "As the initiating party, I choose to begin. Unless you would like to claim aggrieved status."

Cornwallis raised his eyebrows and glanced around at his officers. "Most impressive. I see you are in fact familiar with how this sort of thing is done. Yes, I would like to claim aggrieved status."

"Very well, proceed, sir."

"First, I believe you have in your possession many belongings of mine, including my clothing, wigs, several pieces of furniture, private papers, and various other personal effects of a nonmilitary nature. I would like to have them returned. I'm especially keen to have my journals, over which I have labored for many long hours, and for which I cannot imagine you have use."

"I will do so as soon as possible."

Cornwallis was surprised, and very pleasantly so. He had assumed Martin would ask for ransom and found the offer to simply *give it all back* a bit disconcerting.

"Thank you," he said.

"Please accept my apology for not having done so sooner."

"Apology accepted," Cornwallis said. "Now, on to the next matter—the specific targeting of officers during engagements. I see that you are a man of some cultivation, so I'm sure you understand that in civilized warfare, officers in the field must not be accorded inappropriate levels of hostile attention."

"Here, here," agreed O'Hara.

"And what, exactly, are *appropriate* levels of hostile attention?"

Cornwallis clucked his tongue in disapproval. "Come now, Colonel. Imagine the utter chaos that would result from unled armies having at one another. There must be gentlemen in command, men of judgment and education to lead and, when appropriate, to restrain their men."

Martin's voice turned cold. "To restrain them from targeting civilians, including women and children?"

"That is a separate issue which we can—"

"I consider them linked," Martin interrupted. Without raising his voice, he made it clear that he had no intention of revising his strategy of going after the officers first. Cornwallis tried to explain the difficulty, from his side, of distinguishing combatants from noncombatants. His position was essentially that in an uprising such as this, there were no true civilians, only soldiers. It was inevitable under such circumstances that a few mistakes would be made.

Martin didn't budge. "As long as your soldiers attack civilians, I will order the shooting of your officers at the outset of every engagement." Then he added, "And my men are excellent marksmen."

Cornwallis sighed. "Very well, let us move on to the subject of—"

"Prisoner exchange."

"Sir?"

"Prisoner exchange. You have eighteen of my men. I want them back."

O'Hara leaned in quickly and whispered a piece of advice before stepping away again. Cornwallis stroked his chin, pretending to search his memory. "Let me see. I do have eighteen *common criminals* under sentence of death, but I hold no prisoners of war." Now he was arguing the opposite, that there were no soldiers, only civilians.

"If that's your position," Martin said roughly, "then eighteen of your officers will die. Nineteen if you hang me along with my men."

"What officers? What are you talking about?"

Picking up a spyglass from Cornwallis's desk, Martin

stepped to the nearest south-facing window and checked the view. There was a wooded hillside in the distance. He invited Cornwallis to join him.

"There's a break in the trees, a clearing. Just down from the crest, to the left of that dark patch of pines."

Though difficult to see clearly through the haze, Cornwallis could discern a row of bound Redcoat officers, some of them kneeling, some of them standing with their backs against the trees. Poorly dressed American militiamen stood over them armed with muskets. It was a sight that boiled the Englishman's blood.

"I demand to know their names, ranks, and posts."

Martin shrugged. "They're not as cooperative as I would have liked. They refused to give me their names. Their ranks are nine lieutenants, five captains, three majors, and one fat colonel who called me a cheeky fellow. As for their posts, we picked them up here and there last night."

"I see now that I was wrong. You are no gentleman."

"General, if the conduct of your officers is the measure of a gentleman, I'll take that as a compliment. Now get my men." The men locked eyes as Cornwallis resisted the impulse to strike Martin's impertinent face with the back of his hand.

"General O'Hara," Cornwallis said without looking away, "arrange the exchange."

Martin remained steady. "I thank you, General. I'm sure your officers will thank you as well." He offered Cornwallis a salute that went unreturned, then followed O'Hara toward the door. The two Great Danes started out after Martin until Cornwallis snapped at them.

"Jupiter! Mars! At my heel!"

The dogs glanced at him momentarily before turning to

Martin. He instructed them with a gesture to lay down and stay where they were. They obeyed, but whimpered as he followed O'Hara out of the room and down the staircase.

When the two men emerged from the building, all eyes in the courtyard turned to them. General O'Hara quietly issued a set of orders to his subordinates, and soon a company of Redcoats came and stood for review in formal reception lines as if Martin were a visiting foreign dignitary. The main gates slowly rolled open and then O'Hara, red with embarrassment, shouted to the soldiers standing guard over the militiamen.

"Release the prisoners!"

No one was more surprised by the command than the men locked in the cages. Some of them raised a loud, grateful cheer. Cutting through the sound was the high-pitched gibbering of Billings's laugh. But they all fell quiet again when the ground began to tremble and the air filled with an ominous and familiar sound. As they were being set free, the Green Dragoons thundered up the hill and through the gates.

As they turned and rode toward their barracks, Tavington veered off and pulled to a stop, confused by what he saw. He'd already spotted a young civilian waiting outside the gates with a small herd of spare horses, and now saw the infantrymen standing at attention near the headquarters building in ceremonial lines. His curiosity quickly turned to outrage when he saw the rebel militiamen he'd captured the day before being released from their holding pens. He turned and rode toward O'Hara for an explanation, cutting across the reception lines as he went. In his haste, he rode straight past Martin, who was making his way toward the exit. Tavington dismounted and shoved his reins into the hands of the nearest soldier.

"What is all this?" he demanded. "What are those horses doing outside?"

"Control yourself, Colonel," said O'Hara without meeting his eyes. "It's a prisoner exchange. He has eighteen of our men." He pointed out Martin, who stood just inside the main gates.

"Who is he? I recognize him."

O'Hara flashed him a punishing smile. "He is their military commander. Your Ghost."

Tavington blinked in astonishment. He looked at the man O'Hara had pointed out. He was surprisingly normal. Moderately tall, moderately well dressed, and apparently unarmed, he could have been any colonial civilian. Tavington decided immediately what he would do. He drew his sword and started toward Martin.

"Stay that sword!" O'Hara bellowed. "The man rode in under a white flag and he has conducted a formal parley with his Lordship. He is protected."

Tavington wheeled around. "This is madness! You intend to let him go?"

"If you harm that man, Colonel, you condemn eighteen of our officers."

Tavington used the sword to point vaguely over the fort walls at the embattled countryside beyond. "Eighteen men? Is that all? You're going to turn him free for only eighteen men? Don't you understand he's killed that many of our officers in the last two months alone?"

"It is not necessary for you to agree, only to obey. If you attack him in any manner," O'Hara explained, "I'll have you put in irons. Regardless of what he has done or may do, he has shown no aggression here, hence, he cannot be touched."

The words put an idea into Tavington's head. "Shown no aggression, you say?" He strode past the rows of Redcoats to the front gates just as Martin was going through them.

"You there!"

Martin stiffened when he heard the voice and nearly reached for the knife hidden under his coat. Several of his men were already clear of the gates, lifting their aching bodies onto the waiting horses, but a handful of others, Reverend Oliver and Billings included, were still inside the fort.

"Oh, I know you," Tavington said when he saw Martin's face. "On that farm. You were giving care to those wounded rebels."

The moment they were face to face, Martin felt his self-control begin to slip and the killing instincts rising inside him.

"And there was that boy, that stupid little boy." Tavington came closer and asked, in a voice dripping with mock concern, "Did he die?" He was only an arm's length away, close enough to kill before anyone could come to intervene. He didn't look quite as impressive off his horse and standing on level ground, but still, he was athletically built and looked as if he knew how to fight. Martin's heart kicked in his chest as the image of Thomas collapsing in the yard filled his mind. *Stay the course*, he told himself, *stay the course*.

"Ugly business, doing one's duty," Tavington said. "But sometimes, like that day on your farm, it can be a real pleasure."

The two men were standing close, almost toe to toe, but Martin leaned in even closer, until his lips were inches from Tavington's ear, and whispered a promise.

"Before this war is over, I'm going to kill you."

"Why wait?"

The Englishman responded by putting the sword where Martin could make a grab for it.

It was an offer Martin desperately wanted to oblige, but he stepped back and headed out the gates. When he mounted his horse, he turned back and saw Tavington still in the same spot, taunting him with open arms as the gates began to close. Martin raised his fingers to his mouth and let loose a piercing whistle, then turned to ride away and didn't look back.

The Great Danes came bounding out of the building and across the assembly yard. They sprinted past Tavington and slipped through the gates single file just a moment before they sealed.

"Stop them! Stop those dogs!" Cornwallis thundered from one of the upstairs windows. "Mars! Jupiter!" Everyone in the assembly yard turned to look at him, but the animals did not. They tore after Martin and fell in behind him. It was insult added to Cornwallis's injury. First, Martin had forced him, by means of uncivilized tactics, to exchange his prisoners, and then he had the temerity to abscond with his gift from King George. Furious, he turned from the window and shouted at whoever happened to be standing nearby. It was turning out to be a difficult day, and it wasn't over yet.

An hour later, as agreed, O'Hara led a column of men into the center of the field that separated Fort Carolina from the hillside where the English officers were being held. A drummer beat out a signal, and they waited for the officers to come out of the trees.

When no one appeared, they rode closer and learned they had been tricked. The English "officers" Cornwallis had seen through the spyglass were exactly where they had been, unguarded and unharmed. The only problem was that they were not officers at all, only scarecrows in Redcoat uniforms.

When a red-faced O'Hara tossed one of them onto Cornwallis's desk later that afternoon, the Lord General reacted badly. He cursed and kicked his chair across the floor. But a moment later, his anger changed into ruthless calculation. He walked across the room and brought the chair back to his desk, where he sat down as calmly as a chess player. He drummed his fingers against his lips for a few moments until he came to a decision.

"Get me Tavington."

Late that afternoon, as the sun fell toward the horizon, it appeared to impale itself on the sharpened tips of the fort's perimeter wall. Tavington and Bordon came away from their meeting with Cornwallis looking determined and purposeful. They strode across the assembly yard and marched directly to the Dragoons' barracks house. It was a long, narrow structure with few windows and folding beds against the walls. The men inside were cleaning and maintaining their weapons, reading and playing cards. They parted like the Red Sea to make way for the two officers. Tavington stopped in front of Wilkins, who was polishing his boots with a brush.

"Captain, I have a question for you about one of your neighbors."

"Yes."

"There is a medium-sized plantation, now destroyed, approximately seven miles from Wakefield, over a ridge. It lies east of Black Swamp, alongside a tributary of the Santee River. Who lived there?"

Wilkins thought for a moment, orienting himself to the directions. "Was there a white house sitting on a knoll under an oak tree?"

"That sounds right."

"Benjamin Martin." He turned to Bordon in curiosity. "Why?"

"He is our Ghost," Bordon answered.

"Benjamin Martin?" Wilkins said in disbelief. "I served with him in the Assembly. Are you sure it's him? He's a decent man. Doesn't favor this war, voted against it."

"Oh, I'm sure, quite sure," Tavington told him. "Now, what can you tell me about him?"

"Everything," Wilkins shrugged, holding up the boot he was cleaning. "I can tell you the size of his boot. What do you want to know?"

Tavington sat down on the bed next to him, pleased and excited. "Tell me about his family. I saw a number of children, but what about a wife?"

"Elizabeth Putnam. I knew her well in my younger days. A very fine woman, now deceased."

"Damn the luck," said Tavington. "The children, then. Where do you suppose he might send them? Does he have other family hereabouts?"

Wilkins hesitated to answer. As a young man growing up in Charles Town, he had coveted Elizabeth Putnam, three years his senior, and was jealous of Martin for marrying her first. Later, as assemblymen, the two of them were on opposite sides of nearly every issue. They had never been friendly, but he respected Martin as a man of principle. He had seen enough of how Tavington worked to realize he would be rough with the children.

The two officers and several of the Dragoons were waiting for him to answer.

"His wife has a sister, Charlotte. She has a plantation upriver from his on the Santee."

"Splendid," Tavington said with a grim smile and patted Wilkins's thigh. Then he stood and made the announcement that the Green Dragoons would be riding that night.

14

The war had turned Charlotte Selton's life on its head. She had been a beautiful young widow with more money and time than she knew how to spend. She had lived in Charles Town surrounded by an established circle of friends and family. She traveled frequently and read the broadsheets in the morning and romantic French novels before going to bed. She yearned for children, and a few months before leaving Charles Town, she began asking friends to introduce her to unattached gentlemen.

Then, suddenly, she found herself with not one, but *five* children all at once. Even with Matthew and the other servants to help, looking after them was taxing work—especially since they came to her in damaged condition. Nathan and Samuel, the older boys, withdrew into themselves and couldn't sleep nights without loaded rifles in the room. The younger ones, William and Susan, clung to Charlotte's skirts during the day and came crying into her room during the night, shaken by violent dreams. Margaret did her best to be helpful, but her nerves were on edge and she scolded the others almost constantly. None of the children were allowed to wander from the house, and they had to seclude themselves in their rooms when visitors stopped by unexpectedly. Charlotte discouraged everyone who came from visiting again. The fewer people who knew the whereabouts of Colonel Benjamin Martin's children, the better.

As the days turned to weeks and months, she and the children established a rhythm of living together, and the fear that hung over them subsided. The war continued, but it stayed far from the affluent neighborhood of farms where they lived. Eventually, Charlotte hired a tutor to come once a week, and on Saturday evenings they held dancing parties. When spring arrived, the children pestered Matthew into helping them build a rather grand tree house in one of the oaks behind the horse barn. Their lives had returned, more or less, to normal.

Nathan had fallen asleep in a chair on the upstairs balcony with a blanket and a rifle on his lap when he was roused suddenly by tiny vibrations running through the earth and a noise that sounded like thunder. Nathan recognized it immediately as the approach of the Green Dragoons. A moment later he saw the torches coming through the trees, about two dozen of them, carried by men on horseback. They were coming fast.

The candles in Charlotte's bedroom were nearly burnt to the bottom. She had fallen asleep in a chair, and there was a book open on her chest when Nathan rushed in and shook her awake. He'd spent endless hours in imaginary rehearsals for what he would do if the British arrived, but now that they were here, he was terrified.

"The Dragoons are coming."

In half a moment, she was wide awake and out of her chair. She told Nathan to bring the boys downstairs while she collected the girls, then both of them hurried from the room, shouting the alarm.

"Margaret! Quickly!" Charlotte shouted as she burst into the room and picked Susan up out of her bed. "Quickly!"

They were down the stairs in a matter of seconds, but the Dragoons had already arrived. They were just outside, shouting to one another. Several of them dismounted and strode toward the house with their torches. Charlotte pulled the children around a corner and into the service hallway a moment before the Dragoons put a shoulder to the front door and broke it open with a crash.

Tavington stepped through the door holding a sword in one hand and a pitch-soaked torch in the other. Half a dozen men stormed inside behind him and began to search where he pointed them to go. A moment later, Wilkins stepped through the door almost sheepishly.

Footsteps and men's voices came from just outside the door. It was too late for Nathan to get inside. He shut the door to the shaft as the door to the dining room pushed open. He ducked under the dining room tablecloth that hung almost to the floor.

A pair of black riding boots came into the room and moved slowly toward the table. They stopped only a few inches from where Nathan was hiding, close enough for him to reach out and touch them.

In the darkness of the downstairs kitchen, Charlotte and the children huddled together, staring up at the sound of the footsteps, expecting at any moment to hear the scuffle of Nathan being discovered.

With his heart pounding, Nathan held his breath and waited. The man in the boots stayed where he was, inspecting the items on the tabletop until another man came into the room.

"No one upstairs, sir."

"Very well. Search the outbuildings and the woods. They can't be far."

The voice belonged to Tavington, and when Nathan recognized it, a dread chill shot up his spine. Involuntarily, his fingers moved the firing pin on his rifle into the ready position. He winced at the click it made, realizing he'd given himself away. He took aim as best he could, waiting for Tavington to look under the table. But to his surprise, the boots turned and began marching loudly out of the room.

It was a ruse. When Tavington reached the doorway, he handed his torch to one of his men, silently cocked his pistol, and then doubled back as quietly as a cat. He tore back the tablecloth and took aim, but to his surprise, there was no one under the table.

"I could have sworn—," he said to himself. He gave the room a quick once-over, but found nothing and left.

Nathan, realizing it was a trick, had rolled away to a new hiding place just in time. When it was safe, he went into the shaft and climbed down the ladder to join the others.

Torch light came through the high, narrow windows as the Dragoons came along the side of the house. They found the cellar doors, the only other way out of the kitchen, and tried to open them. Finding them locked from the inside, they moved on.

Charlotte peered out a window and watched the torches move further off. She climbed the set of stairs, unlocked the doors, and led the children outside.

"Here," whispered Samuel, pointing to the hedge plants that grew next to the house.

"No, this way," Charlotte whispered back as calmly as she could, leading them out into the yard at a trot. The Dragoons and their torches were visible on both sides, and the moon was bright enough to give them away. But their only hope was to get some distance from the house. She hurried to a row of camellia bushes fifty yards away and ducked behind them. From there, they watched the group of soldiers near the front of the house and listened to Tavington shouting orders.

"That's the man who killed Thomas," Nathan told them.

The others looked where he pointed and, though it was difficult to see the man's face clearly, they instantly recognized his crisp, commanding voice. He came out onto the front porch and ordered his men to round up some of the slaves for questioning. When Charlotte turned to look for a means of escape, she saw three men creeping up behind.

"Aunt Charlotte?" a voice asked. It was Gabriel, along with Occam and his new partner, Dan Scott. Before the children could make a fuss over him, Gabriel slashed his hand through the air, demanding silence. He and the other men kept their heads up, watching the British search party, but none of them made any movement toward leaving.

Tavington ordered the house and the outbuildings burned, and the men fanned to begin the job. Soon after, several of the slaves were brought before Tavington, half dressed and dragged from their beds. He shouted at them as a group to begin with, but quickly focused his inquiry on Matthew, who had come out in an expensive dressing gown Charlotte had given him. Tavington asked him a series of questions, and each time got exactly the same response: "I do not know, sir."

Tavington heard the defiance in Matthew's voice and didn't like it. He took out his pistol and shot him in the face, killing him instantly, then moved on to question the next slave. Charlotte screamed without a sound when she saw Matthew's body collapse.

A pair of soldiers came to the nearest corner of the house and held their torches to the wall until the flames were established before moving on. The brighter it burned, the more visible the children's faces became in their hiding place.

Tears rolled down Samuel's cheeks. "Gabriel, where is Father?"

All at the same time, Gabriel, Occam, and Dan Scott answered him with the same slashing movement of their hands, telling him not to make a sound. A second shot rang out from where Tavington was haranguing the slaves.

Then a third came from behind them. It was a rifle blast, and the Dragoons all turned toward the sound. When they did, they saw Benjamin Martin, his horse rearing on its hind legs, illuminated by the flickering light of the burning buildings. He fired a pistol in the air and shouted Tavington's name. Some of the Dragoons nearby turned and fired, but their shots went wide.

The next moment he was gone, leaving the British soldiers shouting at one another in confusion. Tavington roared over the top of the noise.

"To your horses!"

It was the signal Gabriel had been waiting for. He waved Charlotte and the children to their feet and whispered to them. "Come, we have to hurry."

Charlotte stole a last glance back at Matthew's body as they hurried away from the burning house and melted into the darkness.

Tavington and his men chased after Martin, following his tracks a few miles into the nearest woods before the trail ended suddenly. The Dragoons spread out and searched almost until dawn without finding a single clue as to which direction the Ghost might have gone.

It was well after midday when the Dragoons, exhausted by their long ride and covered with the red dust of the Carolina earth, returned to the fort. They went directly to their barracks and fell asleep as soon as they lay down. Toward evening, Cornwallis sent for Tavington.

When he reported, still moist from his bath and wearing

a fresh uniform, he found the Lord General in the banquet room, at the head of an elegant table set for one. There was a handsome rib roast on a platter, and enough of everything else to feed five hungry men. Cornwallis invited Tavington to come in and watch him eat. They'd only been talking for two minutes when Cornwallis slammed his palm down on the table.

"The man must be found and hanged! He has insulted me personally and he has insulted the Crown! He is more than half the reason we have not been able to leave for the North."

Tavington stood with his hands behind his back nodding his agreement.

"Rather impressive for a farmer with a pitchfork, wouldn't you say?"

"Our campaign and my reputation both suffer because of your incompetence. I want you to find that man and bring him to me, by whatever means necessary, before my good name is sullied any further."

Tavington immediately smelled the opportunity in the situation. He moved to the table, coming closer than a subordinate ought.

"As you know, my lord, he and his men are elusive. And they have the loyalty of many local people. They protect him, his location, his family, and the families of his men. I can capture him for you, but doing so may entail the use of tactics that might be considered . . . what was the word you used, *brutal*?"

Cornwallis indicated his interest, but he said nothing. He dismissed the valet from the room.

Tavington became bold and poured himself some wine. "I would hate to see your reputation sullied in any way by my actions, especially any that might be thought *brutal*.

There are ways, however, in which I might render you blameless. Ways that would bring your lordship victory without endangering your good name."

"Go on," Cornwallis said.

"My lord, I will do whatever is necessary, and I will assume the full burden of responsibility. When questions are raised about my tactics, and such questions are inevitable, you will say you never authorized them, that indeed you forbid me to use them. I will not argue, but quietly accept the blame. But if I do this, you know as well as I that I would never be able to return to England with my honor. What would become of me then?"

Cornwallis thought it was a fascinating offer, one man trading his reputation for another's. The more he considered it, the more he thought it was the solution to both their problems. The name Tavington was not worth what it had been a generation before. Without military victory, the young officer would find few prospects upon his return home. And the longer they stayed mired in South Carolina, the more the possibility loomed that there might be no victory at all.

"By now," Cornwallis said delicately, "you know it is my opinion that once this war is over, here in the colonies, landowners will form a new and powerful aristocracy."

"I've heard you talk about it," Tavington said with a smile. It appeared that he and the Lord General had already reached an agreement. He sat down in a chair and sipped his wine. "But I wouldn't mind hearing it again. Tell me about Ohio."

Gabriel followed his father's orders exactly as they had been given. From the plantation, he escaped across the Santee at Nelson's Ferry, found the extra horses waiting for him, then led Charlotte and the children past Yaboo Swamp and located the property belonging to an old acquaintance of Benjamin's, Mrs. Dorothy James. Startled awake in the middle of the night, the old woman came to the door cursing like a sailor. She changed her tone as soon as she heard the name Benjamin Martin and quickly took the family in. Gabriel and his men split up and went to the nearest towns to watch for the approach of British troops. They waited for a week before returning with a wagon, again in the middle of the night, to take the children away. They sped south toward the coast, avoiding the larger roads.

They were well past the last British outpost when, near dawn the next morning, the wagon became stuck in the mud of a salt marsh and had to be abandoned, forcing them to continue on foot. The day turned miserably hot and humid. They headed down a dirt road lined on both sides by thick vegetation until they found the sea.

They walked out of the forest at the foot of a saltwater lagoon, a long clear pool of water where the waves had spilled over a thin bar of sand. A cool breeze came in off the water, and after several hours of oppressive heat, low branches, and thorny bushes, the place felt like heaven. The children rushed into the water, splashing and laughing, and waded across the lagoon to the sand bar, which was covered six inches deep with seashells of every description.

Soon they came upon an astonishing site. In a clearing along the banks of the lagoon was a set of grass huts and stick structures that could have come directly from Africa. It was an entire thriving village in the middle of nowhere, isolated from the rest of the world by miles of difficult terrain. Men in wooden boats fished using nets, women were hanging fish up to dry and bringing in firewood, and the children chased one another between the houses.

One by one, everyone who lived there turned and noticed the newcomer, Occam, and wondered why he'd brought the seven white people with him.

It was a Gullah village, one of several along the Carolina coast, a place populated entirely by freedmen and escaped slaves. It seemed a world unto itself, with its own language, music, and architecture, little understood and officially ignored by the white population, which was just how the Gullah people liked it.

As the Martin children wandered uncertainly into the village, a dark-skinned woman in loose clothing with her hair tied up in a bright cloth cried out joyfully and rushed toward them, waving her arms madly through the air.

"Oh, my children! My children!"

William was the first to recognize her.

"Abigale?"

It was her indeed, though she looked much different from how they'd seen her last. They ran forward to meet her, shouting her name, and after a reunion full of happy tears, she took them to meet the others.

When the village people heard Gabriel's story and understood the danger Charlotte and the children were in, they extended an invitation for them to stay. British troops had never visited the lagoon and weren't expected anytime soon. There was some danger in agreeing to hide the family, but many of them had heard of Benjamin Martin and knew his record on slavery.

Abigale showed Charlotte and the children their new home. It was a one-room hut with a dirt floor. The walls were a combination of sapling tree trunks and salvaged wood. The roof was thatched with palm fronds.

"It's not much, I know, certainly not what you're used to," she told Charlotte, "but you're welcome to stay here

with me until we can build you one or two of your own."
Charlotte was moved by the act of generosity.

"Abigale, it's beautiful. Thank you."

That evening, as the children brought armfuls of dune
grass into the hut to make their beds, Abigale sat outside
with Gabriel and Charlotte over a dying fire.

"The Redcoats marched us all down to Winnsboro," she
told them. "They kept us waiting in a field for a few days
without much food to eat. Then they came through and
took all the younger men to fight. They put Father and me
to work in the kitchens at their headquarters on Walnut
Street and we stayed there for a while until the city was
attacked. The shooting lasted from morning to night. I
heard them say it was General Sumter and his Patriot men.
Well, the next day they threw me out. Said there wasn't
enough food. I didn't have anywhere else to go, so I made
my way down here. Before I left, I spent a few days in
Winnsboro trying to find Father, but I never did."

"What's your father's name?" Charlotte asked.

"Abner," Gabriel answered for her.

"God willing," Charlotte said, "your father will be
returned to you."

Abigale pasted a smile on her face, trying to believe it.
Then she headed into the hut to assist the children. Gabriel
turned to Charlotte.

"They won't stop looking for you and the children. My
father would quit this war in half a minute to trade himself
for his little ones."

"We'll be safe here. It's the perfect place to hide." She
stopped and looked around the village, listening to the
waves. "How is your father?"

Gabriel searched himself for an honest answer. "I don't
know," he admitted, "I'm his son." Sensing someone behind

him, he turned and caught Susan studying him with her large eyes.

"Where is Father?" she asked.

Gabriel's mouth dropped open like a trap door. It was the first time he'd heard her speak. "Susan?"

Charlotte laughed. "Speaking now for months."

"Is it true?" he asked his sister, "You can talk? Why have you been so quiet all day?"

"I didn't say she speaks often," Charlotte told him. "It's usually only when she has something worth saying."

"Where is Father?" she repeated. "Why did he go?" She stepped closer to the fire, clutching the same doll Charlotte had given her.

Gabriel leaned forward, still amazed, and did his best to explain. "Susan, he didn't want those men to find you. He led them away so you would be safe."

She shook her head, unsatisfied with the answer.

"He'll come and see you just as soon as he can."

"I don't care," she said. "I hate him."

"You don't hate him," Gabriel said. He knelt down and put his hands on her small shoulders. "He loves you very much. We all do."

"I hate him," she insisted, standing coldly with her arms at her sides. "I hate him and I hope he never comes back."

Tavington lay on his side in the tall grass admiring a handsome sunset and absentmindedly plucking the petals from a handful of wildflowers. A group of his officers stood nearby, awaiting his orders, and behind them was a farmhouse. It was an unattractive structure, flimsily built, and the farm that surrounded it had run almost completely to seed. A few of the Dragoons had entered the house.

"Look at that sunset, gentlemen! Absolutely outstanding. Worthy of a sonnet. Wilkins, you're fortunate to have grown up here." He gestured to the trees and fields surrounding them. "Everything grows here!"

"Yes, it does," Wilkins said, accepting the compliment. "I like it here."

Just then, a hideous scream came from the house and pierced the calm of the evening. Tavington cocked his head and listened to it analytically, as a composer might listen to someone playing his music back to him. He didn't like what he heard and started immediately toward the farmhouse.

He walked inside, still carrying the flowers, and stepped over a pair of dead bodies on his way to talk to Bordon.

"What happened?"

"I'm sorry, sir," Bordon said, shrugging his shoulders over the man tied to the table. "He died."

Tavington sighed. "Did you get anything from him?" Bordon shook his head. "Very well. We'll simply try again. Bring the last one in."

Captain Wilkins surveyed the blood-splattered room and felt his stomach come up in his mouth. He turned and hurried outside just as the Dragoons dragged Rollins in, still carrying one of his haversacks. Bordon cut the straps with a knife, rolled the dead man onto the floor with a crash, then spilled the contents of the sack onto the tabletop. There were gold and silver coins, crumpled handfuls of paper money, British belt buckles, buttons, rings, and all manner of small valuables.

"This one is a rebel and a thief." Rollins stared up at him with one eye and bared his teeth.

"I'm no thief. I'm a Patriot."

Bordon raised the small knife he'd been using, ready to teach Rollins some better manners, but Tavington intervened to stop him. He went to the table and used his fingers to push the stolen treasures thoughtfully through the blood that had collected there before turning to Rollins.

"You've got a small fortune here. How much would you say all this is worth?"

Rollins didn't intend to answer any questions and kept his mouth closed.

"My good man, you appear to be intelligent enough. And you seem the type that understands the value of money. I have a proposition for you. I would gladly pay you triple the price of everything on this table if you were a Loyalist. Help me." Then he gestured at the corpses in the room. "Help yourself. Tell me where I can find Benjamin Martin and his men."

Rollins seemed to consider the offer. His face was bruised from the beating he'd already taken, and he looked at Tavington with his one eye that wasn't swollen shut.

Tavington patted one of the pockets on his belt. "I have enough gold coin with me to satisfy any reasonable demand. Go ahead, man. Name your price."

Rollins shook his head. He wasn't sure what price he'd choose to betray Benjamin Martin, but he was certain that no matter how much he asked, and no matter how much they promised, he would be dead when he rode away. He gathered the saliva in his mouth and spit it in Tavington's face.

"Keep your money and do your worst."

Tavington wiped his face with a handkerchief. "I intend to."

Martin sat with his feet in the swamp water shaving himself with a straight razor, cream, and a small folding mirror he'd found among Cornwallis's personal effects when Billings came and squatted down beside him.

"You shave too damn often. Makes the rest of us look bad."

"You already look bad. It's not my fault you were born ugly."

Billings smiled and pointed to the far end of the island. "They're back. Occam, Scott, and your boy."

"Gabriel?" Martin tossed everything aside, pulled his boots onto his wet feet, and wiped the cream from his face as he ran. Mrs. James had sent him a coded message to say that Charlotte and the children were safe and sound when they left her place, but that had been two weeks before, much too long for Martin to be left wondering. He found himself lying awake nights, imagining all the ways his children might have come to harm.

He greeted Gabriel as a colonel properly greets one of his subordinate officers and asked for his report. When he learned that his five youngest were safe and once again in Abigale's care, he let his military manners lapse and put an arm around his son, offering him heartfelt thanks. He had a hundred questions, and Gabriel did his best to answer them all. He described the escape from Charlotte's plantation, his midnight encounter with Mrs. James, the exotic Gullah village, and the several British outposts he'd seen along the way.

"But wait!" Gabriel slapped himself on the forehead. "I haven't told you the most important thing. You won't believe it."

Worry wrinkled one of Martin's eyes into a squint. "What happened?"

"It's Susan. She's talking."

"No!"

"Yes!"

The news hit Martin like a large whiff of smelling salts. "She talked? My little Susan talked?"

"In full sentences," Gabriel assured him, "just as if she'd been speaking all along."

Even as he smiled, a pang of regret crossed Martin's face. "I'm sorry I wasn't there to hear it. Did she happen to say anything about me?"

"Of course, she . . . well, yes. As a matter of fact she did."

"Sweet girl. Tell me. Tell me everything she said and give it word for word."

Gabriel hesitated as he scrambled to "remember" exactly what Susan's words had been. "She said . . ."

"Come on, son, out with it."

"She said she loves you. She said she misses you and that she understands why you can't be with her. And she can't wait to see you again." Lying wasn't something that came naturally to Gabriel, and he felt as guilty as sin for doing it now. But there was no point in adding to his father's burden, and the smile of joy on his father's face told him he'd done the right thing.

"She said that? Oh, my Lord, she said all that?"

Gabriel nodded.

"Isn't that something? I certainly got better children that I ever deserved."

Reverend Oliver galloped up the trail while they were still standing there and pulled his lathered horse to a halt. Everyone could see by the expression in his eyes that he wasn't carrying good news. He came toward Martin without dismounting.

"Tavington has a list of our men. He's going from one place to the next, burning our homes and killing everyone who resists. Rollins, Cameron, and a few others are dead already."

"Where?" Martin asked.

"Seven homes along the Santee so far."

The moment these words were out of the reverend's mouth, Billings snatched up his musket and ran for his horse. His home wasn't far from the Santee River, and his wife and boy were there with no one to protect them. He didn't stop to ask whether the rest of the men in the camp were coming with him. Whether they did or not, he had to get back to his farm before Tavington did.

He tore away at a gallop, with the others right at his heel. Instead of riding all the way up to Nathan's Ferry, they tried to ford the river near the ruins of a bridge they'd burned months before. Two of the horses were carried away in the water, and their riders were left behind without a backward glance. With Billings leading the way, they rode hard for another thirty minutes, racing along the roads in a pack, ignoring the possibility of meeting a Redcoat patrol along the way.

"Not much further," Billings called. A moment later, he noticed the smoke hanging over the trees.

The sky was gray and threatening. A stiff breeze was blowing in from the coast, strong enough to bring the maple leaves out of the trees and send them skittering across the open ground. As they came into a clearing, they saw what was left of Billings's humble farm. The house was gone, burned all the way down to its foundations. The barn was still standing, but his cows were gone and the henhouse had been flattened. As they rode closer, there was no sign of his family.

But Billings found them soon enough. They were between two trees where the laundry was hung out to dry, half buried in leaves. He dismounted on the fly and ran to where they lay, his long coat flapping behind him like a pair of crow's wings, and threw himself on the ground. He seemed afraid to touch them at first, and only bent over them shouting their names. When they didn't respond, he picked them up one at a time and tried to shake the life back into them. His wife wore a simple white dress, and a blood-soaked bonnet covered her bright red hair. The boy, dressed in a tattered green suit, had been playing with his toy gun, which lay nearby. Martin's men stayed at a respectful distance and averted their eyes from the painful scene when Billings began to scream and wail. There were no signs of a struggle, no indication that either of the victims had been tortured for information. Just one bullet hole in each of their hearts.

Billings staggered back toward the men, weeping and confused. He turned in circles as he walked, searching for something he'd lost. There was a madness in his movements, as if he were a twitching marionette whose strings were being worked by a drunken puppeteer. He pulled a pistol from his belt and began jabbing it through the air at invisible enemies. Reverend Oliver dismounted and came forward to comfort him.

"This is not a time for vengeance, John. It's a time to mourn." He reached out to embrace the man, but Billings's violent, herky-jerky movements prevented him.

With tears streaking down his rough, unshaven face, Billings raised the pistol and pointed it at his own head, cocking the flintlock with his thumb.

"NO!" Villeneuve shouted.

But Billings pulled the trigger and blew his brains out.

Reverend Oliver backed away in horror while the other men sat frozen on their horses, too stunned to move, and listened to the gun's report echo away through the trees. Then everything was quiet except the leaves on the ground and the laundry flapping on the line. It was a long time before Martin pulled himself together and addressed his troops.

"Five days' furlough for all men," he said quietly. "We'll meet back at the swamp. Any man who doesn't come back won't be thought a coward or uncommitted to the cause. Go now. Attend to your families."

After what they'd seen, the men found it impossible to look one another in the eyes. No one spoke as they turned, one by one, and headed off in their separate directions. When everyone but Villeneuve and Gabriel had gone, Martin climbed down off his horse and went to look for a shovel.

15

Charlotte and the children quickly came to feel at home in the marooned world of the Gullah village. With help from the others, they built a sturdy hut of branches and woven grass that stood next to Abigale's, and they pitched in to accomplish their fair share of the daily work. Nathan, Samuel, and Margaret learned spearfishing and how to use the nets, while the younger ones made baskets, brought firewood in from the forest, and helped with the cooking.

Late one afternoon, Charlotte, Abigale, and Margaret were sitting under a simple gazebo, a threadbare cotton tarp tied to a set of poles, to shield themselves from the brightness of the sun. They busied themselves with cutting the cords out of palm fronds with a machete and braiding them into rope. Charlotte was entertaining them with a story of the trip she'd taken to England as a child when Margaret stopped working suddenly and turned to face the sea. A pair of riders was galloping toward them, accompanied by a pair of enormous dogs. Margaret recognized them long before she could see their faces and, putting her work aside, she ran toward the beach to meet them.

"Father! Gabriel!" The other children heard her and came running from all directions.

When Martin jumped off his horse, he lifted Margaret off the ground and wrapped her tightly in his arms. The other children threw themselves at him in a group, knocking him to the sand and piling on top of him, squealing in delight. Martin laughed and wrestled with them until Charlotte and Abigale came to free him. The dogs barked and ran in circles as Nathan led the charge toward Gabriel who got the same smothering treatment.

"Good God, they're huge!" Martin cried out. "What have you been feeding them?"

Charlotte recognized the words and smiled. "They're from good stock on their father's side."

Despite the excitement, Martin quickly realized someone was missing. He looked around for Susan and saw her standing about twenty paces away, watching him with a serious expression. She was a beautiful girl who looked more like her mother than ever. Martin loved all his children deeply, but it was Susan he had missed most of all during the many months he'd been away. He started toward her, eager to hear her speak for the first time, but stopped short when the girl backed away from him.

He dropped to a knee and spread his arms open invitingly. "Oh, Susan, how I missed you."

She examined him coldly, tightening her grip on her favorite doll. Then she turned and ran away, disappearing into the cluster of huts. Martin turned to Charlotte for an explanation.

"Be patient with her, Benjamin. She's had a difficult time. We all have." Then she added, "I'm very glad to see you again." They smiled and gazed at one another before moving closer. Instead of the embrace they both wanted, they settled on an awkward, gentle handshake. The feel of her skin touching his made Martin suddenly short of breath. Embarrassed by the sudden rush of emotion, he escaped from the moment by turning his attention back to the children. They were chasing Gabriel and the dogs along the edge of the lagoon. Martin went to join them, but as he did, he looked back more than once at Charlotte.

He continued looking at her as they sat around the fire

that night eating that day's catch. He looked at her as they went into the hut with the children to make their beds, and continued looking as the others drifted off to sleep and the last fires outside burned themselves out. She looked back at him the whole time, even when it was too dark to see.

The next morning, Martin was in fine spirits. He was given a tour of the village by one of its leaders, a woman about his age with jet-black skin and an abnormally long neck. There were dozens of tiny scars on her forehead and cheeks, a kind of decoration Martin had never seen. Although she spoke only her African language and not a word of English, the two of them laughed a great deal and she managed to teach him how the village was organized and provided for itself.

As soon as breakfast was finished, Gabriel rode away to Pembroke to pay Anne a visit and didn't return until the following afternoon. He arrived just in time to stand at the finish line of a one-mile foot race between the village children. To everyone's surprise except her own, Margaret out-raced all of her brothers and beat several of the village's older boys. Nathan claimed she'd taken a short cut and tried to sulk off, but Martin brought him back and made him congratulate his sister and shake her hand.

The family wandered down to the lagoon, and Nathan immediately called for a spearfishing contest. Martin noticed Susan sitting by herself on the side of a small boat that had been carried ashore. He took the opportunity to go up and sit with her. He took an apple out of his pocket and shined it against his shirt, then pulled out his hunting knife and cut himself a slice. All the while, Susan hugged her doll and looked quietly out at the water.

"Good apple," he said, chewing, "very good, very sweet." He sliced off another piece and offered it to her on the fat part of the blade.

She glanced over at it, tempted. She wanted to reach for it, but didn't want to fall for his trick.

"It's very good," he promised.

She gave in and accepted the gift. She was about to put it in her mouth when she noticed something. A brown flake had come off his knife and was dissolving into a bloodred stain. Susan looked at the foot-long knife, then threw the apple in the sand and walked away.

Martin sighed. He realized too late that the handle of his knife was caked with dried blood. He walked down to the water and scrubbed it clean. When he turned around, Gabriel was sitting exactly where Susan had been a moment before.

"What changed you, Father?"

"Are you so sure I have?" Martin came back to the boat and sat down, cutting himself another slice of fruit.

"Yes, you've changed," Gabriel told him. "You're not like those men you knew before. What did it?"

"That's easy," he said with a smile. "It was your mother."

Gabriel gazed out across the blue water of the lagoon and nodded knowingly. "A woman can certainly have a strange effect on a man."

"You're right about that," Martin said, remembering with a smile. "Why, there were times your mother would look at me and I would have trouble breathing."

"I know the feeling," Gabriel agreed.

Martin stole a glance at the boy from the corner of his eye. He was talking strangely, like a wise old man of the world. He sliced another section off the apple as Gabriel searched for exactly the right words for what he needed to say.

"Father, you once said . . . you said when I had a family of my own, I'd understand. Well, you were right."

Martin looked him over carefully. "You're trying to tell me something, right?"

Gabriel started to explain again, but then noticed the sly smile on the corners of his father's mouth. He understood perfectly. More important, he was happy to learn the news.

"Congratulations," Martin said. He sliced off another wedge of the apple and held it toward his son.

"Apple?"

"I'd love some."

That same afternoon, the Howard family arrived in a beautiful wagon with tall side panels and cushioned seats. Anne rode up front next to her father, while Mrs. Howard sat in the back on a stack of pillows. Trotting along behind them on his horse was Reverend Oliver, armed as usual with both a rifle and a Bible.

That afternoon, they gathered under the thatch roof of an open-sided pavilion for the ceremony. It was crowded with thirty chairs of various shapes, and flower garlands were hastily put together to decorate the four sturdy posts. The Gullah people dressed for the occasion in their most vibrant colors, oranges, greens, and yellows. They streamed out of their houses in high spirits, bringing amulets, carved wooden figures, and other magic objects to put on the ground surrounding the altar.

When Anne emerged from the little hut where she'd gone to prepare herself, the entire village cheered and clapped their hands. She had never looked more beautiful. She wore tiny white flowers in her hair, and a long sea-green dress. She walked on bare feet toward the assembled crowd. Gabriel, dressed in a white shirt and cream-colored jacket, stood at the altar nervously shifting his weight from one foot to the other, awaiting her arrival.

When they were facing one another, Reverend Oliver came to stand between them and lead them through their vows. The young couple hardly seemed to notice him as they stared into one another's eyes.

"Dearly beloved," the reverend began, laying his Bible open on a palm stump, "we are gathered here in the sight of God to join this man and this woman in holy matrimony." He paused and turned to the African priest standing beside him. He was an old man, nearly blind, but with a rich, powerful voice. He translated Oliver's words into the Gullah language for those who didn't speak English.

"Anne Patricia Howard," asked Reverend Oliver, "will you have this man, Gabriel, to be your husband? Will you love, comfort, and honor him for so long as you both shall live?"

"I will."

"And Gabriel Edward Martin, will you have this woman, Anne, to be your wife? Will you love, comfort, and honor her for so long as you both shall live?"

"Yes, I will."

Martin exchanged a glance with Charlotte, both of them feeling every word of the ceremony. Reverend Oliver solemnly raised his hands.

"Then by the power vested in me by His Majesty, King George, I . . ." he broke off, realizing the words had changed meaning since the last time he had used them. Some of the onlookers chuckled when they realized his predicament. ". . . by the power vested in me by our mutual faith in the Lord our God," he went on, "I now pronounce you man and wife."

•   •   •

The party they had that night was an exuberant mixture of African and American customs. The village men brought out drums and hand-carved flutes and played driving, rhythmic tribal songs. Later, a freedman with a fiddle played the Irish folk dances he'd learned on a Piedmont plantation while his wife accompanied him on a wheezing concertina. Everyone danced with abandon, and even old Mr. Howard got into the act, hopping about on his peg leg as he tried to dance in the African style. A pig was slaughtered and roasted over an open fire. There was spiced fruit punch for the children and palm wine for the adults. Gabriel danced with Susan, Abigale danced with Mrs. Howard, and William danced with one of the village girls twice his size. When the party was in full swing, Anne pulled herself away from her new husband long enough to have a word with her father-in-law.

"So you're going to make a grandfather of me?" Martin asked, delighted by the notion.

Anne looked at the ground. "I'm sorry we didn't give you more warning."

Martin laughed. "It *was* rather sudden, but I understand completely. I want you to know how happy I am for you both. I have something here I'd like you to have." He reached into his pocket and pulled out a necklace. "This belonged to Gabriel's mother. I've been holding it all this time, waiting for this moment. I believe she'd be proud to have you wear it."

"Oh, it's absolutely beautiful," she said, examining it. An expertly engraved medallion about as large as a shilling coin hung from a purple ribbon.

"I don't know if you can see it in this light," he said, coming around behind her and pointing to the surface of the medallion. "It shows a little map of the night sky, and this one here in the center is the North Star, the only star in the sky that remains constant and never moves."

She turned around so Martin could fasten it around her neck. Then she touched her hand to her chest.

"I'm honored," she said, visibly moved by the meaning behind the gift. Only a moment later, Gabriel danced up from behind and grabbed Anne by the hips.

"May I?" he asked his father.

"If you must?"

"I must," he answered, tugging the young woman back into the thick of the celebration. Martin, left standing by himself, took stock of the scene and nodded in satisfaction.

"Well done," he said out loud, "very well done." As he watched his son and newest daughter gyrate in jubilation around the bonfire, he retreated into his own thoughts and soon found himself glancing around the village in search of Charlotte. He spotted her sitting by herself near the beach.

"May I sit with you?" he asked, coming up behind her.

She gestured to the unoccupied sand beside her. "It's a free country. Well, it will be."

They sat and watched the waves slap against the sand for a while. It was a lovely, clear night, and when Charlotte turned to look at him, she found him staring up at the North Star. She stiffened and sighed in exasperation.

"What is it?" he asked.

"I'm not my sister."

Martin wasn't sure he understood. "I know that."

"Do you?"

He paused to check. "Yes."

Charlotte waited. "Well?"

"Well, what?"

She rolled her eyes in irritation with how obtuse an intelligent man could be.

"Oh!" Martin said, finally understanding. He leaned closer and kissed her softly on the lips. "How's that, better?"

Charlotte shrugged. She needed further examples before she could come to a conclusion. Martin kissed again, just as tenderly at first but then more and more passionately.

Too soon, it was time to go back. Martin finished tying his gear to his horse, then went to help the Howards load the last of their things into the wagon. When that was done, he came and stood in front of the children, who were somber and silent. He knelt down and called them toward him one by one for a word. He put his arms around each one and kissed them on the head before sending them away, but restrained himself from showing all he felt. He was well aware that he might be seeing them for the last time, but didn't want them to feel it in him. Susan was the last to see him. She stood half-hidden behind her Aunt Charlotte's skirts as he invited her forward with a wave. She came reluctantly to where he was kneeling. She had inherited her mother's good looks and her father's stubbornness, and hadn't said a word to him the entire time he'd been there.

"Just a little good-bye?" he asked her. "One word? That's all I want to hear. Just the word *good-bye*."

She stood with her arms at her sides and didn't move them when he hugged her tightly against him.

Gabriel and Anne stood far from the others, their foreheads leaned together, finding it difficult to say good-bye after too brief a honeymoon. Mr. Howard hobbled over to them on his peg leg and crutches and poked his forehead into their intimate conference, letting them know that it was time to go. He brought them back to where the others had gathered.

Martin stood facing Charlotte with his hat in his hands, fumbling for words. It was an awkward moment, made more so by the audience of children watching their every move. Even Charlotte, normally so poised and plain-speaking, struggled without success to express herself. They stepped toward one another and at first only embraced lightly, feigning chastity. Margaret saw that there was more to it and turned to whisper into the ear of her new sister, Anne. As she was doing so, Martin leaned forward and kissed Charlotte squarely on the lips.

"Ooo," said the children, turning to one another to confirm what they'd just seen. Before they had a chance to make any further noises, Martin stepped away self-consciously. William asked when he was coming back.

"Sooner than you think," Martin answered with a playful scowl, "and when I do it'll be back to farm work for all of you." One of the Great Danes barked in agreement.

William wasn't satisfied with the answer. "You promise you'll come?"

It was a question Martin didn't want to answer, but he flashed the boy a grin so brimming with confidence that William was convinced he'd be back to collect them in a mere fortnight or two.

"Eyah!" Mr. Howard slapped the reins on the horses and the wagon lurched into motion. Martin took a final, sorrowful look at the silent Susan before turning to climb up on his horse. Abigale put a comforting hand on Charlotte's shoulder as the men turned and set off. Before they were out of earshot, Susan cried out.

"Papa!" she started after him, hesitantly at first, but then faster and faster. "Papa! Don't go. I'll talk."

Martin pulled to a stop and saw Susan chasing after him. He jumped off the horse and ran to meet her.

"Please, Papa, I'll say anything. Just tell me what to say. Please, Papa, please don't go."

He wrapped the sobbing girl in his arms and covered her with kisses, fighting back his tears until Charlotte came up beside them to lead Susan away. Martin held the girl at an arm's length and looked into her pleading eyes.

"I'll come back, baby girl. I promise you I'll come back." The words caught in his throat as he said them. With a final embrace, he handed her over to her aunt. In agony, he climbed onto his horse, spurred the animal to a gallop, and rode away without looking back.

16

Black Swamp was shrouded in a blanket of fog that drifted eerily between the cypress trees. Martin led the way along the trail at a cautious pace as Gabriel followed close behind. They crossed over the land bridge and surveyed the deserted encampment they had left less than a week before. Already the swamp had begun to reclaim the island with weeds and tendril vines that came out of the water. As they dismounted, Dan Scott materialized out of the mist to meet them. He seemed to be alone.

"Just the three of us?" Gabriel asked.

"Makes for pretty long odds," said his father.

Scott looked well rested and well fed after his stay in Pembroke, but a bit disheartened by the low turnout. "John Raskin came about an hour ago," he told them, "but he didn't say much. He took a look around, then left. At least that would've made four."

Four would have been better, they agreed.

But slowly, they began to come in. By ones and twos they walked out of the fog, some of them on horseback and others on foot. Ludwell and Moore had spent their entire furlough at the Boar's Head Tavern drinking up their wages, bragging to anyone who would listen that they were part of the Ghost's brigade, and telling the gruesome tale of what had happened at John Billings's farm. They came to Black Swamp leading a group of thirty men, returning veterans and new recruits. Of all the men who made the decision to return, Martin was most surprised to see Occam. When he trudged up the trail by himself, Martin stood up to greet him. Scott, sitting at the fire, asked Occam whether he had any sense in his head.

"You could've been long gone by now. Why'd you come back?"

"Got another two months to go 'fore I get to twelve," Occam answered.

Martin nodded and shook the man's hand.

The men broke open their packs and began to reestablish the camp. Martin walked among them, introducing himself to the new men and welcoming back the others, offering encouragement and suggestions. It was a chance for him to take the temperature of his men, and he was pleased with what he found. Their spirits were solemn, but their conviction remained unshaken. They knew what Tavington's Dragoons had done to Rollins, Billings, and the others, but it hadn't frightened them into submission. It had only hardened their resolve to drive the British out of the colonies. More than ever before, they were a distinctly American army, fighting an American cause.

Still, Martin didn't feel his partisan brigade had put itself back together until a non-American rode into camp, Major Jean Villeneuve. Martin went to greet him.

"Trust the French."

"Yes, trust the French," Villeneuve said as he dismounted. "Where else do I get the opportunity to kill English? Perhaps even a few wounded ones when you are not looking."

As they rolled closer to Pembroke, the Howard family was exhausted by the long hours of traveling, but happily so. The trip had been a great success. The wedding itself had been unusual, unlike anything they ever imagined, but thrilling and deeply meaningful. Mr. Howard bobbed his head in rhythm to the sound of the wheels on the road, still dancing to the African drum songs in his head. Mrs. Howard was asleep in the rear seat, but Anne was still very much awake and brimming with energy. She was busy making plans for her life with Gabriel. As she drank in the beauty of the passing countryside, everything she saw reminded her of him. They had only been separated for a matter of hours, but already she missed him horribly. At last they spotted the spire of their local church above the treetops, and moments later they rounded the last bend and clattered into town.

The Green Dragoons were waiting for them.

The streets were empty and the doors to all the houses, including their own, stood open. Half a dozen mounted Dragoons approached the wagon. Mr. Howard was perplexed to see that he recognized one of them and called him by name. It was James Wilkins, one of his colleagues in the Assembly and a fellow resident of Berkeley County. Wilkins returned the greeting with a tip of his hat and spoke to them gently, politely.

"Everyone has been requested to gather at the church." He saw the concerned look Anne exchanged with her parents and tried to assure them. "Colonel Tavington wishes to address the whole village." He invited them to follow him with a deferential gesture and started in that direction. Mr. Howard was uneasy, but could see no other option. He snapped the reins and followed.

There was no sign of the neighbors, only Dragoons and a few Redcoat infantry. At the church, Tavington sat on horseback and watched as Wilkins helped the Howards out of their wagon and escorted them inside.

When they entered, they found the entire population of the village crowded inside. The Howard's searched the faces around them for an explanation, but their neighbors were as confused as they were. Mr. Howard was outraged and limped toward the soldiers standing guard at the doors.

"By what right are we made prisoners?" he shouted at them. Before they could answer, he hurried to move out of the way. He was nearly run down when Colonel Tavington rode his horse through the opening and into the church.

"This town has given aid to Benjamin Martin and his rebels," he said loudly. "I want to know where they are. If you tell me, you may be forgiven for your treason."

The villagers answered him with a defiant silence.

Mr. Howard stood near the horse, his gaze turned on the people of Pembroke with a sternness that matched Tavington's. Without words, he called on them to remain resolute and divulge nothing. A majority of the villagers supported the Patriot cause, but they were not, by any stretch, political radicals. They went about their daily business and ignored the war as best they could, wishing only that it would end so their lives could return to normal. Many of them didn't care who won the war, but they all knew and respected Benjamin Martin and had no intention of betraying him. Only one man, Mr. Hardwick, looked as if he might speak. The people around him noticed his indecision and stared at him harshly to keep him quiet.

Tavington sat on his horse waiting for someone to answer. When none of them did, he sighed. "Very well." He shook his head ominously and turned toward the exit.

"No," Hardwick said in a panic. He came forward and pointed at Mr. Howard. "This man gives Martin and his men supplies."

"Quiet!" Howard hissed at him.

"He brings them to Black Swamp."

"You damned fool!"

"In the marsh," Hardwick continued, "by the old Spanish mission."

Tavington lifted the palms of his hands to the heavens and smiled gratefully. He had known that eventually he would find someone willing to give Martin up. The astonishing thing was how long it had taken.

"Thank you so much," he said to them all. He steered his horse out of the building, ordering the guards to seal the last set of doors behind him. Hardwick rushed forward.

"But you said we'd be forgiven!"

"And you may well be," Tavington said with a mocking smile, "but that's between you and God."

The doors slammed shut, leaving Hardwick to confront his angry neighbors.

The Redcoats fastened a heavy bar of timber across the entrance as the people inside shouted to demand their release.

"Open this door! Open this door!"

"This is not just!" Mr. Howard bellowed.

Then the shutters over the windows were closed and locked from the outside. As the confusion in the building turned to hysteria, Anne and her mother moved away from the commotion at the doors and sat down on a pew.

Outside, Wilkins brought his horse alongside Tavington's and gestured to a group of the Dragoons who stood nearby holding lit torches.

"Ready to fire the town on your order, Colonel."

"Fire the town?" Tavington asked. Obviously, Wilkins hadn't understood his intentions. "We're going to burn the church."

Wilkins was horrified. "Sir, there is no honor in this," he said, loud enough for the other men to hear. The ones holding the torches followed the conversation carefully, hoping they would not be forced to carry out the gruesome order.

"Captain Wilkins, didn't you say that those who stand against England deserve to die a traitor's death?"

Wilkins struggled with himself. He remembered saying the words, but never imagined a situation such as this. It was one thing, he reasoned, to torture and kill enemy soldiers. It was quite another to put an entire village to death. Unwilling to comply with the order, his first thought was to simply turn and ride away. Then he considered the possibility of taking some action to save the people locked inside. He glanced around and saw that the other Dragoons were waiting on his response. Tavington recognized his distress and studied him in the same curious way he did his victims.

Finally Wilkins relented. He grabbed a torch from the hands of a Dragoon and heaved it high onto the roof. The others followed his lead. They held the torches against the building until the wood began to burn, then lobbed them onto the roof or sent them crashing through the upper windows.

A wild, terrified shrieking came from the desperate people trapped inside the church. The village men made themselves into a human battering ram and crashed their shoulders repeatedly against the doors, trying to force them open, but the bar held. The structure's old wood burned quickly. Flames soon engulfed the walls, and a choking black smoke filled the air.

When Mr. Howard realized all was lost, he moved away from the doors and sat down with his wife and daughter. The three of them closed their eyes and clung tightly to one another as the others made one frantic attempt after another to escape.

Tavington stayed long enough to make certain none of them escaped. As the screaming began to die down, he turned to Wilkins and tried to put the situation in perspective for him.

"The *honor* is to be found in the end, not in the means." He nodded toward the burning building. "This will be forgotten." Then, with a jerk of his reins, he turned his horse and rode away at a gallop.

Wilkins stayed behind, wondering what he had done.

My dearest wife,

I am drunk with happiness to be your husband, but sorely miserable not to have you at my side. Last night I made my bed on the cold ground and dreamed of the day we will make a house together with our child. On our return to this hidden camp, we were glad to see the familiar faces of our fellow soldiers and to find several new volunteers joining us. In our absence, much of our supplies provided a fine banquet for the animals who live here or spoiled with age. Replenishing our stock is our first order of business, it being widely known that an army can do little good on an empty stomach. My father asked me slyly what my opinion would be of going to Pembroke to collect the goods your kind father has set aside for us. My answer was an excited shout loud enough to draw the attention of all the militiamen. I never thought I would be as happy as I was just two days ago on our wedding day, but the prospect of seeing you again tomorrow fills me with unrivaled joy. I am insane with missing you, and this letter is a measure of my madness since I will deliver it by hand tomorrow morning and probably tell you its contents before you can read them. One more thing. I

*have thought of some good names we might give to the child, but
will save them until I see you. Hurry, morning!*

Your most mad, devoted, loving husband,
G.

Martin and his men rode out of the forest on the outskirts of Pembroke. Their faces grew wary when they saw,
ahead of them, a thin column of smoke drifting high into
the air. They spurred their horses and thundered into the
village. The streets were deserted, and the church had been
reduced to a smoldering heap of charred wood. Most of the
men followed Reverend Oliver as he went howling toward
his beloved, ruined church, but Gabriel raced to the Howard
house. He leapt off his horse and ran inside, searching.

"Anne? Anne!"

Martin followed Reverend Oliver to the church. Stepping through deep ashes and still-hot rubble, they walked
into the wreckage and noticed the burnt bodies. The reverend began to reel and leaned against Martin to prevent
himself from falling. The dead were everywhere around
them, hardly recognizable as humans. Many had burned
almost completely away, and those that remained were a
grisly sight. Dan Scott sank to his knees in the dirt outside
and sobbed as he called out the names of his wife and
daughter. Reverend Oliver began to wretch and was
helped away by a pair of the men.

Martin noticed something on the floor where the
pews had stood. He reached down into ashes and
picked up a small medallion, the North Star necklace
he'd given to Anne. His hand closed around it in a tight
fist as he looked up and saw the scorched, broken cross
behind what was left of the altar. He turned and left the

church just as Gabriel came running from the Howards' home.

"Anne?"

Martin motioned to Ludwell and one of the other men. They grabbed Gabriel and prevented him from going any closer to the church.

"Don't go in there," Martin said.

"No," he said, struggling. "No!"

"Don't go in there," his father repeated. He opened his hand to show the blackened necklace resting in his palm, and his son cried out wretchedly, staggering under the weight of a sudden and crushing agony. His eyes darted from one place to another as he struggled to comprehend his loss. Martin went to him and locked him in a rough embrace, trying to restrain and steady him, but Gabriel shrunk from him and eventually pulled free. Lost in grief, he stumbled off. Martin, feeling helpless, stood in the shadow of the church and watched him go. After a few moments of silence, he turned to his men.

"We'll need picks and shovels to dig the graves."

Later that afternoon, Martin was working alongside Dan Scott and some of the other men, helping to bury the dead in the small graveyard near the church. The day was warm and the red clay soil heavy and densely packed. He heard a commotion nearby and paused to lean on his shovel and catch his breath. Villeneuve was waving his arms and shouting at a handful of men in the square. He asked them a question Martin couldn't hear, and they answered by pointing down the road to the south.

Villeneuve turned and hurried toward Martin in a way that signaled trouble. Before the Frenchman reached him, Martin guessed what had happened.

"Gabriel is gone."

• • •

Tavington had sent the main force of his Dragoons ahead to the fort while he tarried in the delightful countryside. He and a small group of his Green Dragoons were enjoying the peace and quiet of the afternoon while their horses watered at a small brook. Insects buzzed through the air, and a few distant birds shouted to one another through the trees. The Dragoons, some of them with their boots off, sat near the water, talking and relaxing.

Tavington was shaving by the water's edge when he sensed that something was wrong and got to his feet. He cocked his head to one side and listened until he heard the sound of approaching horses. He looked to the top of a nearby hillside and saw a group of rebel militiamen coming over the crest, riding toward him at full tilt.

"To arms!"

Gabriel, Reverend Oliver, and a handful of others fired their first round from horseback. They charged down on the Dragoons wildly, staying on their horses until they were well within range of the enemy muskets. Gabriel was the first to dismount. He sprinted down the hill at a dead run, well ahead of his attacking party. Many of the Dragoons adopted the American tactic of retreating behind the trees and using them for cover as they fired. Gabriel ignored the lead balls whistling past him and pushed ahead. He came to within fifty paces before he stopped, leveled his rifle, and fired, hitting one of Dragoons in the chest.

The battle was quick and chaotic. Frightened horses bolted, some of them running into the path of the bullets. Men on both sides shouted instructions to their colleagues as they fired, rushed to reload their weapons, and fired again. Smoke from the guns quickly obscured the view.

One of the English officers strode out of the haze with a

pistol in his hand and shot a Patriot at point-blank range. Gabriel recognized him as Tavington's second-in-command, Bordon. He fired a shot that blew through Bordon's head, dropping him instantly. The Patriots surged toward their enemies.

Tavington defended himself expertly. With his saber in one hand and a pistol in the other, he stood in a clearing, doing battle and yelling words of encouragement to his men. A Patriot charged at him and swung with the butt of his gun, but Tavington sidestepped the blow, then hacked down on the man as he sailed past. When a second attacker came to test him, Tavington stopped the man's momentum with a feint of his sword, then shot him dead with his pistol.

Shots flew through the air, cutting down men from both sides. Gabriel and Reverend Oliver stood near one another, shooting. When a Dragoon came close and dropped to a knee to take aim at them, Reverend Oliver knocked him backward with a bullet. The man fell to the ground screaming, mortally wounded.

Tavington turned toward the sound and spotted Reverend Oliver standing in a cloud of new smoke. Both their weapons were empty. They locked eyes as their hands flew into action, reloading as quickly as they could. Focusing only on one another, it became a race between them, a deadly test of skill that one of them would not survive. Tavington worked with confidence and cold efficiency until he realized the reverend was matching him movement for movement. His hand faltered, and he spilled his cartridge of gunpowder before he had primed his firing pan. He reached for another cartridge, but realized he had lost the contest.

Reverend Oliver lifted his weapon to his shoulder but heard Gabriel come under attack by a sword-wielding

Dragoon only a step or two behind. He wheeled around and saw that Gabriel's gun had been knocked aside and that he had only a long knife to defend himself. The reverend came up behind the Dragoon and delivered a bone-cracking blow to the back of his neck, knocking him forward onto Gabriel's blade.

He spun to face Tavington, but was too late. He felt the bullet puncture his stomach and exit through his back. A cold, burning sensation traveled outward from the wound. As it climbed through his chest and into his head, he knew he was dying. His knees buckled and he fell forward. He tossed the rifle into the air behind him, hoping Gabriel would use it.

He did. Tavington made himself an easy target. Too brave or too foolish to run, he stayed where he was as he reloaded his pistol. Gabriel caught Reverend Oliver's weapon out of the air, took aim at Tavington's heart, and pulled the trigger all in the same motion. The bullet sailed a few inches wide of its intended target, but knocked Tavington off his feet. He spun around and fell facedown with a thud. After shuddering once, his body went completely limp.

Gabriel should have left it at that. But after all that "the Butcher" had done, simply killing him wasn't satisfaction enough. He pulled his knife out of the Redcoat he'd killed and walked down the slope, stepping over bodies along the way. Since he was the last man left standing, there was no need to hurry. He intended to take his time, remembering what his father had said about Fort Wilderness. He hadn't truly understood before, but now he felt the sort of fierce and primitive hatred that made such acts possible. He stood over Tavington's body, debating with himself. Wasn't he too good a man to do what he had in mind? He wanted to believe that he was, but when he imagined what it must have been like for Anne inside the burning church, he felt himself drawn to the deed by an irresistible force. He flipped the knife over in his hand and bent down to begin the work.

As he did, Tavington suddenly flipped himself over and drove the point of a sword into Gabriel's gut, stabbing upward toward the heart. It happened so suddenly, the young man never had a chance to defend himself. Gasping in surprise and pain, he tried to hold himself perfectly still as he searched desperately for some way to lift himself off the sword. But Tavington put both his hands on the hilt of the weapon and gave it a sharp twist.

On the far ridge, another group of American riders crested the hill.

Benjamin Martin, leading fifty of his men, looked down the slope and saw the bodies strewn on the ground. Only two men were left alive, one of them standing over the other. Even at a distance, he recognized them as Tavington and Gabriel. Horrified, he galloped toward the scene at full speed.

As Gabriel slumped to the ground, Tavington ran to a nearby horse and climbed into the saddle. He spurred it hard, riding as fast as the animal would carry him across the brook and up the opposite hillside. He looked over his shoulder, expecting to be pursued, but saw Martin and his men pull to a stop when they reached Gabriel. It was a stroke of incredibly good luck, and Tavington took advantage of it by disappearing quickly into the trees at the top of the hill.

Martin, gripped by agony, pushed himself out of the saddle and stumbled to where Gabriel lay bleeding. Just as he had with Thomas, he scooped the boy up in his arms and held him. Gabriel's eyes were still open, frozen in an expression of surprise.

"Father . . . I'm sorry . . ."

"Ssshhh. Don't talk, son. You'll be fine."

"I . . . I'm sorry, I . . ." Martin tore open Gabriel's coat with one hand and applied pressure to the wound, desperately trying to stop the bleeding.

"Don't talk, don't talk. You're going to live, you hear me? I'll take care of you."

Gabriel nodded his head, but he was fading fast. Martin could feel him dying. He gave up on the wound and cradled the boy in his arms, comforting him as best he could. All of his restraint and self-control disappeared. He stroked the boy's face with his hands, brushing the hair back, and pressed his son's face tenderly to his own.

"I'm sorry, Father," said Gabriel, fighting for air. "I'm sorry about Thomas."

"Oh, son," he said trembling, "that wasn't your fault. It was mine." The tears rose up in his eyes, but when he felt Gabriel come to the end, he didn't want that to be the last thing the boy saw, so he tried to force a thin farewell smile across his lips.

Gabriel was dead.

Martin continued to hold him, rocking him back and forth just as he'd done when he had first come into the world. He felt a strange sensation, a numbness, spread through his body like snakebite poison. It was the life draining out of him, just as it had drained from his son. He was crushed under the weight of the loss and his own guilt. He knew that ultimately, he was the cause of Gabriel's death. It was the curse he'd brought on himself before the boy was born. He'd avoided it for so many years, he let himself believe it was gone. But now it had found him and was making him pay.

His men gathered around him, silently watching him

grieve. They had been there only a few minutes when they heard a low, rumbling sound beyond the horizon. It came toward them slowly until they realized it was the rat-a-tat-tat of military drums.

A narrow slash of blue appeared on the horizon as an army topped a distant hill and started down into the valley. They were Continental Regulars and they came by the thousands, marching down into the valley as thousands more moved to the crest of the hill. They blanketed the green valley with blue, and Martin's militiamen waved their hats to them in greeting.

Martin looked up and watched them for a while without reaction, then turned his attention back to Gabriel.

17

The Continental Army made their camp that night in the elbow of land between the Broad and Pacolet rivers. There was a thin sheet of cloud in the sky that caught and amplified the moonlight, casting a blue glow on the skins of the tents.

Men from all thirteen colonies were there, a mix of Continentals and militia. Some slept in tents, while others spread themselves on the ground and used their haversacks as pillows. Hundreds of small fires burned, and everything was tense and hushed. They realized the British were nearby and aware of their presence.

Two hours before dawn, Burwell rode through the camp on horseback until he found where the South Carolina militia had set themselves up. A pair of men sat at a fire playing melancholy tunes on fife and violin.

"Colonel Martin's tent, where is it?"

The men pointed toward the largest oak Burwell had ever seen, an ancient tree with massive branches that traveled parallel to the ground like a set of welcoming outstretched arms. When he moved closer and dismounted, Jean Villeneuve came up to meet him. In the dim light, each man saw the stress and fatigue etched into the face of the other. Burwell had come when he heard that Gabriel was dead and Martin had quit the war. Without being asked, Villeneuve nodded to say it was true.

They hadn't seen one another for many months, but there was no reunion. They said good morning somberly; then Villeneuve led the way under the branches of the giant tree. He stopped several paces from Martin's tent and motioned for Burwell to continue by himself, wishing him luck with a nod.

A single candle burned inside. Benjamin Martin sat on a campstool, his clothing disheveled and his face resting in his hands, staring at his dead son. He had washed Gabriel's body, combed his hair, and laid him out under a blanket so that only his face was showing. His skin had already turned gray and shrunken.

Burwell had grown fond of Gabriel during the two difficult years they had spent together in the North under Washington. Looking after the young man, as he had promised to do, never become the burden he feared it would. In fact, his intelligence and steadfast dedication made him a valuable asset, and within a few months he had risen to become the colonel's most trusted aide-de-camp. But Burwell inspected the body now without emotion.

"I'll help you bury him."

"No," said Martin in a quiet, croaking voice that made it sound as if he were the one who had died.

Burwell turned to him. "How many men have we seen die?"

"I've seen only two," Martin told him, "Gabriel and Thomas. They were in my charge and I lost them."

As a friend, Burwell was moved by Martin's wretched condition. As a general on the eve of battle, he wanted none of it. "My wife in Alexandria is with child, my first. I fight for that child."

Martin said nothing.

"Benjamin, nothing will replace your sons, but if you come with us you can justify their sacrifice to the *cause*."

Still he said nothing.

"Benjamin, we finally have a chance! We've chased Cornwallis out of Fort Carolina and have him running toward the Chesapeake. He still has us outnumbered, but Nathanael Greene and Dan Morgan are down here from Virginia. If we can win this next battle, victory in the war is within our grasp."

"Go seek your victory. I am small issue to it."

"You're wrong," Burwell said, trying one last time to make him see. "You matter to your men and you matter to others as well. Your victories and your losses, they are shared by more than you know. Stay with us, Benjamin. *Stay the course!*"

His use of the phrase was a coincidence. He didn't know it was a motto Martin had been reciting since his transformation during those hard first years with Elizabeth, a way of reminding himself not to sink back into being the sort of man he had been before. Burwell only thought to use the words because he'd heard Gabriel use them from time to time.

Martin lifted his head and looked into Burwell's eyes. *Stay the course?* The meaning of the words had changed somehow and now they sounded hollow. Drained of energy, he shook his head.

"I have run my course."

There was nothing more to say or do. Burwell went to Martin and laid a hand on his friend's shoulder for a moment, silently wishing him well. Then he turned and walked out.

The militiamen had gathered around Villeneuve's fire, anxiously waiting to learn the outcome of the meeting, hoping Burwell would be able to raise the spirits of their devastated leader. But when he came toward them with his head down, they knew he had failed. He came and stood among them, staring quietly into the fire, wishing he had something encouraging to say.

"When we head out, you men will be coming with me," he said tersely. Then he climbed on his horse and hurried away.

Within two hours, the great patriotic army had broken camp and marched away, leaving Martin's tent standing alone in an empty field of smoldering campfires. It was still dark when he came outside, stripped off his jacket, and began the painful task of digging another grave at the foot of another oak tree. As he worked, his own body felt brittle and unfamiliar. He carried Gabriel outside, laid him gently in the ground, and covered his body with earth. He pushed a crude cross into the soil and knelt to say a final good-bye.

Bowing his head, he spoke directly to God, commending Gabriel into His care. He explained that although the young man had died at war, he had been fighting in the service of his ideals, hoping to make the world a finer place. He asked for the salvation of Gabriel's soul and, if possible, that he be reunited with his already-departed loved ones, especially his new bride, Anne.

Next, he tried to say a few words to Gabriel, but the only thing he could think to say was how very, very sorry he was. His two primary reasons for joining the war had been to avenge Thomas's death and to keep Gabriel away from harm. He had failed on both accounts and blamed himself for both boys' deaths. When he thought of the butcher Tavington, he felt none of the thirst for vengeance that had motivated him before. Feeling utterly shattered, he could find no reason to go on.

When he looked up, it was dawn. A pale streak of yellow was rising on the eastern horizon while overhead the sky was still dark and full of stars. He went back to his tent and began to strike it, but quit when he realized he wouldn't need it where he was going.

He slipped on his coat, picked up his own gear and Gabriel's haversack, and went to his horse. As he was packing his saddlebags and preparing to ride away, he noticed something sticking out of the haversack, a white star on a blue background. It was the Old Glory his son had spent so many hours stitching back together. He remembered what it had looked like, tattered and muddy, after the disastrous battle at Camden, and how the disheartened Patriot soldier had advised Gabriel to leave it where it was, saying it was a lost cause. But Gabriel, the idealist, had refused to believe it.

He pulled a corner of the flag out of the haversack and ran his fingers over the material, thinking about Gabriel's dedication to "the Glorious Cause." What a shame, Martin thought, that his son would never get a chance to see the new world he had been fighting for—especially now that it seemed so close at hand. He remembered what Burwell had told him that night about victory being within their grasp.

He went to put the flag away, but hesitated to do so and held it out in front of him instead. He studied Gabriel's rough stitching job in the dim light, and the longer he looked at it, the more he imagined his son's spirit coming through the mended material and speaking to him.

Stay the course, it seemed to be saying.

Martin looked from the stars in his hands, up to the stars in the sky. Although the new day continued to grow on the horizon, the North Star was still visible. In fact, it seemed to be shining more brightly than usual, almost as if it were urgently trying to tell him something.

• • •

Lumbering and mighty, the Patriot forces were on the march. Under the command of General Greene from Rhode Island, they followed a seldom-used road through a field stubbled with dead grass. The leaves on the distant trees were erupting with the colors of fall, brilliant reds and yellows. Thousands strong, the army moved quietly. Some of the men traveled on horseback, some rode in wagons, but the vast majority of them were plodding along on foot. They marched three and four abreast in a line that stretched for miles.

Leading the procession was a mixed unit. Burwell's blue-uniformed Continentals marched alongside the rough-looking civilians who had spent the last year fighting under Martin. Normally, Continentals disdained the company of militiamen, but Burwell's troops understood what the grizzled veterans of the swamp had accomplished and were proud to have them along. Villeneuve rode side by side with Burwell, leading them along the trail.

About two in the afternoon, Burwell happened to look off to the east and saw something moving behind a shallow ridge that ran parallel to the road. It was an American flag, an Old Glory, being carried on horseback. Villeneuve saw it, too, and he smiled when he recognized Gabriel's flag, almost completely repaired, trailing a single strip of loose fabric as it fluttered closer.

When Colonel Benjamin Martin topped the ridge, the men who had fought under him were the first to raise their voices, glad to have him back. He was the leader they knew and trusted, the only man they wanted to follow into battle. But they were not the only ones who raised a shout. The entire army began to roar in approval, shouting *huzzah* and waving their hats in the air. Martin encouraged them. He cantered up the long line of men, showing the flag and urging them to make more noise.

"Huzzah! Huzzah!" they thundered, shaking the ground below their feet.

When he arrived at the front of the line, Burwell and Villeneuve made room for him on the trail, greeting him with soldierly nods.

The army continued trudging forward, but it had a new bounce in its step.

Cornwallis was on the move, but not on the run. His slow October retreat across South Carolina was a tactical maneuver. Even with all his heavy artillery, Cornwallis could have easily outpaced the Patriots if he had tried. Instead, he maintained a deliberately slow pace, staying just beyond his enemy's reach, luring them forward while he brought his far-flung forces back together and searched for a suitable place to turn and engage.

A few days after Martin rejoined the Patriot march, Cornwallis found a very acceptable battlefield. It was a place called Cowpens, so-named for the livestock yards that had once stood there but had been gone for some years. The terrain was not as perfectly level as he would have liked, but it offered broad open fields surrounded by natural obstacles—precisely the type of place he needed to fight an orderly, European-type battle.

At sunset, as his men were establishing camp for the night, Cornwallis was in fine spirits. Impeccably dressed, as usual, in his red uniform jacket dripping with gold adornments, he stood in his spacious command tent, surrounded by his staff of officers. He had spread a set of topographical maps on a folding table and seemed well pleased with what they showed him. Everything was falling effortlessly into place.

When General O'Hara came to the tent and relayed the

latest intelligence reports, his Lordship's good mood improved still further. The Americans had done exactly what he suspected they would. They had followed him into Cowpens and trapped themselves. He drummed out a little tune on the tabletop with his fingers, then made an announcement.

"Gentlemen, our little game of cat and mouse with these colonials is over. With the Broad River at their rear and open fields on both flanks, they have nowhere to run. I have maneuvered them *precisely* where I want them. They are tired, hungry, outmanned, and outgunned. Tomorrow, at long last, we will destroy them." He smiled almost giddily at his staff, already imagining hundreds of London's church bells ringing in his honor as he returned home victorious. "We engage at dawn," he said crisply. "Ready your men." Applauding his Lordship's cleverness and congratulating him in advance, the officers filed out of the tent brimming with confidence.

Cornwallis followed them into the brisk early evening and strolled toward the field hospital. He ducked under the tent flap and found Tavington, disheveled and only half dressed, sitting on an examination table as his wound was treated by one of the doctors. His hair was out of its queue and hung uncombed down to his shoulders. His shirt was not tucked into his trousers, and there was a nasty bloodstain on it where he'd been shot. Cornwallis stood by quietly and watched Tavington grimace as the physician rubbed alcohol into the wound. A moment passed before he cleared his throat to announce his presence.

"You will be missed tomorrow, Colonel," Cornwallis said with a fair amount of irony in his voice.

Tavington turned to him, startled. "*Missed*, my lord?"

"Your wound."

"It's nothing, my lord!" To prove it, he slapped the doctor's hands away and sprang to his feet. "I am ready to serve you."

"Very well," Cornwallis said with a wicked smile, "but make sure *I* am the one you serve. I stand on the eve of the most important victory of my career. Do not fail me."

"Fail you?" Tavington felt insulted by the suggestion and stepped closer. "*My* efforts, in no small measure, have brought you to the brink of this victory."

Cornwallis shrugged. "I grant you that *small measure*, in spite of your failing to deliver the Ghost to me."

Tavington hung his head. "Thus far."

"Throughout history," Cornwallis went on, "the greatest generals have always had subordinates who believed that they themselves won the wars. But this is *my* victory." He moved menacingly close to Tavington and stared coldly. "I will not tolerate another of your premature charges borne of your eagerness for glory. Wait for my orders to charge, Colonel."

"Yes, my lord," Tavington said obediently.

Satisfied with the response, Cornwallis turned to go, but gave Tavington one last thought to contemplate. "If not," he said over his shoulder, "you may abandon any hope of Ohio."

Less than five miles away, another staff meeting was taking place at that same hour. After a strenuous day's march, the Patriot army had stopped for the night in a place that had once been a large plantation. A ruined mansion stood at the top of the nearest hill, completely gutted by fire. As the sunlight faded from the sky, the men began to build fires and gather around them, Continentals and militiamen segregating themselves from one another.

General Greene, the army's commander, called a strategy meeting with the handful of men he trusted most under an open-sided tent. His scouting parties had returned with distressing new information about the size and position of Cornwallis's forces.

Twelve officers were invited. Benjamin Martin, Harry Burwell, and Jean Villeneuve were present. General Daniel Morgan and cavalry leader William Washington were also in attendance.

Nathanael Greene was a clean-shaven man forty-five years of age with thinning hair and a razor-sharp mind. A Quaker, he had been excommunicated from the Society of Friends for supporting armed resistance to England. Until 1775, Greene was blissfully ignorant of all matters concerning warfare, but by the summer of 1776, he had taught himself nearly all there was to know about the subject. Impressed with the man, George Washington appointed him brigadier general. The next year, he was promoted again. After repeated urgings from both Washington and the Congress, he reluctantly accepted the difficult post of Quartermaster General and succeeded in finding money and supplies where his predecessors had found none. He was popular with the men who served under him and was considered by the British to be as dangerous an opponent as General Washington himself.

"Unfortunately, gentlemen," Greene began in a doleful voice, "it seems Cornwallis has us cornered. Not only does he outnumber us, but more than half our force is militia, unreliable at best." As the other men nodded their heads, Martin stepped up to disagree.

"You underestimate our militia," he said to the group. "All of you do."

"You've done wonders with them, Colonel Martin," Greene allowed, "but we've seen our militia lines break again and again. At Kips Bay, at Princeton . . ."

". . . at Camden."

". . . and Brandywine."

Martin heard them, but remained steadfast. "The British have seen the same thing," he pointed out. "Cornwallis's own letters bear out the fact that he has no respect for militia. None whatsoever."

"What are you suggesting, Ben?" Burwell asked.

"I'm suggesting we use that."

Greene was interested. He asked if Martin was speaking only in general terms or whether he had some particular strategy in mind. Villeneuve and Burwell smiled at the question. They knew Martin well enough to guess that he already had an entire plan of battle sketched out in his head, which, as it turned out, was true.

It was a daring plan, and as he explained it to the other officers, it met with more than a little skepticism. Dan Morgan shook his head and said he doubted it could work. But in the end, even he agreed that Martin's plan was the best one available to them and decided to give it a try.

Soon after the meeting broke up, Martin began moving from campfire to campfire, speaking with no more than a handful of militiamen at a time. He had been at it for half the night by the time Villeneuve, who was polishing the boots he planned to wear the next day, noticed him sitting down among a group of men nearby. He put the boots aside and went to listen.

". . . and I know you men have already sacrificed a great deal," he heard Martin saying. "All I'm asking is that the militia fires *two* rounds." The men were from

Maryland and had fought in a handful of skirmishes.

"I don't know," said one of them, "plenty can happen in the time it takes to fire two shots."

"'Specially against British Regulars," another man agreed.

"Which is why I'm not asking for three," Martin said. He stayed with them a little longer, explaining some of the particulars of the plan before moving off to let them consider his request. Villeneuve watched him go immediately to the next campfire, where he introduced himself to a new group of men and had the same conversation again.

It was well past midnight before Martin returned to his own men, exhausted. As soon as he laid his head on the ground, he went out like a pinched candle.

18

The next morning began like any other. A soft pink dawn broke across the eastern horizon, casting a tranquil glow on the fire-blackened bricks of the ruined mansion at the top of the hill as the American camp stirred slowly to life. Birds began to sing in the distant trees, but they were interrupted by the sound of British signal drums in the distance.

General Greene and a handful of his officers took their horses up the hill and stood on the front steps of the mansion, between the marble columns that had once supported a roof, and looked across the field with their telescopes. A few miles away, they saw the British making their preparations.

Martin used these last quiet minutes before the storm to look after some unfinished personal business. He led his horse into an empty field away from the tents and cleared a place in the tall grass to build a fire. Once it was going, he dug through his saddlebags until he found something he'd been saving—the last of Thomas's toy soldiers. The little man was armed with a pike and had been painted Patriot blue. Martin melted it down in a long iron spoon, then poured the liquid into a mold.

There was only enough lead for one bullet.

He plunged the mold into a small pail of water to cool, clipped off the sprue of excess lead, and then tucked it into a special pocket on the front of his weapons belt. He would need to find it quickly if he happened upon Tavington.

When that was done, he turned to a harder task. He found pencil and paper in Gabriel's haversack and sat down to compose a farewell note to Charlotte and his children. He stared down at the empty page for a few minutes, searching for the right words but soon realized there was no easy way to tell them what he had to say, so he plunged into it, writing as quickly as he could. He finished quickly, folded the page up without reading it over, and tied it closed with a string. On the front of it, he wrote, *To Family of Col. B. Martin, S. Carolina.*

As he came back into the camp, he was struck by the sight of a large, rather gaudy, French military flag waving in the breeze outside Villeneuve's tent. Red, blue, and white, it was decorated with golden fleur-de-lis and the words *PER MARE ET TERRE.* A moment later, Villeneuve stepped outside to greet the morning wearing a spectacular white battle uniform. It was a finely tailored suit of clothing with gold buttons, blue epaulettes on the shoulders, and matching blue lapels. He wore a white cravat tied over his throat, and the lacy cuffs of his shirtsleeves showed at his wrists. To complete the outfit, he had put on an enormous black hat with a brim that folded up at the front and back.

Martin, who wore a simple cotton shirt under a leather vest, thought Villeneuve looked like a man who was planning to have high tea with the Redcoats, not one who was planning to kill them. When the stocky major caught Martin staring at him, he lifted his chin defiantly in the air.

"If I die," he declared, "I will die well dressed."

The American drummers began beating out the order to assemble. The Continentals from the various colonies fell into their formations and went up the hill in disciplined groups behind their company flags. The militiamen went with them, but they straggled up the hill however they pleased, some in talkative groups and others quietly alone. Mounted sergeants galloped back and forth along the crest of the hill, shouting orders and directing the men to their positions.

Martin and Villeneuve rode their horses to the very center of the assembling army and looked out across the broad alley of land. The British made an impressive and frightening sight. Stacked twenty rows deep, they formed a solid wall of red jackets that extended nearly the whole width of the giant field. In the gaps between them were cannon emplacements protected by earthworks.

As the militiamen continued to arrive and take up their positions, Burwell rode up to the spot wearing a black cavalry cap with horsehair trim. He spotted a group of Virginia militia standing behind a large red banner embroidered with a black rattlesnake and the familiar motto DON'T TREAD ON ME. A Virginian himself, Burwell stopped to offer the men a few words of encouragement before coming to see Martin and Villeneuve. The three men acknowledged one another with nods, then turned and watched with grim expressions as the first wave of Redcoats began marching toward them.

"God be with you," Burwell said to them.

"And with you," replied Martin. He reached into his pocket and withdrew a folded paper tied in a string. "Harry, will you give this to my children?"

Burwell only stared at the letter. He could guess what it said, and accepting it seemed the same as accepting Martin's death. He looked Martin over carefully for a moment, trying to read his intentions before reluctantly taking the paper and putting it into his coat. When he rode off, Martin and Villeneuve dismounted and went to take their places in line with the other men.

The militiamen stayed somber and silent as the distant Redcoats marched closer. Without meaning to, Dan Scott and Occam ended up standing next to one another. As he watched the enemy advancing, Scott's face twitched with a mixture of hatred and fear. Though he was eager to pay the English back for what they'd done to his family at Pembroke, there was a part of him that wanted to turn and run. He glanced up and down the line, wondering how many Americans would be dead by afternoon, when an idea occurred to him.

"You know, it's October."

"I know," said Occam in his deep, gravelly voice.

"That's more than twelve months. You're free now."

"I'm here on my own accord," he said, turning to look Scott in the eyes, one free man to another. When he did, Scott felt ashamed of the way he'd acted in the past.

"I'm honored to have you with us," he said. "Honored."

The words meant a great deal to Occam, but he only looked back at Scott without changing expressions.

Then, before anyone felt ready, a shout was relayed down the line and the drummers tapped out the cadence for the advance to begin. Villeneuve, who carried neither musket nor rifle, stepped out in front of the militia line and put his sword high in the air. He waited for a sign from Martin so he could relay the order to the men, but Martin surprised him by shouting it himself.

"Forward!"

Like a heavy ship lurching away from its moorings, the one thousand men of the militia set out in two staggered rows to face an enemy force nearly twice as large. Villeneuve led the way down the hill, marching in an exaggerated fashion to help the men behind stay in step, but it was a futile gesture. While the Continentals to the right and left kept the pace and their formations, the citizen soldiers at the center had difficulty with both and, after the first fifty yards, gave up altogether. They didn't see the point of marching in step, as long as they got to where they were going. According to plan, they marched at a slower than normal pace.

As they got underway, Martin kept an eye on the fierce Frenchman marching half a step ahead, looking him over carefully head to toe. He knew the chances were good that Villeneuve would die that morning, a long way from home.

"How old were your daughters?" Martin asked him.

Villeneuve had made it clear in the past that his family was not a subject he wished to discuss. He turned and shot a look at Martin, ready to tell him to mind his own business when, to his surprise, he realized he was willing to answer the question.

"I had two daughters. Violette was twelve and Pauline was ten." He marched along a few more steps before adding, "They both had green eyes."

"I'm sure they were lovely."

"Yes," Villeneuve answered gruffly, "they were."

On the opposite side of the field, Cornwallis sat on horseback surrounded by his flags, his officers, and a body-guard of six hundred infantry reserves. As always, he was fastidiously groomed and attired. He had risen from bed half an hour earlier than normal to have his valets wash and powder his hair. His sidelocks were tightly curled above his ears, and he wore a new hat trimmed with gold ribbon an inch wide. He was aware that the day marked an historic occasion, and his only regret was that there were no distinguished persons of rank present to witness his victory. With O'Hara sitting at his side, he surveyed the field through a spyglass, anxious for the action to begin.

When he saw the Americans begin to advance, he imme-diately ordered his cannons into action. The very first shot was an exploding cartridge shell that flew an extraordinary distance. It streaked high above the heads of the Americans, trailing fire the entire way, and smashed through the topmost bricks of the ruined house. The shell exploded a second later, raining more bricks and debris on the ground. Though no Americans were hit, it seemed an auspicious beginning.

"Unless I'm dreaming," Cornwallis said, peering through his glass, "I believe I see militia forming at their center."

O'Hara quickly unfolded his own telescope and lifted it to his eye. It was true. On both sides of the advance, there were compact groups of Continentals, but the middle was defended by a ragged line of civilians only two lines deep.

The two generals looked at one another, delighted and slightly amazed, wondering what in the world the Americans were thinking. Protecting one's flanks was crucially important, of course, but it was not to be done at the expense of a weakened center. It was an egregious violation of the laws of military strategy, not to mention common sense. Having been tricked by the Americans before, Cornwallis immediately suspected a trap of some sort, but quickly waved the possibility away. Cowpens was not an overgrown swamp or a densely wooded forest where the Americans could surprise him with their tricks. He had settled on the place precisely for that reason.

He told O'Hara he wanted the cannon fire concentrated on the American center and ordered the use of exploding shells. They were less lethal in the open field than cannonballs, but the noise and flying debris they caused tended to spread panic. Cornwallis thought he stood a good chance of breaking their lines before his infantry had fired a single shot.

As the shells began to pound the field, the militiamen behind Martin and Villeneuve began to curse and pray.

They faltered a bit, but none of them turned to run. The earth was soft enough from recent rains to partially absorb the shells. They buried themselves where they fell and exploded straight up into the air.

They had gone only a few hundred yards when Martin ordered the men to halt even though the British front line was still well out of range. Cornwallis saw nothing unusual in this, attributing the sudden stop to the natural cowardice of the militia in the face of the cannon fire.

For several minutes, Martin's men waited in tense silence as the British marched menacingly closer, their feet lifting and falling in perfect rhythm. As the distance closed, they began to notice a fair number of Africans among the Redcoat ranks, slaves and freedmen who had been pressed into service. And then they began to distinguish the officers from the enlisted men. And then they saw the individual faces of the enemy.

"Ready arms!" Villeneuve shouted, and the Americans lifted their guns to the their shoulders. The Redcoats were within range, but continued to advance until the Americans could see the whites of their eyes. When they were seventy paces away, some of the militiamen began to lower their rifles to fire, but were ordered to wait. The British commanding officer was a handsome captain, tall and thin, who wore a powdered wig under his hat. He appeared utterly calm and confident. He led his men to within sixty paces, then fifty, and then forty.

"Platoon halt!" he finally cried. The moment the words were out of his mouth, Martin gave an order of his own.

"Take aim!" All one thousand of his men responded at once. The men of the rear line rested their guns on the shoulders of the men of the first line to steady their aim. The Redcoats stared back unflinchingly. Seeing that the

Americans would have the first volley, they planted their feet and waited for it to come as patiently as a row of Thomas's lead soldiers. Villeneuve lifted his sword high in the air, then he and Martin shouted in one voice.

"Fire!"

The militiamen squeezed back on their triggers and turned their heads away to avoid the flash of powder in their pans. Smoke and fire blasted from their guns, sending a volley of bullets into the Redcoat line that instantly cut down almost two hundred men. As the sound echoed away, smoke billowed into the space separating the two armies, partially obscuring the view. Gagging on the thick odor of burned powder, the Patriots began to reload even before Villeneuve shouted the order.

The Redcoat captain was still standing. As calmly as could be, he waited for his second-liners to step forward and replace the fallen before sounding the order.

"Present arms!"

Martin hadn't fought a battle like this since his early days in the French and Indian Wars, and now he remembered why. Struggling to keep his mind focused and his hands steady, he went through the steps of reloading his weapon, but he couldn't help listening. The British sergeants were shouting, the wounded were screaming, and the drums were relaying the captain's orders to the men at the sides.

"Take aim!" shouted the Redcoat captain.

In a few heartbeats, Martin knew, he would be either dead or alive, and there wasn't a thing he could do about it. It was a simple roll of the dice. He glanced up from his reloading only once, to make sure the lines were still intact, and saw that they were. So far, not a single militiaman had turned to run. That would change a moment later.

"Fire!"

The British muskets cracked and sent a hailstorm of lead flying at the Patriot line. Some balls winged past their ears or splattered the dirt at their feet, but many others found their marks. Everywhere there was the soft thud of bullets penetrating flesh. The impact knocked some men backwards and dropped others straight to the ground. Blood and handfuls of clothing spattered through the air. All up and down the Patriot front line, men were mowed down like blades of grass by a great, invisible sickle.

The militiamen, even the veterans, looked around in horror at the magnitude of the slaughter. Some of them froze stiff with panic while others backed away, then turned to run. This was the moment Martin had known would come.

"Hold the line!" he shouted. "Hold the line!"

"Hold the line!" Villeneuve joined in. The two of them bellowed the command over and over, "Hold the line!" until the men around them took up the cry. Soon nearly every volunteer on the field was shouting the words, including some of those who were themselves running away. "Hold the line! Hold the line!"

Generals Greene and Cornwallis, watching from opposite sides of the field, were both impressed when they saw the breakaway militiamen turn and rejoin the battle. If a Redcoat or a Continental decided to run, there were officers stationed behind to shoot them, but militia were free to come and go. At that moment, it became clear to both commanders that this was no ordinary group of militia.

It was clear to Tavington as well. He and his Green Dragoons watched the battle's opening moves from a nearby hilltop. They remained out of view behind a stand of sugar maples and oaks gone brilliant with autumn color, their horses shifting below them nervously with each blast of the cannons. Tavington itched to attack but remembered Cornwallis's stern warning. He was less than two hundred yards from where the New York Continentals had squared off against a division of Redcoats, but he hardly noticed the battle between these groups. His attention was focused on the remarkable battle for the center. Like Cornwallis, he was astonished by the stupidity of the American decision to use volunteers to face the brunt of the attack and was equally astonished to see them hold their ground.

Following the action through his spyglass, he couldn't help but notice a man in a French uniform standing brazenly in the space between the two armies, waving his sword and shouting instructions. The brilliance of the man's uniform made him an easy target. Just beside him was someone Tavington recognized—Benjamin Martin. The notorious Ghost, the one who had eluded and embarrassed him for so many months, was standing in plain view, far from any protection except for his own feeble militiamen.

Tavington's hatred and killing instincts boiled to the surface. He pocketed the spyglass and drew his sword.

"Prepare to charge!" he called, much to the surprise of his men. Captain Wilkins was sitting beside him.

"Sir, we haven't been given that order."

Tavington barely heard him. Suddenly nothing else mattered to him.

"CHARGE!"

The Dragoons bolted into the open behind a company of their own infantry, one that was marching to outflank the New York brigade. In his haste, Tavington nearly trampled them as he raced down the hill at a full gallop, taking the shortest possible route toward his prey.

Cornwallis hoped the Patriot center would collapse after the first volley. He was disappointed but not overly frustrated when they did not. A second round from the Patriots would cost him several more of his infantry, but that was a relatively minor problem. But when he saw the Dragoons enter the fray before his command, he flew into a sudden rage.

"Damn Tavington," Cornwallis shouted, "damn that man!"

With a victory at Cowpens, Cornwallis expected to smash the American resistance and take his place among the great English military heroes of history. He assumed that Tavington, despite their agreement, was rushing in to steal the glory and make a name for himself. Cornwallis wasn't going to tolerate it.

When Martin looked up and saw the Dragoons roaring closer, he was not exactly surprised. He had seen Tavington charge too early at the Battle of Camden and read about Cornwallis's frustrations in the captured journals. But surprised or not, the English Light Cavalry was an awesome and frightening sight. He glanced behind him, gauging the distance to the ruined mansion at the top of the hill. Not all the militia had finished reloading, but there was no time. The Dragoons were within a thousand yards.

"Take aim! Take aim!" Martin shouted, and then, "Fire!"

The Americans' second volley ripped into the Redcoats, but this time not as many of them fell. The shots had been poorly loaded and hastily aimed. Almost immediately, the Redcoat infantry was finished reloading and ready to answer.

"RETREAT!" Martin shouted, leading them away. Before the drummers could tap out the order, the entire line of militiamen had turned. They ran as fast as they could, shouting as they went. The Redcoat front line fired when ready, hitting several Americans in the back.

"Order the bayonet charge," Cornwallis shouted to O'Hara as he watched Tavington's horsemen rush into the action. "We will see who takes the glory from this field."

The British drum corps beat out the order and within seconds, the Redcoat front lines had lowered their weapons to become a solid wall of foot-long knives. They surged forward with a thunderous cry, pursuing the Americans. At the sides of the field, the British ran into the American Regulars, who firmly held their ground, but the center opened completely and Redcoats poured into the breech by the hundreds. The foot traffic was so thick, the Dragoons were unable to catch the fleeing Americans.

"Congratulations, my lord!" cheered O'Hara when he saw the result. The early use of bayonets, while not part of the original plan, had blocked Tavington's path and arrested his progress.

Cornwallis was not finished. Tavington's early charge had aroused his ego and his pride. Having begun this new course of action, he was determined to press forward with it.

"Infantry reserve into the center," he said in an offhand way. General O'Hara was surprised by the order and hesitated to relay it.

"But, my lord," he pointed out, "you have already taken the field."

"Yes, and now we shall take their spirits. Send the entire battalion over that hill and crush them. It ends today."

O'Hara thought it unwise, especially when they couldn't see what might lie beyond the hilltop. But Cornwallis would hear no arguments. Soon another group of several hundred men began a double-time march toward the front.

Winded from the long run, Martin paused at the crest of the hill to look behind. Huge numbers of British infantry were charging up the hill and gaining ground. Some of the older militiamen and the wounded stragglers were falling under the steel blades. The Dragoons were beginning to shoot through the gaps, filtering their way to the front of the charge.

"Faster!" Martin shouted, waving his men urgently over the top of the hill. As they started down the other side, they came face to face with an army of five hundred men—Burwell's Continentals. This force had been held in reserve, their muskets primed and ready.

As the British stormed over the hill in pursuit, Tavington quickly realized he'd rushed into a trap. He pulled back on his reins and frantically shouted to hold the charge, but it was too late. The Redcoats' momentum carried them down into the small valley.

Martin's men raced toward the Continentals and threw themselves to the ground, giving Burwell's men a clear shot at the Redcoats. The general chopped the air with his sword and shouted.

"Fire!"

A powerful volley tore into the Redcoat infantry, leveling a great many of them. At the same time, cannon and mortar emplacements hidden in the wings roared to life. They sent iron balls flying and skittering across the ground and into the British ranks, breaking men in two and knocking the legs out from under the Dragoons' horses.

Amid this sudden confusion, many of the Redcoats continued to advance while others turned and scattered. Burwell's second line stepped forward and fired another punishing round. Before their smoke had cleared, Martin's troops rose from the ground, freshly reloaded, to fire yet a third. Their volley concentrated on the hated Dragoons, knocking many out of their saddles.

Despite these heavy losses, the Redcoats still had nearly equal numbers. Before they could reorganize themselves, Martin ran out in front of his men and shouted another order.

"Charge!"

He started forward at a dead run, and before his men had time to consider the danger of the situation, they followed him. With a fresh shout, they stormed to the attack, stepping over the bodies of the fallen.

Martin pointed himself like a rocket at an English soldier carrying a Union Jack. He lowered his shoulder and crashed into the man, flipping him into the air. Then he swung his musket like a broadsword and cracked a second soldier across the face. Villeneuve matched him step for step, slashing and hacking his way into the enemy ranks. With no bayonets of their own and little training in hand-to-hand combat, Martin's men waded into the melee and fought with an energy that surprised and frightened the enemy.

The Redcoat captain in charge of the infantry stood his ground, fighting with his sword. Martin pulled a pistol and shot him, then rushed past as the man sank to his knees clutching his chest.

Burwell's men closed their ranks and surged uphill through the mayhem, bayonets lowered. Occam and Dan Scott moved alongside them, reloading on the fly. As they did, they came under attack by a pair of Redcoats. Occam knocked his man down with a quick, crushing blow to the head. When he turned to help Scott, he came face to face with a black man in a Redcoat uniform. It was Joshua, one of Benjamin Martin's freedmen, a man Occam had never seen before. They stood muzzle to muzzle for an instant, surrounded by the chaos of the battle, neither one of them willing to fire on the other. The color of their skin reminded them that this was not *their* war. As they lowered their weapons slightly, one of the militiaman, trying to help Occam, used a pistol to shoot Joshua in the stomach. He collapsed to the ground with a huge wound as the man pulled Occam away to a different part of the battle.

Behind their bayonets, Burwell's men were an unstoppable force. They marched through the mayhem, pausing briefly to help the militiamen where they could, but their primary objective was the top of the hill. Once there, they would have the Redcoats surrounded and could double back on them.

But in a stroke of bad luck, they came to the back side of the mansion at the very moment Cornwallis's reserve infantry arrived at the front. Several hundred strong, they came around both sides of the building and quickly formed a firing line. The two armies faced one another at a distance of only twenty paces.

The Continentals were stunned. Their guns were empty, and there was no opportunity to retreat. There was not even time to begin reloading. Burwell stood gravely beside his men as the British muskets lowered into position and fired.

The destruction was horrible. The close-range shot shredded the Continentals, killing dozens and injuring many more. As the smoke and noise of the blast began to clear, Burwell immediately ordered a charge. He could see two more full lines of Redcoats standing on the far side of the ruins. His men were badly outnumbered, but under the circumstances, a charge seemed to be their only hope. The two armies threw themselves at one another behind their razor-sharp bayonets. With loud screams and a clattering of blades, they began cutting and spearing one another.

As the militia gained control over the Dragoons and the first wave of Redcoat infantry, they began hurrying up the hill to support the Continentals. But the fresh British units fought well, and the commanders on the other side of the mansion began sending groups of reinforcements into the fray at a steady pace. The tide of the battle shifted decisively in the British favor.

Martin was still with the main body of the militia when he caught sight of Tavington. The colonel was on his horse nearby, skillfully defending himself with his curved saber. The moment Martin spotted him, he started in that direction, reaching for his pistol and the special bullet. Completely focused on his goal, he hardly noticed the Redcoat who stepped into his path and slashed at him with his bayonet. Martin ducked away just in time, broke the man's jaw with a powerful punch, and kept moving.

"Colonel!" Villeneuve's voice cut through the noise and caught Martin's attention. He turned and looked. Villeneuve pointed to the ruins with his sword. "The line is faltering!"

Martin saw that he was right. Continentals and militia alike were pouring away, retreating in the face of the superior British numbers. For a brief moment, Martin stood frozen by indecision. Tavington was less than fifty yards away from him. But if the lines broke, the battle, and possibly the entire war, would be lost. After a last glance at his enemy, Martin turned away and started up the hill.

"NO!" he screamed at the retreating men, "NO!" He held his arms wide as if he could hold back the flood, but the men continued past him. "NO!"

One of the Continentals came toward him holding an

Old Glory. Martin jumped into the man's path and ripped the flag from his hands. He then continued uphill, moving against the tide, shouting, "No! No! No!"

From every corner of the battle, men looked up and saw the Old Glory unfurled, moving to take the hill. The sight gave new courage to the Patriots. Those who were running away stopped where they were in order to watch and then, a moment later, turned to follow. Martin plowed through the Redcoats, oblivious to the danger on all sides. He pushed forward until he came into the yard of the ruined mansion and then fought his way up the marble stairs, where the English numbers were the greatest. With the flagpole as his only weapon, he battered men out of his path, leaving them for the Patriots following behind him. When he reached the top of the steps, he used his free hand to grab a Redcoat by the crossed white sashes over his chest and throw him roughly aside.

With Villeneuve standing guard, he stood between the stone pillars and waved the flag back and forth through the air. The sight of their flag and Martin's bravery inspired the men to make a new offensive. Raising their voices and their weapons, they surged toward the top of the hill and overwhelmed the British infantry. Within a few minutes, they were once again in control of the small valley.

Cornwallis and his entourage could see nothing of the battle taking place behind the hilltop. Though anxious, they were confident that they would soon see the British signaling flags relaying the news of the victory. When instead they saw the American flag waving impudently from the steps of the ruins, they were appalled. Cornwallis had heard the American cannons sound shortly after his men had disappeared over the crest, but was positive he had sent a sufficient number of men to overcome any obstacle. For the first time, it occurred to him that he might not prevail.

The situation became even more dire when the Patriots rushed forward to engage the rest of his reserves. They attacked so suddenly and so swiftly that his men didn't have a chance to fire their weapons. Alarmed, Cornwallis turned to desperate measures.

"Have the artillery concentrate on their center. Drive them back!"

O'Hara's face blanched when he realized the order meant they would be firing not only on the enemy, but on their own men as well. He pointed this out, but Cornwallis remained adamant. The order was relayed, but it did little good. The Americans fought like avenging angels, smashing into the reserves and cutting them to pieces before the cannons could find their range. The Redcoat lines disintegrated in a matter of moments, and the soldiers turned and began to run back across the field.

"My lord," O'Hara said, "if we wheel right and reform, we may be able to turn their flank."

"You dream, General," Cornwallis said, utterly disheartened. Although the fighting continued in pockets for several more minutes, he could see that the outcome had already been decided.

Martin, still holding the flag, stood near the ruins urging the Patriots on when he heard a horse neigh behind him. He turned and saw Tavington again in the distance. He had rounded up a handful of Redcoat deserters and was leading them back to the fight, but forgot about them completely the moment he noticed Martin.

As the two men locked eyes and stared hatefully, all the heat and noise of the battle going on around them seemed to recede into the background. Nothing mattered now except settling their personal score.

Martin gripped the flagpole in both hands and began to advance. Tavington spurred his horse forward, raising his saber into the air. They ran at one another at full speed, impelled forward by the mutual need to kill. When they were about to collide, Tavington's sword arm whipped around behind him, building momentum for a killing blow. But as he swung, Martin veered into the path of the speeding horse and planted one end of the flag firmly against the ground. He raised the sharp tip at an angle, and the horse crashed into it chest first. The pole snapped in two as the impaled animal screamed and crashed to the ground. Tavington was sent flying through the air and landed hard fifteen yards away. By the time he struggled to his feet, slightly disoriented, Martin was loading the bullet he'd made that morning into his pistol. After picking up his saber, Tavington started toward Martin to finish him off, but he stopped when he saw the pistol pointed at him.

Martin took careful aim at Tavington's heart, but as he pulled back on the trigger, a cannonball exploded into the earth just behind him and the shot went awry.

It hit Tavington in the left bicep and lodged there after spraying blood. As debris from the explosion rained down on Martin's head, he saw that Tavington was still on his feet. The Englishman looked down at his wound as if it were nothing, a minor annoyance. Then he came forward, his eyes bright with hate, waving his sword menacingly through the air in front of him.

Martin ducked under the first blow and plowed forward, lifting Tavington off his feet and throwing him down on his back. In a flash, his boot pinned Tavington's wrist to the ground and he swung down with his pistol, using it like a hammer.

Tavington rolled himself over and took the blow between the shoulder blades. He tried to grab Martin's foot, but was too slow. Martin kicked him in the face, snapping his head back violently and splitting open his lip. It was a powerful blow that should have knocked him unconscious, but Tavington showed no sign of being affected. When he tried to stand, Martin cracked down again with his pistol, this time hitting Tavington hard on the back of the neck. Still he tried to rise to his feet. Martin kicked him savagely in the stomach and then again in the face. The blow was strong enough to lift Tavington partially off the ground and flip him over onto his back.

Reaching into his weapons belt, Martin tossed away his pistol and drew his Cherokee tomahawk. Before he could use it, however, he heard a horseman behind him and wheeled around to see his neighbor, Captain James Wilkins, holding a pistol at him from close range.

The two men froze, looking at one another.

"Shoot him, Wilkins!" Tavington shouted, his speech distorted by his swollen lips. His mouth was full of blood and broken teeth. Wilkins stared down the barrel of the gun at Martin. "KILL HIM!" Tavington raged.

Still, Wilkins hesitated. He had long been Martin's enemy, but had always considered him a decent and respectable man. The same was not true of Tavington, whom he considered a butcher. After a long, derisive look at his commanding officer, he lowered the pistol, yanked on his reins, and rode away.

Tavington sprang to his feet and attacked again, slashing with speed and power as Martin backed away, using the blade of his tomahawk to deflect the blows.

When Tavington stumbled, Martin regained the advantage and pushed him backward with a series of quick strokes of the hatchet. As the battle continued around them, they chopped at one another, each gaining and losing the momentum. Despite Tavington holding the better weapon, they were evenly matched.

Eventually, however, Tavington won out. When their two weapons clashed and held at tight quarters, the Englishman freed himself first and brought the handle of his sword crashing into Martin's face. In the same motion, he slashed deep into the flesh of Martin's left arm.

When Martin retreated in pain, Tavington knelt and, without giving up his sword, quickly retrieved a bayonet from the ground. He held it in his left hand and tried to wave it in a threatening way, but it appeared that the bullet wound to his arm would prevent him from using it effectively.

Martin, breathing hard and covered in sweat, countered by pulling out his six-inch knife and using both weapons at once. The two men came at one another again and fought at close quarters. But the tomahawk proved to be less useful than the saber, and the longer they fought, the more control Tavington asserted.

The tip of his sword nicked Martin several times across the arms and thighs until he was able to strike a more powerful blow, one that cut deeply into the back of Martin's legs. When Martin stumbled and fell to the ground, Tavington swung hard, and the force of the blow knocked the tomahawk away.

Left with only his hunting knife, Martin was in a hopeless situation. He deflected several blows from Tavington's sword, but knew it was only a matter of time. His only hope was to step in close and try to disarm his opponent. When he did, Tavington speared him with the bayonet. He drove the point of it into Martin's stomach and out through his back.

Martin doubled over in pain, and his hands fell to his sides. As he looked up, he noticed Tavington was smiling, pleased with own cleverness. It seemed that his arm was not as badly damaged as he had pretended.

Staggering backward, Martin tried to move away to safety, but his legs failed him after just a few steps. He sank to the ground, sitting on his feet, and stared wide-eyed out across the battlefield. Making no move to defend himself, he watched his fellow Patriots pursuing the Redcoats across the field. An Old Glory fluttered past him, and he heard his men cheering as they followed it.

Martin saw an English musket with bayonet affixed laying nearby and crawled forward painfully to pick it up, the bayonet cutting his insides as he moved. Refusing to give up while there was any life still in him, he rose to his feet once more. Tavington, who had already left him for dead, seemed almost amused by his stubbornness. He came to where Martin was standing and swung at him again with the saber, but he was only toying with him now. When Martin pushed the musket out in front of him to deflect the blow, Tavington immediately struck downward across Martin's back, pounding down on the exposed tip of the bayonet.

Like a bolt of lightning, the hideous pain shot through Martin's body, arching his back until his face pointed at the sky. His arms shot out to the sides as he wheeled around and collapsed once more to the ground. His limbs all went limp as he fell, but he somehow managed to keep hold of the musket. He heard Tavington come up behind him to deliver the killing blow.

"Kill me before the war is over, will you?" he said, remembering the promise Martin had made at Fort Carolina. He snorted. "It appears you are not the better man."

Martin, kneeling like a condemned man on an executioner's scaffold, sat perfectly still with the musket across his lap. He could feel Tavington measuring the final stroke, and knew that in a moment he would feel the flash of the blade against the side of his neck, but he made no effort to resist.

But when he heard the blade slicing through the air, he ducked to the side with surprising speed and, in the same motion, brought the musket up and around. He buried the bayonet in Tavington's gut and pushed it through him. Tavington's swollen face opened wide in surprise.

"You're right," Martin said, struggling to his feet and pulling the blade out of his own stomach with a grunt. "My *sons* were better men."

He put the tip of the bayonet against Tavington's throat and stared into his icy blue eyes. Both of them were covered in blood and dirt, weakened by their injuries. But Martin was stronger. He plunged the blade into Tavington's windpipe and, a moment later, gave it a sharp twist. He stood there looking into the monster's eyes until the last drop of life had drained out of them.

When he staggered away, Tavington was dead, but still on his feet. He had slumped forward on the musket, which kept him propped up. Martin left him that way because it seemed an undignified way to die, a gruesome end for a gruesome man.

Dizzy and barely able to stand, he turned and surveyed the field. The British infantry was now in headlong retreat, running back in the direction they'd come and tossing their weapons aside as they went. Cornwallis and his entourage had lowered their flags and were riding away in haste. As Martin watched them flee, he told himself it was time to go home.

19

Villeneuve had found Martin on the ground, halfway between the mansion and the Patriot encampment. He had tried to walk off the field under his own power and had gotten more than halfway before he collapsed. The doctors who examined him gave a grave prognosis, saying he would probably be dead before sunrise. Tavington's bayonet had done too much damage to his internal organs. When Martin stirred the next morning, there were dozens of visitors lined up to come and pay their respects. Dickey Ludwell and Jack Moore were the first to come in. They found Martin laying flat on his back, his head propped up slightly on two pillows. He seemed perfectly alert, but the doctors had warned them about that.

The moment they ducked under his tent flap, hats in their hands, Martin knew something was wrong. Not just by the doleful expressions on their faces or the way they hung their heads, but because both men had bathed, shaved, and combed their hair. It had to be more than mere coincidence that both of them looked like they were headed to either a wedding or funeral. He demanded an explanation.

"Ain't you heard?" Moore asked, glancing nervously at Ludwell.

"Heard what?"

Ludwell bent solemnly to a knee. "You got wounded mighty bad, Colonel Martin. They say you're not going to, well, that there's a chance you might not make it." It was painful news to deliver, and Ludwell's face crumpled in grief. He was so moved by the plight of his fallen commander that he began to sob. Behind him, Moore turned away and wiped his eyes with his sleeve.

"Oh, bull's pizzle!"

The men turned to him at the same time. "Pardon?"

"You heard me. I said bull's pizzle! I'm well enough. Army doctors are quacks."

"He showed great courage in the face of the Grim Reaper," Moore said as if he were reading from a gravestone.

"Jack, I'm serious. I'll be fine." To show them what he meant, Martin pushed himself, painfully, very painfully, into a sitting position. "You see?"

They were still unconvinced when Burwell came in. He was as gloomy and melancholy as the other two. He was also astonished to find Martin sitting up.

"Harry, these men tell me I am to die. I say they're wrong. I'd like your opinion."

A smile spread slowly across the stony landscape of Burwell's face. He had always taken Martin at his word and had never yet been disappointed. "I'd wager ten crowns you'll be on your feet in less than two weeks."

Martin asked Moore and Ludwell to give him a moment with his old friend and they left, more confused than comforted by what they'd seen.

"I don't think you should be sitting up, Ben. It looks painful." The blanket had fallen away, and the bloodstained bandage wrapped around Martin's middle was visible through his shirt.

"I resign, Harry. I've done what I came here to do. Now I'd like to go back to my family."

"I can't do that, Ben. Cornwallis still has an army, and he'll call the rest of the troops together. We still need you." He said

Greene was already making plans to go after Cornwallis and finish him off and that Martin should bring his militiamen with him in a month or so, as soon as he was able. When Martin insisted, Burwell started playing dirty. "All right, I'll accept your resignation, but only under one condition."

"Which is?"

"Write it down on paper and put it in my hand."

"Agreed," Martin said. Someone had stacked Gabriel's haversack, along with the rest of his gear, near the foot of the bed. "You'll find pencil and paper in that sack. Hand them to me, please."

Burwell kept his feet planted and shook his head.

"How do you expect me to write out the letter?" Martin asked, noting the sly look Burwell was giving him.

"Remember, Benjamin, you've got to personally put it in my hand. Now lay down and get some rest." He turned on his heels and walked out. Martin shouted for him to stop and come back, but Burwell was gone.

No sooner had Martin laid his head back on the pillow than Dan Scott stepped through the doorway with eyes gone red from crying. Martin stopped him before he could begin expressing his condolences and asked him for something to write with.

Burwell, satisfied with the clever trick he'd played, walked across the camp to his headquarters tent where his staff, as usual, had several matters requiring his immediate attention. There were questions about repairs to the cannons, requests from the English officers captured during the battle, and an angry local farmer who had come to demand repayment for a cow and nine chickens he claimed were taken from him by Continental soldiers. The colonel was dealing with such matters when he saw something that froze him dead in his tracks.

Benjamin Martin stood at the entrance to the tent, leaning on Occam's strong arm. He had scratched out his letter of resignation and had come to deliver it. Understanding the severity of Martin's wounds, Burwell was flabbergasted. He could see that Martin's mind was made up and quickly came forward to accept the letter. Still, he urged Martin to reconsider.

"Take a month. Go see your family. I'll hold this letter and if, in six weeks' time, you haven't caught up with us, I'll make it formal."

Martin agreed.

Less than ten days later, he arrived at Saint Helena and rode into the Gullah village in the back of a wagon. His wounds were still tender, but the trip was not overly difficult for him. His children restrained their exuberance and hugged him delicately in welcome. The way he put his arms around Charlotte made it clear how much he had missed her embrace. All of them were overjoyed to see him, but immediately began asking about Gabriel. Martin sat them all down and explained what had happened, then spent the next week trying to console them.

During that same week, Charlotte began several times to tell him something, but each time changed her mind and stayed quiet. The third time it happened, they were sitting on a bench outside their hut at night.

"What is it you want to say?"

Charlotte smiled mysteriously and changed the subject. "I think you're starting to regret your decision. I think you want to go back to the war." Martin looked at her, alarmed to realize she could read his private thoughts as accurately as her sister had done in years past.

"I only went to try to look after Gabriel. And part of me . . ."

"And part of you wanted to kill that man who killed your sons."

"Yes."

"And did you?"

Martin nodded that he had. He had killed Tavington just as he'd wanted to, at close quarters while looking him in the eyes. But there was less satisfaction in it than he had imagined. "I think I caught some of what Gabriel and Anne were sick with."

"Patriotism?"

He nodded again. "And I keep wondering what they would want me to do."

"They'd want you to do your duty."

The two of them fell silent for a time. They stared out at the lagoon and watched the way the moonlight moved across its surface as they pondered what duty called for in the present situation.

"I believe in this cause," Martin said at last.

"Then you must go."

When Martin spoke to his children the next day, Margaret was the first one to make up her mind. She wanted the British kicked out of the country and sent back across the Atlantic where they belonged. Nathan, Samuel, and William put their heads together in a private conference and agreed that it was best way to honor the memory of their two brothers. Susan was reluctant to see her father leave them again, and asked him to swear an oath that he would return to them safely. When he did, she nodded her head to make the decision unanimous.

He rode north, found the army, and reassumed command over his company of men. Burwell had given him six weeks, but he'd returned in only three. Along with the rest of the Patriot army, the South Carolina militia began to engage Cornwallis at every opportunity.

Nearly five months later, a pair of Martin's men rode into the Gullah village to deliver a letter and several small gifts to his family. Charlotte was, by that point, visibly pregnant. She had not known for certain during Martin's visit and despite the temptation, decided not to tell him of the possibility. She gathered the children around her in a circle near the shoreline and read the letter to them.

Cherished Family,

It has now been some months since I have seen you. I am sorry to have gone so long without writing, but had no means of delivering letters to the place you are in. The fact that I can spare the two men who will carry this letter to you is a sign of the progress we have made. During these last months, wherever the English tried to stop and regroup, we have engaged them in skirmishes and driven them further on. Eventually, Lord General Cornwallis took flight with his army and moved out of the Carolinas. God willing, we will never see him there again. He has moved north into Virginia and entrenched himself here at Yorktown. We were surprised to see the extent of his fortifications when we arrived here only a few days after him. He has constructed several redoubts on the commanding ground and dug an entrenchment at the head of the Wormley River. We guess he has about sixty-five cannons in the town. Attacking him now is out of the question for us, so we play a tense game of waiting. Cornwallis has appealed to Sir Henry Clinton to bring the English navy and several thousand reinforcements from New York. If they arrive soon, Virginia will certainly fall into their hands and our sacrifices over the last months will have been in vain. We Americans anxiously await the arrival of General Washington, who has left the north with stealth and is marching the bulk of his army to the south. Even if he should arrive ahead of Clinton, I fear our chances of forcing a surrender are minimal. All our hopes now rest with the French. Admiral de Grasse has been promising for some months to bring his fleet into the Chesapeake, but there is still no sign of him. Will they arrive in time? Will they bring sufficient troops and ships? Or will they arrive at all? These are questions we ask ourselves many times each day.

I have not forgotten my promise to you, and if all goes well I expect to see you soon. In the meanwhile, pray for me but most of all pray for our cause.

Your loving father,
Benj. M.

Just three days after the letter was sent, Martin led his South Carolina militia on a hike to the top of the highest hill overlooking Yorktown. Villeneuve, Occam, and Scott were among the group that accompanied him. When they reached the peak and turned around, they were treated to a magnificent vista. Seven thousand French troops had arrived, some by land and some by sea, to support the Americans, who were now nine thousand strong. The flags of the two nations flew side by side in great numbers. The tents had been pitched in a massive semicircle that surrounded the town and touched the York River at both ends. The comte de Rochambeau's army had joined Washington's troops on their rapid southward march while Admiral de Grasse had carried others in his fleet of warships, which now formed a barricade across the river, preventing Cornwallis from bringing in fresh supplies.

Almost from the moment they arrived, the allied army's cannons had pounded the British defensive works mercilessly, and they continued to do so as Martin and his men watched from the hill. It was a grand and impressive sight.

"*Vive la France,*" said Martin, drinking in the view.

Villeneuve smiled and quietly replied, "*Vive la liberté.*"

Cornwallis's situation deteriorated dramatically over the next few days. His men had only putrid meat and wormy biscuits to feed themselves, and soon fever began to spread. They turned to slaughtering their horses for food and dumped the carcasses in the river. And all the while, the allies kept up a continuous bombardment with the ninety-two cannons in their arsenal, firing more than a thousand shots each day into the fortress town. The British returned fire as best they could, but in time they began to run low on munitions.

The siege continued for several more days.

From his damaged headquarters building, Cornwallis looked out at his shattered defensive works and cowering troops, wondering how much longer they could hold out. He stopped sending messages to Clinton appealing for help. Even if his messengers slipped through the cordon, by the time they got to New York, it would be too late. O'Hara joined him near the window, and repeated what he'd been saying for days.

"My lord, I beseech you, you must order the surrender."

"Has it come to this?" Cornwallis said dismally. "An army of rabble, of *peasants* . . . everything will change. Everything *has* changed."

That same afternoon, the South Carolina militia was standing guard over one of the forward cannon emplacements, keeping their heads low and their eyes alert. Every few minutes a Redcoat popped up from behind their earthworks to fire a musket ball at the gunners, and each time they did, Martin's men fired back at them. There was a commotion among the men farther down the road. A group of American officers was coming toward them on horseback.

"It's him," shouted a soldier, "it's Washington."

All the Patriots, militia and Continentals alike, stopped what they were doing to come and catch a glimpse of the man who embodied the hope of American liberty. He was instantly recognizable by his blue and yellow commander's uniform and the large hat he wore on his head. There was a gravity about him, a certain soldierly grace in the way he moved, that set him apart from the officers surrounding him. The road was easily within range of British snipers, but he rode along serenely, ignoring the danger.

When he came to the place where the South Carolina militia banner flew beside Gabriel's Old Glory, he dismounted and stood face to face with Colonel Benjamin Martin. Washington, who had painfully bad teeth, worked his jaw back and forth habitually as the two men exchanged hard stares. After a moment of this, Martin shook his head and smiled.

"Your hair's gone gray."

"I've earned it," Washington said. "I wanted to personally greet you and the South Carolina militia. This country owes a great deal to you." The men beamed with pride when they heard him say it.

"Thank you," Martin said on behalf of the entire group.

"I was sorry to hear about your son," Washington said, looking out over the British-held territory.

"I lost another a little more than a year ago, Thomas. He was only fifteen." A cannon was fired nearby, ripping the air with a loud explosion.

"I've had no sons to lose, nor daughters," said the general. "I lose the sons of other men." He looked around at the thousands of men laying siege to Yorktown, knowing that each one of them was someone's son, or brother, or father, or husband. He sighed under the weight of the responsibility, but then smiled crookedly. "Life was easier when we only had ourselves to get killed."

Martin nodded amen, then turned his head suddenly when he heard an unfamiliar noise coming from the British position. Washington and everyone else looked the same way.

A small, solitary figure appeared atop the British horn-work, a drummer boy no more than fourteen years old. Martin could see him beating out a parley, but it was impossible to hear beneath the sustained noise of the bombardment. A moment later, a British officer stepped tentatively into the open, climbed up next to the drummer, and raised a white flag. As he began to wave it slowly back and forth, the artillery units took notice, and the shelling slowed and then stopped.

One roar replaced another. As the cannons fell quiet, the French and the Americans began to cheer. It began slowly, a few men at a time, but as the full meaning of the surrender flag sank in, it grew louder and louder and louder until all sixteen thousand men were shouting at once. They threw their hats into the air and threw themselves into one another's arms, laughing and dancing in mad circles. They cheered so loudly that farmers living ten miles away knew immediately that Cornwallis had given up.

They had every right to make so much noise. It was the most improbable of victories, as far-fetched as David besting Goliath. Poorly trained, ill-equipped, and usually out-numbered, the Patriot forces had defeated the most powerful nation on the face of the earth.

Washington, expressing his enormous satisfaction with only a thin smile, shook Martin's hand but did not try to speak over the noise. They understood and respected one another too well to require many words. Washington hurried back to his horse and spurred past his officers, riding hard back to his headquarters.

The articles of capitulation were drawn up as quickly as possible. Washington was aware that every passing hour represented another chance for Sir Henry Clinton to sail in and break the siege. Once the particulars had been settled, a ceremony was scheduled for the following afternoon. Tens of thousands of civilians, far outnumbering the allied armies, poured in from the countryside to attend the event.

By noon, only two hours before the formal surrender was to take place, Martin had packed his saddlebags and was ready to leave. He spent a while talking with the men who had served under him, telling them of his intention to go home and rebuild his farm. He invited them all to visit and promised that there would be a square meal and a decent bottle of wine waiting for them when they came.

When he walked back to his horse, two other men were waiting to wish him well, Villeneuve and Burwell. In Burwell's hand was the letter Martin had written on the morning of the Battle of Cowpens.

"War's over," he said. "I guess this won't need to be sent."

Martin recognized the letter he had written to his children, still tied shut with the string.

"Thank you," Martin said, reaching out to accept it and shake the man's hand. "And where will you go now?"

"Home, to start over."

"Is there any news about the child you were expecting?"

He was pleased that Martin had remembered. "My wife gave birth to a son three weeks ago."

"Congratulations, Harry, that's wonderful news. What are you going to call him?"

"We named him Gabriel."

Martin was honored, and deeply touched, by the gesture.

"A good name for a farmer," Villeneuve said. He stepped up to Martin with his chin pushed forward in a pugnacious way and offered his hand. As Martin reached out to shake it, both he and Villeneuve changed their minds at the same moment and moved into an embrace. They stepped back and looked one another in the eyes. Like their countries, the two men had moved from suspicion and hostility to trust and mutual affection. After working so closely together for so many months, saying good-bye was difficult. There was no use in prolonging the moment.

Martin climbed onto his horse and rode away.

When he entered the Gullah village at St. Helena, he was amazed at the sight of his children. They seemed to have doubled in size during the few months of his absence. But he was doubly amazed to see the dramatic change that had come over Charlotte. She was seven and a half months pregnant and her long, thin frame made it look as if she were carrying twins or maybe triplets. She smiled warmly as he came toward her. He held her for a long while before kneeling down and gently stroking his hands over the child inside her.

He had planned to start back to Fresh Water as soon as possible, since there was so much work to be done there. It would take him many months to build the family a new house, and years until the place was running as it had been. But they stayed until the child was born. It was a little girl, and they named her Rose. By the time mother and child were able to travel, it was late spring. Leaving the lagoon was a bittersweet experience for the children. They were excited about going home to resurrect the magic place they remembered, but they were leaving behind many new friends. They had learned to speak Gullah and to weave sweetgrass baskets and catch fish with spears—language and skills they knew they would lose over time. Many tears were shed as the wagon rolled away early one morning.

The journey home seemed especially long to Martin. He said very little as he drove the rickety old wagon onward. His mind was occupied with planning the new house and organizing all the various tasks that would need to be accomplished before the next rainy season. Nathan and Samuel were growing into sturdy young men, but even with their help, Martin didn't see how he could finish everything that needed to be done.

It was late in the afternoon by the time they rounded the final bend in the road and saw the brick pillars that marked the property line. The berry brambles had completely overgrown the fence, and the elements had turned the wood a silvery shade of gray. When they started up the road, Martin was alarmed to see that someone was building a two-story house on *his* property. The framing work was more than half finished, using the foundations of the house that had burned. He supposed it had to be one of his neighbors who had mistakenly assumed him killed in the war. He slapped the reins against the horses and hurried up the slope to deliver the bad news that he was still very much alive.

As he came closer, he began to recognize the crew of men doing the work: Dan Scott, Occam, Dickey Ludwell, Jack Moore, Jean Villeneuve, and a handful of others. They had split and roughed out a large number of beams and had set up a portable mill beside the structure. Like his previous home, it was a traditional four-over-four and, from a distance at least, the frame seemed quite solidly constructed.

He pulled the wagon into the yard not far from the oak tree and came toward the new building with his family following behind him. Occam had come out into the yard to bring in another timber. Martin was too moved by what he saw to speak, but he used his hands to ask Occam for an explanation.

"Gabriel said if we won the war, we'd build a new world. We figured we'd start right here."

Villeneuve waved to him briefly before going back to his hammering. Dan Scott paused from his work on the upper floor to nod down at the family.

Martin was overwhelmed. He tried desperately to think of something to say, some words that would express his gratitude to these men he regarded as brothers, but his feelings at that moment were stronger and deeper than he knew how to describe.

"A new world?" he asked, beginning to roll up his sleeves. "Sounds good. Let's get to work."

About the Author

This is Stephen Molstad's seventh book for Centropolis Entertainment. Along with the novelization of the blockbuster *Independence Day*, he has written a pair of related novels—*ID4: Silent Zone* and *ID4: War in the Desert*. A graduate of UC Santa Cruz, he lives in Los Angeles with an old VW Bug, a lazy cat, and a patient wife, Elizabeth. He invites your comments at molstad@centropolis.com.